KU-531-577

DEADLINE AT DURANGO

Allan Vaughan Elston was a prolific author of traditional Western novels and many more short stories and novelettes, memorable for the complexity of their plots and the flamboyance of the villains who are often more interesting than either the heroes or heroines. He was born in Kansas City and spent his summers on a Colorado cattle ranch owned by his father. He was educated as a civil engineer at the University of Missouri and worked in various engineering companies in South America as well as his own in the United States before, in 1920, turning to ranching. Times were hard financially at the ranch so in late 1924 Elston tried writing his first fiction. His first story was "The Eyes of Teconce" in *The Frontier* (2/25), an adventure tale set in the rugged Andes, but his second was "Peepsight Shoots High" in *The Frontier* (6/25), marking his debut as an author of Western fiction, in which henceforth he specialized. His second Western story was "Triggers in Leash" in *The Frontier* (7/25), subsequently adapted for the third episode of "Alfred Hitchcock Presents" in 1955. His first Western novel was *Come Out and Fight!* (1941) followed by *Guns On The Cimarron* (1943) prior to his re-entering the U.S. Army during the Second World War. Following the war, he found his stride with *Hit The Saddle* (1947) and *The Sheriff Of San Miguel* (1949). In the 1950s he would average two books a year, an impressive accomplishment for any writer and Elston was already into his sixties. His novels tend to be precisely situated as to year and place and often contain an intriguing mystery. *The Landseekers* (1964) was Elston's final novel to appear in a hard cover edition. Henceforth, he confined himself to writing paperback originals. At his best, Elston was a fine craftsman who could unite novelty of setting and events with a plot-driven complexity to produce a generally entertaining narrative.

DEADLINE AT DURANGO

Allan Vaughan Elston

GUNSMOKE

First published in the UK by Ward Lock

This hardback edition 2010
by BBC Audiobooks Ltd
by arrangement with
Golden West Literary Agency

Copyright © 1950 by Allan Vaughan Elston.
Copyright © 1951 by Allan Vaughan Elston in
the British Commonwealth.
Copyright © renewed 1978 by the Estate
of Allan Vaughan Elston.
All rights reserved.

ISBN 978 1 408 46265 2

British Library Cataloguing in Publication Data available.

MORAY COUNCIL LIBRARIES & INFO.SERVICES	
20 30 19 19	
Askews	
WF WF	

To the ... days at
Duran ... er, and
J. Luna ... nt Creek

Printed and bound in Great Britain by
CPI Antony Rowe, Chippenham and Eastbourne

1

THE CONCORD STAGE, trace chains rattling, lurched to a stop in front of the Grand Central Hotel in Durango. It had been snowbound for a day and a night on Cumbres Pass, coming over the Divide from Alamosa. The driver now plunked his whip in the whip socket and yelled throatily, "End of the line. Everybody out."

It was sundown of the eleventh of April in the year 1881.

Actually only one passenger disembarked. The others had already dropped off at the West End and Windsor hotels, a few blocks down Main Street. The man who got off now was tall, broad-shouldered, darkly handsome in spite of his weariness, and with an air of being supremely sure of himself. He wore a center-creased felt hat of pearl-gray which matched his gloves and his Ascot tie. His fur-collared overcoat hung open, exposing a heavy gold watch chain which spanned his double-breasted vest. His eyes were a light, calm brown, his skin tight and young. Because he was clean-shaven in a land of bearded men, he looked even younger than he was.

The walk he stepped out on was of new pine boards. A plump Mexican boy appeared and took his valise inside. The hotel itself was of new pine boards, two-story, box-shaped, unpainted. Before going in, the traveler turned and took his first, careless appraisal of the town.

This side of the street, he observed, was lined with respectable shops, restaurants, and hotels. But the other side seemed to be a solid chain of saloons and honky-tonks. Some had false fronts. Others had second-story windows, lamplighted. From one of them, directly across the way, a rouged woman smiled seductively at the newcomer.

Up the street creaked a freighter's wagon pulled ponderously by four yokes of bulls. Saddled horses and packed mules lined the hitchracks. From the saloons came a metallic discord meant for music. Loud talk, shrill laughter, the clink of coins on bars. It looked, the newcomer thought, like a town of about three thousand which had sprung up overnight. More than half the buildings were brand-new. The rest were old with new underpinnings, as though they'd been torn down at some abandoned townsite and hastily re-erected on this street. Was it because the Denver and Rio Grande Railway was building a narrow-gauge line into Durango?

The traveler now entered the hotel and found a carpetless lobby with a sheet-iron stove in the center. He took off his pearl-gray gloves and warmed his hands by the stove. A kerosene lamp hung from the ceiling. Candles flickered by a registry book on the desk.

The name the arriving guest wrote in it was:

Jefferson Davis Lantry, St. Louis.

Half an hour later Mr. Jefferson Lantry was seated in front of a steak supper in a restaurant up the street. On coming in he'd purchased the latest issue of the *Durango Daily Record*. Lantry read idly as he dined. Since he was looking for an opportunity to make money, he was more interested in the advertisements than in the news. Yet the main item of current news was so boldly headlined that it impelled his attention.

Last night, the item related, there'd been a killing at the Coliseum Theater in Durango. Without known provocation, and apparently in a mood of sheer bravado, a man named Adam Smith had shot and killed a popular citizen named Pringle. The entire audience having witnessed the murder, Smith had been promptly arrested and jailed. The town was incensed about it.

Scraps of talk came to Lantry from two stock hands at the next table.

"It'll take a tight jail to hold that guy, Ed."

"Sure will, Jake. Tighter'n anything we got here. The way I hear it, the boys are organizin' right now."

Lantry finished his supper and strolled back to the hotel. A distinguished gentleman who appeared to be in his late fifties was seated facing the lobby windows, looking out at the street. He wore a long black coat and a cavalryman's campaign hat. Lantry judged him to be a retired army officer, was sure of it when the clerk brought a cigar and said, "Here you are, Major. Anything else?"

Lantry took the next chair. This major looked like a man of substance and might be worth cultivating. When the man fumbled for a match and failed to find one, Lantry offered a light himself.

"Thank you, suh. Don't believe I've had the pleasure of meeting you. Talcott's my name. Carey Talcott."

Lantry smiled. He had even white teeth, and his smile always made an impression. "I'm Jeff Lantry. Just got in from St. Louis. Here to make my fortune, Major." He laughed pleasantly.

"In what line, suh?"

"What lines are there? I'm new to the Basin. That's what they call this country, isn't it? The San Juan Basin?"

Major Talcott nodded, puffing his cigar. "The San Juan Basin," he said, "like all Gaul, is divided into three parts. Grass, timber, and ore. Take your choice, young man."

Lantry glanced down at the major's spurred boots. "Your choice, I take it, was grass."

Again the major nodded. "It's God's best cow country, suh. Calves grow bigger out here than they do back in Tennessee, where I came from."

"You range close by?"

"Seventy miles northwest of here, suh. On the west fork of the Dolores."

"I haven't decided," Lantry said, "which line I'll take a whirl at. Might be grass, might be timber, might be ore."

Pawns of those three industries—cowboys, timbermen, and miners—were milling along the opposite walk. Major Talcott remained silent for a while, looking out the window, watching the customers weave in and out of the vice traps over there. The sight brought a grim smile to his lips. "There's a fourth line, suh. It lives off the other three." He thumbed a bit sadly toward saloon row.

Lantry smiled. "You mean the fourth line in the end gets all the money earned in the first three."

"Most of it," Talcott conceded with a sigh. "I paid my crew off last night. They're all in town, and most of 'em, God bless 'em, 'll be broke by mawnin'."

Lantry said good night and went upstairs to bed. The jolting ride over Cumbres Pass had left him too weary for anything else. For a while he lay awake, mulling over the major's terse summary of Basin opportunities. You could go out into the wilderness and make money from cattle, from timber, or from mines. Or you could stay right here in town and let them bring the money to you.

Which should it be? Scruples had never handicapped Jeff Lantry. He was an opportunist. He was here to make a fortune the quickest and easiest way.

Why not let fate decide it? He could sit tight for a while and then take the first inviting break. It had worked before, back on the Mississippi river boats. "Lucky Lantry," men had called him in St. Louis. Would his luck hold here in Durango?

He slipped into sleep.

Two shots from the street awakened him. He sat up in the dark, struck a match, and looked at his watch. It was still only eleven o'clock.

Heavy boot treads thumped along the boardwalks. Lantry got up and looked from his window. Saloon lights across the way made the scene plain enough. Men were on the move. A long line of them on each walk, two abreast, all moving purposefully in one direction. And Lantry could see that they were masked.

It looked like a vigilante committee. Lantry remembered the news story. A wanton killer in jail and feeling running high all over town. Was this a lynching? Perhaps those two shots had been the signal for assembly. It was no concern of Lantry's. With a slight shrug he went back to bed.

At dawn he was awake again. Always he'd been an early riser. What he wanted right now was a pot of black coffee.

Lantry dressed and went out for it. Main Street, at this dawn hour, should have been empty. But it wasn't. People were abroad, most of them with awed and strained faces. Some stood in whispering groups. Others were moving south along the walks.

Curious, Lantry followed them.

Two blocks south down Main Street brought him to a corner dignified by a solid frame building with grilled windows. The sign over it said *First National Bank*. People were turning to the right at that corner.

Just back of the bank, facing a side street, was the town's one-room post office. Most of the crowd had assembled there. Lantry joined it and saw why. A tall pine tree stood in a vacant lot directly across from the post office. And a man's body swung from a limb of the pine.

Morbid whispers buzzed about Lantry. "Ain't it awful, Sadie?" This from one of two pale bawdyhouse girls at Lantry's elbow. And he was quite willing to agree. Here was grim evidence of the raw, rough readiness of Durango.

A sign on the pine tree, signed *Citizens' Safety Commit-*

tee, warned that the body must not be cut down till daylight.

It was broad daylight now. And Lantry could plainly see the face of the hanging man. It was hideously distorted, and yet to Jefferson Lantry it seemed oddly familiar. A feeling he'd seen the man before somewhere persisted.

He moved a few steps nearer. Last night's *Daily Record* was still in his pocket. He took it out and read the murderer's name. Adam Smith.

Two mounted men whirled around the bank corner and rode up. They were stern men who wore badges. The county sheriff, Lantry assumed, and the town marshal. One of them stood on his saddle and cut the body down.

As it fell in a grotesque lump under the pine, Lantry closed in for a better look. No one paid him any attention. For an intense minute he studied the dead man's face.

Then he was sure. Here was a man he'd seen more than once in St. Louis. His name wasn't Adam Smith. It was *Frank Foster.* Durango evidently thought he was Adam Smith. But a fugitive like Frank Foster would, of course, change his name. Lantry stared again at the dead man's left ear. Cauliflowered. Just like Frank Foster's.

"Stand back, everybody," the sheriff shouted.

And Lantry discreetly withdrew. His brain was tingling. They'd bury this man as Adam Smith. No one would ever dream he was Frank Foster, desperately wanted by the St. Louis police. In a mushroom town like this, walled off from the world and without even a railroad, with its law forces only half organized, it wasn't too strange that Foster could have concealed his true identity.

The strange thing about it, Lantry thought, was that he himself had happened along at this moment. Yet, after all, there were three thousand people here, most of them from east of the mountains. It made three thousand chances for someone to be here who at one time or another had crossed the path of Frank Foster. If Lantry hadn't recognized him, it might have been someone else.

Was this the break he'd been waiting for?

Two hundred thousand dollars! That was what Foster had made off with. Lantry's wits fastened on it, turned the possibilities of it inside out. What had Foster done with that fortune? Where was it now?

Details of the coup came back to Lantry. The big transfer of funds in St. Louis, from bank to bank. The three men who'd held up the guards. The pursuit by police. A running fight in which two of the robbers had been killed. But the third, Foster, had faded into thin air. And every dollar of the loot with him.

Lantry walked back to Main Street and turned into a saloon there. The place was deserted except for a bartender.

"Whisky," Lantry said.

"Have they cut that guy down yet?" the bartender asked.

Lantry nodded. "Was he around here long?"

"He showed up at Animas City," the barkeep said, "late last fall. Coupla mile up the river. When they moved the town down here, durin' the winter, Ad Smith came along with the rest of us."

"Came to Animas City by stage, I suppose?"

The man back of the bar thought a minute. "Nope. I recollect he rid in leadin' a pack mule."

"From which direction?"

"I didn't notice."

"Which hotel did he put up at? I mean here in Durango."

"None of 'em. Took a room at Amy Driscoll's boarding-house up on Second Avenue. Reason I know, everybody in here last night was talkin' about him."

Lantry dropped a coin on the bar and went out. Which way to the Driscoll boardinghouse? He inquired of a passer-by and was told, "Two blocks south, mister, then turn a block up the hill."

Jeff Lantry hurried that way. He was a persistent opportunist, and this could be the chance of a lifetime. A thin chance, he admitted. Frank Foster wasn't likely to hide two hundred thousand dollars, or any sizable part of it, in his boardinghouse room. But it was worth a look. And he must beat the sheriff there. Right now the sheriff was busy with the body. In the end it would be his duty to collect Adam Smith's clothing and personals for delivery to whatever heir or connection, if any, should claim them.

Lantry quickened his pace down the trash-littered walk. Durango, this early morning, had an ugly, frowsy look, like a harpy awakening after a debauch. He crossed from the saloon side of the street to the side of respectable shops. On every horizon loomed high, pine-clad mountains. Beauty was there, painted by the sunrise on those snowy summits, but Lantry didn't see it. His mind was a single track, now. Was he still Lucky Lantry?

Turning a block up the hill at F Street, he had no trouble finding the Driscoll boardinghouse. It was a pleasant place, by comparison, neatly fenced with pickets. Lantry knocked, and a tired, aproned woman opened the door.

He gave her his most engaging smile. "Adam Smith had a room here, I believe. Was he related to the Herkimer Smiths of Pueblo?"

"I haven't the slightest idea, sir." The woman made a grimace of distaste. "For *their* sake, I hope not. It's a disgrace to my decent house to have a man like that—"

"If you'd let me look over the things in his room," Lantry suggested, "I could soon tell. I hope I'm wrong about him being a cousin to the Herkimer Smiths of Pueblo. It would be quite a shock to them."

"I'm sure it would," Amy Driscoll agreed. "It's the second-floor rear. Whoever he was, I hope they take his things away at once. I can't bear to have them around."

She stood aside. Lantry went upstairs and to the rear second-floor room. Adam Smith's things were scattered about it. There was a carpetbag in the closet, a roll of saddle blankets, an old slouch hat, and an extra pair of boots.

He went through the carpetbag and found nothing of interest. His hand delved into each boot. He spread the blankets out and shook them. What about the mattress? It was a narrow straw tick on a cot. Lantry looked it over carefully. If Foster had hidden money in it, there'd be a seam. And there wasn't. Lantry tapped the walls, looked in the oil lamp, gave minute inspection to the floor boards.

Nothing to suggest a cache. It was clear that two hundred thousand dollars, or any important part of it, wasn't hidden in this room. Foster might have gambled it away before arriving this far west. Or other outlaws might have taken it from him.

His hand on the doorknob, Lantry turned for one last look. His gaze swept the cot, the blankets, the carpetbag, the boots. One of the boots had a heel which didn't match its mate. Once he'd heard of a smuggler hiding jewels in a heel.

But he wasn't looking for jewels. He was looking for money in bulk. And it wasn't here. He set the boots upright in the closet, just as he'd found them. He rerolled the blankets, straightened the cot. No use leaving the room with the appearance of having been ransacked. He picked up the old slouch hat to rehang it on a hook.

The merest afterthought inspired him to look under its inner sweatband. A strip of paper was there, folded. His first thought was that the hat might have been a size too large and the wearer had inserted the fold to make the hat fit snugger on his head.

But when he spread the paper out, what he saw made

him draw a quick breath. He stood frozen for a moment, staring at it. Here was the answer. The key to fortune. The pot at a rainbow's end. With this to guide him, he could go unerringly to it.

The scrap from the sweatband showed a simple sketch drawn in pencil. There were only four lines on it. Three streams and a trail.

Four lines and a penciled cross!

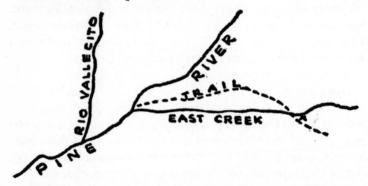

The cross, Lantry could hardly doubt, marked a spot where Frank Foster had buried his loot.

Two hundred thousand dollars would be bulky. In twenties it would be ten thousand bills. Two hundred packages of fifty bills each. More than could be stuffed into a man's pockets.

But not more than could be enfolded in a bedroll and packed on a mule. According to the bartender, Adam Smith had ridden into town leading a pack mule. No doubt the pack saddle was empty by then, the fugitive having already buried his loot in the woods.

He'd be afraid, Lantry reasoned, to do otherwise. Circulars might be out for him. And if he took that much cash to a bank, he'd immediately arouse suspicion. Over the Divide he'd come, by dim back trails, perhaps hiding in the wilderness a long time before presenting himself in the Basin settlements. To make certain he could return to his cache, he'd made a sketch referenced by three streams and a trail.

Leaving everything as he'd found it, and retaining only the sketch, Lantry quit the room and went downstairs. The landlady met him in the lower hall. "He wasn't the Smith I thought he was, after all. Sorry I bothered you."

Lantry gave her one of his charm smiles and went out. His step was jaunty as he headed for a Main Street café. The trail was blazed now. Straight to fortune. He could dig it up at will. Lucky Lantry!

2

SIPPING HIS MORNING COFFEE Lantry recalled the shooting in a theater night before last as described by the *Daily Record*. According to the paper, Adam Smith had shot his victim "without provocation and in a mood of sheer bravado." If intoxicated, the killer might have done just that. But it didn't seem quite in character with a cautious fugitive like Frank Foster. Having been shrewd enough to bury his loot in the woods before coming to town, why would he spoil everything by an unprovoked gunplay in a public place?

A possible answer was that the victim, Pringle, had recognized Smith as Foster. Or perhaps he'd asked some question which led the fugitive to think Pringle was suspicious. Fearful of exposure, and with his nerves on hair trigger, Foster might unleash a bullet on the spot. Maybe it had been that way. Maybe not. No one would ever know.

After breakfast Lantry returned to the Grand Central Hotel. As he entered the lobby he saw a plump, comely woman of about forty. She stood at the desk looking at the latest registrations. The desk clerk said, "Here he is,

Mrs. Romney. Mr. Lantry, meet the editor of the most enterprising newspaper in the Southwest, Mrs. C. W. Romney."

Lantry bowed. "A pleasure, madam."

"I make it a point," she said briskly, "to interview new arrivals. You are from St. Louis, Mr. Lantry?" Her pencil was poised over pad.

"I am."

"How long will you be with us?"

"Permanently, I hope."

Her eyes appraised him from his polished boots to his vest-spanning watch chain and on up to his strong, self-assured face. She could see at once that he was no ordinary drifter. He looked capable, purposeful, and certainly he was good-looking. Durango needed men like this one. "You couldn't do better, Mr. Lantry. Opportunities here are unlimited. Have you any business plans?"

Lantry smiled, and the evenness of his unstained teeth wasn't lost on her. "I haven't quite decided," he said, "whether to tackle ranching, lumber, or mining. I was discussing it with Major Talcott only last night."

Her pencil flashed. He saw that he'd impressed her by mentioning such an outstanding citizen as Talcott. Then he realized that here was a chance to make his planned excursion to Pine River plausible.

"First," he announced, "I'll explore the country out east of here on horseback. Look things over, I mean. Get the lay of the land. Perhaps stop at a few ranches and mines and lumber camps. Later, I'll do the same thing out west of here. In the end I shall invest in some attractive Basin enterprise."

The editress beamed her approval. "Splendid! One other thing, Mr. Lantry. You have a family, I hope. You'll be sending for them?"

His smile broadened. "Sorry to disappoint you, Mrs.

Romney. I'm a bachelor."

"What a shame! Ours is a crude culture, Mr. Lantry, and needs the softening influence of women. Ranches and sawmills and mines aren't enough. We must have *homes*. We can't have them without women. The right kind of women, I mean."

Lantry said jocularly, "Why don't you put in a call for them, Mrs. Romney?"

Her eyes sparkled. "An excellent suggestion, Mr. Lantry. I'll do it at once. I'll write an editorial addressed to single women of the Midwest and East, inviting them to the San Juan Basin. Watch out for it, sir."

He chuckled. "You bet I'll watch out. If you succeed in a mass importation of old maids, every man in Durango had better watch out."

"Good morning, Mr. Lantry. And thanks for the idea." Mrs. Romney bustled out of the hotel.

An hour later Lantry was at the government land office looking over maps and plats of the county. The confluence of Pine River and the Rio Vallecito, he discovered, was some thirty miles by trail in an easterly direction. From there, according to Frank Foster's sketch, he'd have to follow Pine River upstream to the mouth of East Creek. An old Indian trail led up East Creek toward the Continental Divide. Eventually this trail crossed East Creek at a spot marked by a cross on the sketch.

"I'm thinking of trailing up Pine River to look over grazing possibilities," Lantry said to the land-office clerk. "Much snow over that way?"

"I wouldn't risk it before May," the clerk said. "It's been a mild winter—not much snow last month or two. But enough to give you trouble, I'm afraid."

It forced Lantry to wait three weeks. The delay chaffed him, but there was no help for it. He couldn't risk getting bogged in drifts.

Early in May Lantry paid his hotel room rent for a week in advance. "I'll be out of town for a few days," he announced. "But I want to keep the room permanently."

At the livery stable he purchased a fully equipped saddle horse and pack mule. "I'll have my camp outfit delivered here," he told the liveryman. "At six tomorrow morning I want you to pack it on the mule. Then send the packed mule and the saddled horse to the Grand Central Hotel."

He didn't dare take a guide. He must travel alone, and must seem merely to be inspecting the country's natural resources.

An outfitting store sold him a bedroll, a prospector's pick and shovel, a light camp kit, and food for four days. Lantry then bought a suit of corduroys, riding-boots, and a high-crowned felt hat. After changing into them at the hotel, he went across to a saloon for a drink. Customers there were all gun-slung. Toughies, most of them. The miners, cowboys, and gamblers drifting in and out all seemed to be walking arsenals. Nearly every pony tethered at the hitchracks showed a carbine stock protruding from the saddle scabbard. This was a gun country. It would do a man no good to dig up a fortune unless he was prepared to protect it.

So Jeff Lantry went out and bought a forty-five gun, a gun belt, a holster, and cartridges. The minute he put them on he ceased being conspicuous in Durango.

Early morning found him trailing easterly out of town. The horse was a rangy bay, the mule a blocky little calico. It was the first calico mule Lantry had ever seen. The liveryman had put him on the right route. It ascended sharply into piñon and cedar foothills. The main San Juan range reared in snowbanked bulges beyond.

A keen exhilaration gripped Lantry. Riding into a wilderness leading a pack mule was new to him. Yet the very newness of it excited and challenged him. The unknown lay ahead, locked in silent mystery. Sentinels of pine and spruce and rocky tors stood guarding it. It beckoned rather than repelled Jeff Lantry. Many weaknesses had warped his character, but timidity wasn't one of them.

This was a wagon trail of deep ruts. They'd told him he could make Pine River by sundown if he kept pushing on. Pushing on meant a fast walk, at best. For miles Lantry saw no life except a bounding deer.

Unexpectedly the trail dipped downward. It led to a grassy valley through which a clear stream riffled. Cottonwoods lined the stream, and Lantry saw grazing cattle. A little way upstream he could see a log ranch house and a pole-fenced meadow. He remembered the plats he'd studied at the land office. This would be Florida Creek. There was still another hump between here and the Pine.

After fording the Florida the trail again went steeply up. The calico mule, tired now, dragged at the lead rope. Lantry had to rest it at the first bench. Then he pushed on to an aspen summit. Here the sheltered spots still held snow.

The sun was low when Lantry descended into the broad, lush valley of Pine River. Here again he sighted a log ranch layout and grazing cattle. The river, swollen by melting snow, awed him a little. It was a swift torrent and looked hock-deep to a horse. Lantry turned up it, exploring for a ford. Shortly the river divided into two forks, and he knew that the leftermost must be the Vallecito.

He dismounted stiffly, unsaddled, and hobbled his horse. Then he turned it loose to graze in the high, cured, last year's valley *vega*. Before unpacking the mule he studied the hitches carefully. He'd be awkward in repacking tomorrow. But he'd have to chance it. So Lantry took off the pack and pack saddle. The liveryman had assured him he needn't hobble the mule, because it wouldn't desert the horse. Lantry didn't quite believe it. He had no lore of wrangling. Playing safe, he tethered the mule at the end of a long rope.

That night Jefferson Davis Lantry slept under the open sky for the first time in his life. It was bitter cold. He heard the yapping of coyotes. A weird screech awakened him, and he wondered if it was a panther. The champing of his own grazing animals, the wind in the pine boughs, and the rushing riffles of the river, these and other unfamiliar sounds challenged him from the night. They were voices he didn't know. But he'd met harsher challenges than these, and mastered them. As a ten-year-old runaway from an orphanage; as a stripling in the slums of St. Louis, unwanted, parentless; as cabin boy on Mississippi river boats; as a roustabout on the cotton docks of Memphis; as a waiter in an elegant New Orleans café, watching enviously as he served the wealthy, modish patrons; and later as a night-school student, as a bit-part actor in a road show, every minute fighting to be somebody, to get ahead, to get ahead— The rushing river echoed it back to him now, get ahead, get ahead.

He crawled from his blankets in a shivery dawn and made a fire. Breakfast was coffee and a can of peaches.

Packing the mule baffled him. It needed more skill than he'd thought. Whatever hitch he tried, the load still seemed insecure and unbalanced. Then a Mexican boy came upvalley, herding a small band of sheep. Lantry called to him, tossed him a dollar. "What about lending me a hand, kid?"

He was soon on his way again, securely packed. Fording the Vallecito wasn't too hazardous. Above the fork, Pine River was cut to half size but still turbulent. Lantry followed its west bank through a canyon and emerged, after a few miles, in a wide bluestem valley. From piney hills on the river's opposite bank tumbled a small creek. It was certain to be East Creek, shown on Frank Foster's sketch.

Sight of it brought an exultant flush to Lantry. He forded the Pine, the pack mule floundering through deep, swift riffles behind him.

And, yes, here was a trail leading up the little creek along its north bank. Just as shown on the sketch. Lantry followed it eagerly. He was on the last lap now. Treasure lay ahead. He was supremely sure of it. Frank Foster wouldn't have concealed that sketch in his sweatband unless it meant something.

This was a narrow trail, rutless. A mere byway of the wilderness. Perhaps a short cut over the Divide beaten out long ago by Ute moccasins. It led Lantry upward into a forest of primeval pine. Its grade steepened. Horse and mule were soon blowing hard. The trail veered from the creek, but Lantry could still hear the tumbling cataracts to his right.

How far was it now? The sketch didn't say. Wherever this trail crossed the creek, there would be the place.

Snow lay in patches, and the patches became more frequent. A little farther on Lantry stopped in dismay. A drift three feet deep lay athwart his path. He detoured around it, found the trail again. It kept veering to the left, climbing higher and higher. Lantry reined to a halt with a lost feeling. He could no longer hear the creek.

Was this the wrong route, after all? He pressed on and came to another snowbank, longer and higher than the last. Again he circled and again he found bare ground beyond, and the trail.

But he was far from the creek, too far either to see or hear it. Giant conifers, silent and inscrutable, walled him in. Above them the sun shone warmly, and its rays made the snow patches glisten. In every glade the ground was bare.

This trail, Lantry reasoned, would be impassable to a horseman in midwinter. And that fact could easily explain

Frank Foster's overwinter stay in Durango. Having buried his loot in late fall, he would need to wait until late spring to retrieve it. The thought encouraged Lantry, and he pushed on.

After another steep climb the terrain leveled off. The trail began veering to the right. In that direction lay the creek. In a little while Lantry again could hear the hum of its racing water.

Quite suddenly the forest opened into an almost level mountain park. The timber here was tall but not dense. Snow patches were infrequent, and in the bare spots last year's grass grew stirrup-high. And now the creek could be both heard and seen. It rippled gently through the park from pool to pool.

Lantry spurred his mount. He pulled impatiently at his lead rope, dragging the laggard mule on.

Trail and creek converged to a crossing. Lantry fished Frank Foster's sketch from his pocket. Its cross marked a spot on the other side of the stream, exactly in the V between stream and trail.

He splashed his animals through the riffles. Dismounting, he offsaddled the horse and unpacked the mule. His heart was thumping with high hope as he tethered both beasts to a sapling. The ground in the V had about four inches of snow on it. Lantry took his shovel and began scraping it away.

For a sweating hour he labored there. It rewarded him by exposing a black circle of earth and chunks of charred wood. Someone had made a campfire here. Who if not Frank Foster?

Lantry tested with his pick, first here, first there. Here the ground was solid, sewn with roots. There it was rootless and loose!

Cut roots meant the site of an earlier digging. Furiously Jeff Lantry dug there himself. He struck loose stones but no roots. Roots, he reasoned, would have been chopped away by the first digger and not thrown back into the hole. This was the place. The end of the rainbow! Lantry swung lustily with his pick. Roustabouting on a river boat had hardened his muscles. When his pick struck something which was neither earth nor stone nor root, he knew that his gamble had won.

The thing was soft, yielding, spongy. Lantry scraped away dirt and exposed canvas. A tarpaulin or perhaps a bedroll. Would the money be mildewed? Lantry kept at it, scraping, prying. It was a roll of canvas, tightly roped. He dragged it triumphantly from the hole.

When he unrolled the bale of canvas he exposed a yellow oilskin slicker. Thongs of rawhide were wound around it. Lantry slashed through them, and inside the oilskin he found money. Beautiful money. It wasn't mildewed. It was banded in packets of fifty bills each, bank-style. Packet after packet of it, fives, tens, twenties, fifties. This, Lantry thought, could be the entire stake intact. The same caution which had impelled Frank Foster to hide the money here, late last fall, could also have made him afraid to spend it on his flight west.

In bulk it was enough to fill an ordinary suitcase. Lantry didn't stop to count it. He must get out of this altitude before another snow blew up. Quickly he rerolled the money in the oilskin slicker and then bound all inside his own bedroll.

He tossed Frank Foster's mildewed tarp into a pool of the creek. Into another pool went his own pick and shovel. The pack saddle was still on the mule. Lantry balanced his bedroll on it and made the best hitch he could manage. No time to quibble over the right knot.

It was still only noon when he started down the mountain. His animals traveled faster now, sensing a homeward direction. Drifts on the trail no longer worried Lantry for he knew his way around them. He could camp again where he'd camped last night. By sundown tomorrow he'd be back in Durango.

What then? He wouldn't dare take this money to a bank. Even if the serial numbers hadn't been advertised, a deposit of such size would invite inquiry. He must keep the money in his room at the Grand Central. He could buy a stout, brassbound trunk with a lock on it. No one would have reason to break into the trunk.

Gradually, he'd invest the money. Many small investments, he decided, would be safer than a single big one. He'd limit any one investment to ten thousand dollars. A cash deal for two hundred thousand would cause raised eyebrows, but a deal for ten thousand wouldn't.

A deal in what? Cattle? Timber? Mining stock? He still didn't know.

That night Jeff Lantry camped on Pine River and by noon the next day had crossed the Florida. A few more hours should take him to Durango.

He was climbing his last ridge when he saw two horsemen riding toward him. They were bearded men, each belted with a gun. A type common enough in the San Juan Basin. One of them was short and thick-shouldered, with a broad, flat face. The other had a lank build and rode with a rifle held crosswise over his pommel. As they came nearer, Lantry saw one of them speak in a guarded voice to the other. Then they stopped, blocking the trail.

It might be trouble. "Howdy, men," Lantry said genially. He tried to lead his mule past them.

"What time you got, mister?" the lanky man asked.

It gave Lantry no choice but to look at his watch. The watch was solid gold and had cost him a hundred dollars. "Four o'clock," he said.

He saw them exchange glances. The thickset man gave

a slight nod and whipped out a forty-five gun. "I could use that ticker myself, mister. Hand it over."

"And don't start nothin' you can't finish," the lanky man advised. His gaze fastened alertly on Lantry's right hand. Lantry's left was occupied with the lead rope.

A draw would be suicide. The odds were too hopeless. "You're one too many for me," Lantry said, and handed over the watch.

"Thanks." The thickset man leered. "Allers like to know what time it is. I could use yer wallet, too. Just happens we're busted, me and my pard." He kept the forty-five pointed at Lantry's chest.

There wasn't much in the wallet. Lantry had spent most of his funds outfitting for this pack trip. Bitterness boiled inside him, but he held it in leash. He took out the wallet and tossed it to the gunman.

"That's usin' yer head, mister. This here gun goes off mighty easy, sometimes. Now you can climb down and start walkin' to town."

So they were taking his horse and mule, too! It came with a mocking irony to Lantry. They had no idea what was on the mule. Just blankets and a camp kit, they'd think.

The thickset man cocked his gun. "It goes off easy, I said. Don't keep us waitin', mister. Climb down."

Lucky Lantry! The name backfired now. He'd picked up a fortune only to lose it to these cheap highwaymen. Nothing he could do about it. With a grim despair Lantry took his right boot from the stirrup to dismount.

A casual voice from the hillside startled them. "Hi, gents! What's goin' on, a hoss trade?"

Both the outlaws whirled that way. So did Lantry. A black-chapped rider was sitting his mount not thirty yards away, uphill from them in a fringe of cedars. He had a young, smooth face, copper-tinted by the sun, and dark curly hair. His lips and eyes were smiling. There was a gun at his hip, but his hand wasn't near it. He held his reins high.

The thickset man fired from his hip. In the same split second the lanky man whipped his rifle stock to shoulder. The shock of surprise petrified Lantry. He forgot, for the vital moment, that he was armed himself.

At the shot, the black-chapped rider disappeared from his saddle. Lantry thought he was unhorsed by a bullet. He knew better only when he heard two quick shots from the ground. The cowboy was hunkered on his heels, beyond his mount, shooting under its belly.

Lantry remembered his own gun and drew it. There was no use. The stocky outlaw was already slithering from his saddle, arms outflung. The lanky man had pitched forward. He clung desperately to his horse's mane, then slid sidewise to the trail.

The black-chapped cowboy rode his horse downslope to Lantry. "Bad hombres." He grinned. "Hope they didn't skin you up any."

"No," Lantry said. "And thanks. They only took my watch and wallet." He dismounted and recovered them.

"Gifford's my name. Tom Gifford." The cowboy looped a leg over his saddle horn and rolled a cigarette. "From over in the Mancos Valley. You headin' for Durango?"

"That's right. I'm Jeff Lantry."

"*Bueno*. I'm pointin' that way myself. Soon as I rope these gents up, I'll ride along with you."

Stepping gracefully from his saddle, Gifford made a quick job of it. Both outlaws were dead, each with a bullet through the brain. Gifford draped them over their own mounts. "They're Ab Coleman and Chick Webb," he explained. "Knocked over the bank at Telluride not long ago. The sheriff'll stand us a treat for bringin' 'em in, Lantry. Let's ride."

With Lantry leading his calico pack mule, and Gifford leading two corpse-laden horses, they resumed the trail to Durango.

3

FROM A CORNER OF HIS EYE Lantry studied the other man. He was young, not much over twenty-five. His face was strong, a little too angular to be handsome. His hips were slim, his shoulders broad and sloping, and he rode like a part of his horse.

"I'm new around here, Gifford. You say they're a couple of stick-ups named Coleman and Webb?"

Gifford nodded. "Some folks say they used to run with the Blue Mountains gang. Maybe they did and maybe they didn't. Nobody knows for sure just who's in that Blue Mountains outfit."

"The Blue Mountains are just across the line in Utah, aren't they?"

"That's right. Gang of raiders holes up there. If you ever see any of 'em, see 'em first."

"What do they raid? Cattle?"

"Not as a rule. They'll butcher a yearlin' now and then for beef, that's all. Their specialty's holdups."

"Do they come openly into Durango?"

"Nope. They wouldn't dare do that. But they got a spy in Durango. Somebody who passes 'em tips."

"What makes you think so?"

"Because they always seem to savvy where to strike. And when. Say you're a cowman. You sell a bunch of heifers for cash. As you ride home with the money, you get held up. Or say you're a gambler. You make a cleanin' at faro some night. Right away the Blue Mountains boys know all about it. How could they know unless they keep a lookout in Durango?"

"You have no notion who this spy is?"

"Not the foggiest," Gifford said.

"You say you're from the Mancos Valley? Where's that?"

"About sixty mile west o' Durango," Gifford said. "I was over this way looking at some cows."

"You have a ranch of your own?"

Gifford's grin made him look boyish. "Call it that if you want. It's just a creek-bottom homestead with a cabin and corral on it. All it needs now is about three hun'erd good heifers."

"You couldn't run that many on a quarter section, could you?"

"Nope. But you could run 'em on the open range, near by. Million acres of it over that way, with the best grass in the Basin."

Lantry drew him out. In the next mile or so he learned a few basic facts about cattle ranching. A quarter-section homestead wouldn't support more than twenty cows. But by using the homestead merely as a headquarters to ride herd and brand from, and depending mainly on free government grass beyond your own lines, you could run as many head as you had time and help to look after.

"Trouble is I'm fresh outa cash," Gifford said frankly.

"How much would three hundred cows cost?"

"That many cows and about six good bulls'd cost around ten thousand dollars."

"Can't you buy them on credit?"

"Maybe. But I don't like the idea o' goin' in debt. That's why I rode over this way to look at Dave Garlow's stuff on the Florida. Dave offered to let me have three hundred head on shares."

"Shares? What kind of a deal would that be?"

"Dave offered to let me take the cows over to my range and keep 'em there for a year. For takin' care of 'em, I'd get half the calf crop. At the end of the year he'd get all his cows back and half the calves. But after lookin' at his stuff, I turned the deal down."

"Why?"

"It's Mexico stuff. Southerns, I mean. Runs mostly to horns and legs. I'm lookin' for a share deal like that, Lantry, but it'd have to be good native stuff."

Lantry was thoughtful all the rest of the way to Durango. He himself had cash to invest. And here was a way to get into the cattle business without owning an acre of land. He could let men like Tom Gifford run cattle for him. No doubt there were lots of Tom Giffords in the San Juan Basin. Men with savvy and energy, each with a cabin and a corral on a quarter section.

"How much of an annual calf crop," Lantry inquired, "could a man figure on?"

"Around sixty-five percent," Gifford estimated. "Three hundred cows oughta drop about two hundred calves in a year. The share man'd get a hundred of 'em, worth fifteen bucks a head at weanin'. Fifteen hundred a year's more'n he could make punchin' for some big ranch."

"But wouldn't he have to hire help?"

"Not with just three hundred head to look after. With a penny-ante herd like that, he could do all the work himself. At the same time he'd be improvin' his own homestead and addin' to it."

Shadows were long when they rode into Durango. Four horses and a pinto mule made a grotesque file as Tom Gifford and Jeff Lantry guided them down saloon row. The boardwalks were swarming with the usual evening crowds. Men stared, nudged each other, pointed. Lantry caught a phrase or two.

"Looks like Ab Coleman and Chick Webb."

"Sure does. Deader'n buzzard bait, both of 'em. I allers figgered they'd wind up like that."

"They'd orter known better'n to monkey with Tom Gifford."

"Who's that with Tom? Some U.S. marshal, I betcha."

A lady, shopping on the nice side of the street, hurriedly dragged her child out of sight. A freighter yelled from his wagon seat, "Hi, Tom. Looks like you been wolf huntin'."

Lantry reined in at the Grand Central. "If you don't mind, Gifford, I'll take my duffel up to my room. Join you later at the sheriff's office."

Gifford nodded. He continued on down the dusty street, leading the two death-laden horses. Lantry dismounted on the walk and unpacked his mule. A boy came from the lobby and offered to help him with the bulky bedroll.

"I can handle it," Lantry said. "You take this horse and mule to the livery barn." He heaved the bedroll to his shoulder and went up to his room with it. He didn't relax until it was locked in a closet there.

He met his own eyes in the mirror, grimaced at the haggardness of his face. A close call, that one. The grimace softened to a smile. It looked like he just couldn't lose. He could thank Tom Gifford for it. But for Gifford he'd've been picked clean.

He brought a quart of brandy from his valise and poured himself a drink. He needed it. Then he washed, shaved, changed his shirt, locked his room door, and went out. In the lobby they told him the sheriff's office was four blocks south down Main, at the corner of E Street.

On the way there Lantry stopped at a supply store. After selecting a small, brassbound trunk with a stout lock on it, he ordered it delivered to his hotel.

When he arrived at the sheriff's office he found that Gifford had already made a complete report. The sheriff shook hands with Lantry. He was a tired, sallow man, oldish, with low-hanging jowls and a discouraged mustache. "Looks like you fellers done a right good job," he said. "A job I fell down on myself. Been ridin' the skin off my saddle tryin' to ketch up with them hombres, ever since they pulled that stage job on Otto Mear's toll road. Tom, you can have my badge any time you want it."

Tom grinned. "No, thanks. I'll stick to ranchin'."

The sheriff turned back to Lantry. "Here's Tom's statement all wrote out. Just fer the record, you better sign it yourself."

Gifford's statement was overly modest. It shared the credit evenly with Lantry. . . . . *had already taken Mr. Lantry's watch and wallet when I came along. That made the odds even, so we shot it out with them.*

Lantry saw no point in amending it. He signed his name under Tom's.

Tom flipped away his cigarette and stood up. He mopped trail grime from his face and ran a hand through his thatch of curly black hair. "My mamma wouldn't know me." He grinned. "Reckon my next stop'd better be the barbershop."

As he started out, Lantry called him back. "If you're not busy tonight, Gifford, drop in at the Grand Central about eight o'clock. I've got something on my mind."

The cowboy eyed him curiously, then nodded. "Sure, Lantry. I'll be there."

When he was gone Lantry turned thoughtfully to the sheriff. "Do you know anything about the cattle business?"

"That's about all I *do* know," the officer said. "Why?"

"This man Gifford's looking for a small herd of cows to run on shares. Say three hundred head. Suppose I buy that many and turn them over to him. For handling them a year he gets half the calf crop. Would it be a sound investment for me?"

The sheriff didn't hesitate. "It sure would, mister. You could trust Tom with your shirt. He's a top hand with stock. Uster punch fer the Jess Jallison outfit. Now he's got a right nice little claim of his own on the Mancos."

"What about the loss to rustlers? You've got 'em in this country, I take it?"

"Plenty. But a smart rustler wouldn't fool with Tom Gifford's stuff. He throws too mean a gun."

"Is that all that would keep rustlers away?"

The law officer rubbed his jaw and took a minute to think it over. "No," he offered finally. "There's another angle. Rustlers do most of their raiding on the big brands. Like Major Talcott's, on the Dolores. Or the Jess Jallison outfit in Mancos Valley. Or Buck Shaw's Dove Creek spread. Or Sax Consadine's on Cherry Creek. Those four outfits run about ten thousand head each, scattered all over the Basin. They run so many cows they can't keep a close tally. They never see their stuff 'cept at spring and fall roundups. So if a rustler wide-loops one of their calves, it ain't missed."

"I see. So a man like Tom Gifford, with only three hundred head to look after, could keep a closer tab."

"That's right. He'd know every cow by sight. He could keep a little bunch like that within two-three miles of his cabin. Count 'em twice a week, if he wanted to."

Lantry thanked him and went out, stopping in at the first bar for a bracer. It was one of the bigger saloons with gaming and dance rooms connecting. Roughshod men lined the bar, some of them paired with gaudy women. A tall, slender siren wearing polished gold nuggets for earrings hooked an arm in Lantry's. "It is for you I have been waiting, Handsome. While you buy me a small wine, you may tell me about your fight with the *bandittos*."

Usually Lantry brushed off women like this. Before he could brush off this one she said to the bartender, "Didn't you hear Mr. Lantry's order, Pablo? A red whisky for him and a white wine for me."

So they already knew his name! From certain glances of

respect cast his way, and from the general undertone of the bar talk, he realized that the story of the gun fight had spread all over town. And that Tom Gifford's modest version of it had cast him, Lantry, in something of a heroic light. They were under the impression that he'd helped Gifford shoot it out with desperadoes. All of which, by the code of Durango, made him a man among men.

Pablo set out the drinks. "At your service, Señor Lantry."

The girl picked up her glass, smiled at him. "I am Ruby," she said. "Ruby Costello. I hope you like me?"

Some unusual quality in her voice made him look at her. Slightly to his surprise she wasn't as overdressed and over-painted as fancy girls usually were. In fact she was rather stately and stunning. Ruby, she called herself. And her hair was like that, ruby-red. It showered in a mass of fire about her white throat. Her beauty was hard, ruthless, but in no way common or cheap. Meeting her anywhere else Lantry would have tipped his hat. "Why," he asked curiously, "did you come to Durango?"

Her eyes met his with a frank challenge. "For the same reason you did, Mr. Lantry. To get ahead."

"How can you get ahead in a joint like this?"

"Some day I will own it. It will not be a joint then." The calm confidence of her response amazed him. "It will sparkle with brilliance," she said. "I will change its brass to silver and make it the show place of Durango. Many men like you will come here, Mr. Lantry, and bring me the fortunes they make in the Basin."

Had the wine gone to her head? Then he looked at her again and saw something of himself—a reflection, it seemed, of his own ambition and purpose. Get ahead, get ahead— It was the theme song of *her* life, too.

Her tone changed to banter. "I see you do not approve of me, Mr. Lantry. You believe in the double standard. You think only men may be bold."

Lantry gulped his drink and set the glass down. "I think only men can get away with it," he said. "So long." He turned brusquely from her and left the bar.

Ruby's teasing laugh followed him. "Come back and see me, Mr. Lantry."

At the door he collided with a bushy-browed cattleman coming in. The man clapped him heartily on the shoulder. "You Jeff Lantry? I'm Buck Shaw of Dove Creek. Just saw Tom Gifford at the barbershop. You fellahs sure did a good job. It's the only way to stop jaspers like that. Throw a few slugs through 'em."

"Thanks," Lantry said.

It was the same when he crossed to the Chuck Wagon Café for supper. The girl at the cigar counter gave him a look of adulation. The café man stepped up with alacrity, affording him the welcome of a celebrity.

"Good evenin', suh." This time the voice was Major Carey Talcott's. He was seated with a younger man who looked strangely like him. "Won't you join us, suh? Meet my son, Bruce."

Lantry sat down with them. They'd heard all about his exploit with Tom Gifford. Lantry didn't disillusion them. Not that he was out for unearned plaudits. At the same time he couldn't forget a fortune in loot hidden in his room. During the next year he'd have to ride about the range investing that money, a little here, a little there. So a reputation for being able to protect it wouldn't come amiss.

The major inquired, "Have you decided what line you're going into?"

"Cattle, in a small way," Lantry said. "I may stake Tom Gifford to a few cows and let him run them on shares. Is it a good idea, Major?"

"Excellent," the elder Talcott answered promptly. "A dependable young man, Tom is. You agree, Bruce?"

"I sure do," Bruce Talcott echoed warmly. "When Tom quit the Jallison outfit, we offered him a job on the Bridle-bit. But he said he'd rather go it alone."

The Talcotts, Lantry noted, differed only in age and dress. Each had wavy hair of a reddish tinge, the same lean, fine-featured face, with lazy gray eyes under a high forehead. Each had the same courteous speech and slim, six-foot build. But while the son was rigged out like any other hard-riding cowboy, the father wore a long black coat, and the hat on a rack near him was the headgear of an army trooper.

"You won't lose on Tom Gifford," the major repeated.

It was enough for Lantry. He went back to his hotel with his mind made up. Ten thousand in twenty-dollar bills, passed in a cattle buy, wouldn't be too conspicuous. Perhaps by making a chain of similar deals he could gradually put the entire loot into circulation.

Lantry found the brassbound trunk in the hall outside his room. He moved it in, locked the door, took the bedroll from his closet, and unrolled it. He spread the oilskin slicker on his bed.

Packet by packet he counted the money. It lacked only a little of two hundred thousand. The feel of it thrilled Lantry. The wheel of fortune, after a single dizzy whirl, had stopped at his own number.

He locked the money in the trunk, locked the trunk in his closet, went out, and locked his room door.

Down in the lobby he found Tom Gifford waiting.

"I'm offering you a contract, Gifford. If you like it, we can sign it right away."

Tom rolled a cigarette, licked it, looked up quizzically. He was clean-shaven now, his curly dark hair neatly trimmed and brushed. Not as tall as Bruce Talcott, Lantry noted, and a bit rougher-hewn. It was easy to see he'd led a less sheltered life than young Talcott. He looked like a boy who'd swum upstream from childhood, taking whatever hard knocks might come. Lantry himself had traveled that road. It gave him a sense of kinship with this leathery young rangeman.

"I'll register a brand in my name," Lantry offered. "You find three hundred young cows that suit you and put that brand on them, I furnishing the money. You handle the cows for one year. You then return them to me, plus half the calves, at the Durango stock pens. You retain as your own the other half of the increase."

Tom Gifford jumped at it. "I know right where to get the stock," he said eagerly. "Some fancy, two-comin'-three-year-old heifers down at Farmington. You'll throw in six good bulls?"

"Yes."

"You've made yourself a deal." Tom's rope-scarred hand shot out and gripped Lantry's heartily.

They moved to a lobby table, and Lantry made out an agreement in duplicate. The desk clerk was called over to witness the signatures. Lantry kept one copy and Gifford the other.

"You're in the cow business now." Tom grinned.

To celebrate it, Lantry took him to the nearest bar. The man from Mancos ordered only a plain soda, explaining, "Liquor spoils a guy's aim, Lantry. For all we know, might be some friends of Coleman and Webb in town."

The bartender laughed derisively. "Don't let him kid you, Mr. Lantry. He's like that allatime. Won't even take it fer snake bite, Tom won't."

Something else was on Lantry's mind. "Look, Gifford. What if I make the same contract with some other homesteader? Would it cause any complications?"

"It sure would," Tom said, "unless you took out a second brand."

"Can I do that?"

"Yeh, you can register as many brands as you want provided you pay a one-dollar registration fee for each one."

Lantry nodded thoughtfully. "I see your point. If I furnish Jones a herd of cows with a certain brand, I don't dare furnish Brown a herd with that same brand. Both herds would be my property. But if they mixed on the same range no one could tell how many calves were due Jones and how many were due Brown."

"In a nutshell," Tom said.

"Very well. So if I make several of these share deals, I'll take out a separate brand for each one."

Lantry left him and went back to the Grand Central lobby. Discarded on a chair there lay a recent issue of the *Daily Record*. Recalling that the editress had interviewed him, Lantry looked through it to see what kind of an impression he'd made. He found the item. It was brief but quite complimentary, stating that Mr. Jefferson Lantry was out looking over the Basin's resources with an eye toward investments.

Turning a page he saw a bold-faced editorial with the heading:

WANTED IN DURANGO.

The text below, penned in Mrs. Romney's stilted journalese, brought a smile to Lantry. He remembered her promise to send out a call to unmarried women of the East and Middle West. Lantry skimmed through it, reading only snatches.

WE WANT GIRLS. Girls for sweethearts, girls for wives, so that when we get an arm shot off, or get kicked by a mule, or thrown from a bucking bronc, we may hear a gentle voice and see the glitter of a crystal tear. Girls who'll go to a dance on Saturday night. Girls who'll go to church on Sunday—and take a buggy ride afterward. Girls who'll build Durango and boom the sale of homes and lots. Girls who aren't afraid to work, who'll wait on table until the right man comes along. We want fat and funny girls, lean and fragile girls, petite blondes, and stately brunettes so beautiful in the twilight. Silver and gold are ours, grass and timber and the richest ore on earth. But without true women we're still a wilderness. With them, wilderness were paradise enow.

Hear ye, Girls of AMERICA, come to DURANGO.

It amused but failed to impress Lantry.

Nothing would come of it, he was sure. Even if young women east of the Rockies should read the article, it wasn't likely that any of them would be stupid enough, or bold enough, to take the advice. This was a man's country. As far as Lantry was concerned, they could leave the women out of it.

4

MAY AND JUNE WERE BUSY MONTHS for Lantry. For a starter he registered three cattle brands—JL; Half Diamond Slash; and Flying N. Three hundred young cows hand-picked by Tom Gifford were branded JL. Gifford took them to his little ranch on the Mancos.

Lantry looked the field over cannily before making his next contract. In the end he made it with a solid, middle-aged homesteader named Luke Carmody. Carmody was from Kansas and had a spade beard. He also had a wife and two teen-age boys. His claim was up Lightner Creek, only a dozen miles from Durango. The man was highly recommended by the local bank. Lantry furnished him three hundred cows branded Half Diamond Slash, under an agreement similar to Tom Gifford's.

His third applicant was Gerry Ashton, a cowboy who'd filed on Disappointment Creek some thirty miles north of Major Talcott's ranch. Lantry rather liked Ashton's looks and learned that he'd once punched cattle with Tom Gifford. Ashton's homestead was remote, and Lantry had never seen it. While he was debating the matter dubiously, Jess Jallison came to the hotel to see him.

"Hear yuh staked Tom Gifford and Luke Carmody to some cows," Jallison said. He was an enormous man, neckless, with the shoulders of a bullock and a booming voice. His Circle K spread, out in the Mancos Valley, was the biggest in the Basin.

"That's right," Lantry admitted. "Share deals. Why shouldn't I?"

Jallison took out a cigar, bit the end off it, and struck a match on his *chaparejos*. Suddenly he bellowed, "Tom and Luke are all right, I reckon. But I wouldn't go into it wholesale, if I was you, Lantry."

"No? Why?"

"Because if you'd stake every Tom, Dick, and Harry like that, you'd soon overstock the range. Every shoestring settler in the brush'd come lopin' in, soon as they heard you was settin' people up in the cow business. I was talkin' it over with Buck Shaw and he—"

"Suppose you and Buck Shaw run your business," Lantry cut in coldly, "and let me run mine." He'd half expected something like this. Some of the bigger stockmen, he'd been warned, would be hostile to a scheme of chain ranching.

Jallison glowered. "You mean you aim to do it? Wholesale? You'd scatter a mess o' shoestringers all over my range, crowdin' my stuff off it, butcherin' my beef, gormin' up my roundups!"

"I'll do what suits me," Lantry retorted, "without any advice from you."

Jallison's eyes contracted. He spoke quietly. People said that when Jess Jallison talked loud he was harmless, but that when he spoke low he was deadly. "Have it your own way, Lantry. But the first time one of these peanut brands of yours wide-loops a slick-ear o' mine, I'll hold you to account." Abruptly he turned and went clanking out to his horse.

It angered Lantry. A stubborn streak made him jump instantly to a decision. Just to prove he couldn't be bullied by Jallison, he'd look up Gerry Ashton at once and make that third contract.

Ashton was in town. Lantry called him to the hotel and signed an agreement. Three hundred cows branded Flying N went to Ashton's remote claim on Disappointment Creek.

Succeeding days proved Jallison right on one score. A dozen other young rangemen, some of them quite irresponsible, heard that Lantry was setting people up in the cattle business on shares. They came loping into Durango to make application themselves.

But Lantry turned them down. He'd proved his defiance to Jallison. And now he'd better go slow. If he put out too much cash in one season, people might wonder where it came from.

"I've invested every dime in my poke, boys," Lantry told the applicants.

Up in his room the brassbound trunk still held nearly one hundred and seventy thousand dollars. Stored with this were three contracts, one with Gifford, one with Carmody, one with Ashton.

The money worried him, made him reluctant to leave town for any lengthy inspection. He couldn't risk anyone prowling his room.

Best to mark time for a while, Lantry decided. He'd already put out thirty thousand dollars, scattered among three cattle sellers. There might or might not be a record of the serial numbers. Lantry spent a nervous season, waiting, alert for a challenge. But every passing week made his coup seem more secure.

Durango, with its smells of dust and sweat and liquor, roared about him. Day by day it expanded, hammers clacking and saws screeching, tents overflowing the vacant lots. Animas City, a short way up the river, became a ghost town as the last of its shacks were torn down to be re-erected in Durango.

But in the raw night life of the town Jeff Lantry took no part. The Soiled Doves of Durango—a term used editorially by Mrs. Romney whenever she referred to the women of saloon row—made no time with him. Neither did the gamblers. Lantry had learned about house games, faro, chuck-a-luck, and roulette, on boats along the Mississippi River. So in Durango he gave them a wide berth. Sucker traps, he considered them. Once a week he sat in at poker with sober businessmen on the right side of the street. Usually he won, but not conspicuously. Respect and dignity were things he wanted almost as much as fortune. No reason, if he watched his step, that he couldn't have all three.

To Lantry's surprise, the *Daily Record's* call to young women of the East began bearing fruit. The stages from Alamosa began bringing them in. They came shyly to the hotels, generally in pairs, primly correct in their bonnets and long-flounced skirts, and immediately inquired where they might find respectable employment. Most of them found it as restaurant waitresses. But not for long. Men were fifty to one woman in the Basin. The bell of the new Episcopal church on Second Avenue rang, now, with an increasing frequency. Trim frame homes, family-style, began to appear on Third Avenue. "The Boulevard," Durango called it proudly. In a July issue Mrs. Romney wrote an article triumphantly entitled *The Matrimonial Boom*.

All of which amused but failed to interest Jeff Lantry. What *did* interest him was a new service now being offered by the First National Bank. The bank had installed private safety-deposit boxes for rent to customers.

Lantry was prompt to rent the most commodious box offered. A few packages at a time, he carried his cash two blocks down Main and crammed it in his bank box. He was safe, now. Even the bank wouldn't know it was there.

And safe, most of all, from the notorious though almost legendary Blue Mountains gang. Twice during early summer a homing rancher, after a successful play at the Durango gambling-palaces, had been held up on the trail. Lantry couldn't forget what Tom Gifford had told him. That no one knew who composed the gang. That they struck swiftly and surely, with an amazing foreknowledge that the victim carried a fat wallet, and then faded toward dim blue peaks just beyond the Utah line. They could only do it, Tom had said, by having a spy in Durango. A lookout who could tip them to juicy prospects. What, Lantry often thought grimly, if they'd known of the fortune in his room?

His bay saddle horse and calico mule were still at the livery stable. "See if you can find me a guide," Lantry said to the liveryman. "I want to take a little *pasear* around the Basin."

"They's a half-breed Piute hangin' 'round here. Name's Charlie Sheep. He can pack a mule and cook victuals. And he knows every game trail in the county."

"Tell him to be ready in the morning."

At the next dawn Lantry headed west toward Mancos. Charlie Sheep led the way on a mount of his own, a raw buckskin branded Y7. The pack mule carried supplies for a week.

"You stop first Lightner Crik?" Charlie asked.

"That's right. Luke Carmody's place. He's running one of my brands, and I want to look it over."

The guide turned to the right up a small stream fringed by cedars. However, it wasn't as a guide that Lantry mainly needed him. By an occasional inquiry he could have found his way even to Ashton's remote claim on Disappointment Creek. But it was a nuisance to make camp and fumble for the right hitch on a pack animal. Let Charlie Sheep do it. Moreover, it seemed to Lantry he'd present a better front if he traveled with a servant. He'd be more in character as a tycoon of the range.

Also there was the angle of defense. Today Lantry didn't have any important money on him, but the Blue Mountains gang might think he had. Their spy at Durango might tip them off that Lantry sometimes bought cows for cash, in ten-thousand-dollar lots, and they might assume he was on such a buying trip now. So Charlie Sheep could also serve as a bodyguard. Charlie carried a carbine in his saddle scabbard. A stolid, flattish face and a cast eye made the man anything but prepossessing. He wore a battered felt hat with a frayed feather in it. His small coal-black eyes never smiled, and the hilt of a knife protruded from his boot.

Lightner Creek widened to an oblong swale, and in this Lantry saw a new log cabin. Near it a teen-age boy was plowing. Dots of red and white on a hillside were grazing cows. The place looked peaceful and industrious. A blocky man with a spade beard emerged from a shed and walked toward them.

"I been expectin' you," Luke Carmody greeted. "Time you was lookin' me over."

At the cabin Lantry met his wife and two sons. The place had three rooms and a fresh, scrubbed look. Neatness gleamed from every pot and pan. Here was a family who knew nothing but work. A glance assured Lantry he'd made a wise choice in Carmody.

"Stuff's all close by," the homesteader said. "Want to check it?"

Checking the little herd didn't take long. The Carmody boys, on ponies, bunched the cows and drove them proudly by the cabin. There were three hundred of them, and six bulls, all branded Half Diamond Slash. The earmarks were underslope right and swallowfork left. They were Lantry's chattel, all of them, and the inspection brought him an odd sense of pride and elation. Half their increase would accrue to him, and the other half to Carmody.

Carmody's wife served a lunch of side meat and cornbread. "We have to push on," Lantry said. "Want to make Tom Gifford's before dark."

Carmody showed them a short cut through the hills, and it took them to the main trail at Hesperus by midafternoon. Here they forded the La Plata River and continued northwest toward Mancos.

Over a piney ridge then, and down into Cherry Creek. The country beyond opened into a vast, circular valley, lush and green. On the far rim of it Lantry saw the roofs of an imposing ranch.

"That Jallison place," Tom Sheep grunted. "Him got plenty cattle."

"I don't think he likes me." Lantry grimaced.

Their route missed the Jallison ranch and took them across the Mancos to Tom Gifford's. Cottonwoods obscured Tom's cabin until they were within a stone's throw. It was compact and homey, with log walls and gable. The ring of an anvil hammer guided them to a shed where Tom was shoeing a horse.

"The boss himself!" Tom welcomed. "About time you were showing up."

"Any grief yet?" Lantry asked.

"Nary a carcass. In the morning we'll take a tally."

Tom walked to the cabin with them. On the way he proudly pointed out twenty acres of oats enclosed by a pole fence. "Winter feed," he said.

Twilight was too far advanced for any further inspection. Tom made supper while Charlie Sheep put up the stock.

"Heard you made another deal like this with my old side-kick, Gerry Ashton. Haven't seen much of Gerry since we punched cows for Jess Jallison."

"Is Jallison a good neighbor?"

"He treats me all right."

"How many cows does he run?"

"Too many. They drift clear down into New Mex and off east to Utah. And sometimes they don't come home."

"Rustlers?"

Tom nodded. "By the way, did you hear what that son-of-a-gun Gerry Ashton did? He went and got himself married."

"Why shouldn't he?"

"No reason at all. Except that claim of his on Disappointment Creek's a helluva lonesome place to take a woman. Especially one like he picked."

"What kind did he pick?"

Tom chuckled. "Did you hear about those tenderfoot females comin' in from the East? Seems they read about a girl shortage out here. Well, one of 'em tossed a loop around Gerry Ashton. He can't say I didn't warn him. I told him to stay out of Durango."

To Lantry the news seemed mildly favorable. While a wife was the last thing he wanted for himself, he was aware that they usually caused a man to settle down. He'd just seen an example of it, over at Luke Carmody's.

"She'll sure get the shivers next winter," Tom predicted, "when she hears the wolves howlin' up there. That valley's a sweet range for cattle, but it's no place for a woman that's not farm-bred."

"Why," Lantry asked, "do they call it Disappointment Creek?"

"Because you'd expect to find more water there, in a valley that long, heading out of high mountains. There's enough for stock and a small ditch, but no big river like the Dolores or the Mancos."

Early in the morning Lantry tallied the three hundred JL cows in Gifford's charge. They were all present in good flesh. With Charlie Sheep he rode on, bearing north toward the remote homestead of Gerald Ashton.

5

WHAT HE'D SEEN SO FAR WAS REASSURING. It was better than operating a big ranch of his own. A ranch would mean overhead, equipment, payrolls, buildings, and taxes. It would mean grueling work and long rides through the blizzards of winter. This way he avoided all that. Let the other fellow do the work. By putting cows out on shares, Lantry himself need own no land, build no cabins, plant no winter feed, hire no men. His profit, half the increase, could be shipped directly to market.

He had funds for seventeen more share deals like the three already made. Eventually he'd make them. A normal calf crop, they told him, was sixty to seventy percent. Which meant that his own share from a full investment would be about two thousand calves a year. And weaning calves, they said, brought fifteen dollars per head.

Daydreaming pleasantly, Lantry rode on behind the calico mule which plodded at the end of Charlie Sheep's lead rope. Topping a rise they dropped down into the valley of the Dolores River. Lantry heard the plash of its current, through the pines, long before he saw it. The village of Dolores sprawled at its big bend, on the southerly bank, and soon Lantry could see its adobe walls showing drably through the trees. There was a single street with three saloons, a post-office-store, and a few flat-roofed mud houses with hollyhocks at the gates. This place, unlike Durango, had been a settlement of the early Spaniards.

A pounding of hoofs and a cloud of dust made Lantry aware of riders loping into town from the opposite direction. He saw three cowboys whirl up and dismount at the main saloon. One of them was crossbelted, a gun butt glinting at either thigh.

Quite abruptly Charlie Sheep dropped the pack mule's lead rope. He wheeled his buckskin and spurred it into timber to the left of the trail. Lantry heard him crashing off through the creek-bottom brush.

Why? Was he afraid of that crew of riders? Lantry waited for minutes. The half-breed didn't come back.

Puzzled, Lantry picked up the lead rope. He rode on into Dolores leading the mule. Three saddled horses stood hipshot at the rack. Lantry noted the brand on them. Y7. The same brand was on Charlie Sheep's buckskin.

An inkling of the truth came to Lantry. He went into a bar and found the three riders there. They were gaunt, sun-blackened men. The one with crossed gun belts nodded.

Lantry ordered beer and said, "Howdy. Care to join me?"

"Don't mind if we do."

The bartender, a bushy-haired Mexican, set out four beers.

"How far to Major Talcott's place?" Lantry asked. His plan was to stop there on the way to Gerry Ashton's.

The man with the two guns said, "Ride up the river ten mile to the fork. Then take the west fork five mile more."

"Do you ride for the major?"

"Nope. We're Buck Shaw's men from over Dove Creek way."

Lantry recalled Shaw as one of the Basin's four big cattlemen mentioned by the sheriff.

The man with two guns asked, "You just ride in from Mancos, mister?"

"That's right. I'm from Durango and I came by Mancos Valley."

"Didn't happen to see a buckskin gelding with Y7 on the left hip, didja?"

It gave Lantry the answer to Charlie Sheep's sudden flight. They were obviously out looking for a horse thief. Men of this stripe, he'd been told, made short shift with horse thieves. In this case the thief was his own guide, Charlie Sheep. Should he tell them?

If he did, they'd chase Charlie and string him to a tree.

Lantry shook his head. "No. Didn't pass any horse like that on the trail. Have another one?"

"Thanks, but we gotta be ridin'. *Hasta la vista,* mister."

Their spurred boots clanked out. Lantry heard them gallop off down the Dolores.

He found a cantina next door where they served him soup and tortillas. As Lantry finished eating he saw Charlie Sheep peering in. Out on the walk he found the Indian waiting with his saddle slung over his shoulder.

"What did you do with the buckskin?"

Charlie shrugged. His small black eyes avoided Lantry's. "Me no like him. Turn him loose in the woods."

Lantry smiled grimly. The buckskin would drift back to the Y7 range and eventually be recovered by its owners. It was better that way.

"You know anyone in town here, Charlie?"

Charlie nodded. "Blacksmith, him friend o' mine."

"Okay. Borrow a nag from him for a few days. I'll buy you a better one at Major Talcott's."

Charlie's eyes lighted gratefully. He went off down the
street. In ten minutes he was back astride a bony, thin-
hocked pony.

From that minute the half-breed's attitude toward Lantry changed. It was more than grateful. It was worship-
ful. He was stupid, but not too stupid to know Lantry had
saved his neck. His reaction became a doglike devotion to
this master who didn't even rebuke him for stealing a
horse.

They rode on up the river trail. This was pine country,
the giant conifers banking steeply toward towering peaks.
Here the river plunged through boxed narrows, there it
broadened into a ribbon of silver threading through a
park. Here it roared; there it whispered. Willows and mul-
berry arched it. Clematis and columbine grew by the trail.

A long way yet, Lantry knew, to Gerry Ashton's place.
He'd worried no little about his judgment in selecting
Ashton. He'd seen the man only twice, and his land not at
all. Lantry knew nothing about him except that he'd once
punched cattle with Tom Gifford. Ashton had offered no
references. Turning over ten thousand dollars' worth of
cows to him, Lantry thought, might prove an unsound
investment.

Up the west fork the country opened. And late afternoon
brought Lantry to the best-appointed ranch he'd ever seen.
There was a lush alfalfa meadow. A brimming ditch circled
it and a wide-verandaed ranch house stood invitingly at
its upper end. Lantry crossed a pasture with fine cattle and
still finer horses. Some of the gentle culture of Tennessee
had been magically transported to this remote Western
ranch.

In a paddock back of the barns Lantry found Major
Talcott and his son, Bruce. Bruce was trying out a skittish
colt, breaking him expertly to the saddle. Other horses in
a near-by corral looked like racing stock. Lantry saw a

track sulky under a shed.

"Bless me if it's not our friend Lantry!" the major exclaimed. He climbed the paddock fence and shook hands warmly. "We were hopin' you'd drop in on us, suh. Come up to the house and I'll mix you a cool one."

Bruce was no less cordial.

Charlie Sheep was sent to a bunkhouse and told to make himself at home. A Mexican boy came up and took charge of the horses.

Minutes later Lantry was sipping from a tall glass on the veranda. "On my way to Disappointment Creek," he explained. "How far is it?"

"Thirty mile north of here, suh. You'll be our guest for the night."

Most of the crew, Lantry learned, were off delivering a drove of beef to an Indian agency in New Mexico. A servant girl came out, pushing a wheel chair. In it was the major's wife, frail, gray-haired, her back permanently injured from a fall. The fall, Lantry later learned, had been from the saddle of a jumper. Running horses, trotting horses, jumping horses—these seemed to be the main interests of the Talcott household.

The major talked nothing but horses. Lantry wondered how they found time for running cattle.

That night he slept in a high, four-poster bed with a mattress of eiderdown.

"You're in the business of selling horses, Major," he said after breakfast, "and it happens I want to buy one."

"We can fix you up, suh. Bruce, show him that string you brought down yesterday from Groundhog Creek."

Bruce showed Lantry a penful of saddle horses. One of them, a long-limbed sorrel with a starred forehead, immediately caught Lantry's eye. He decided to buy it for his own use, and turn his bay over to Charlie Sheep.

"That's the one I want." Lantry pointed.

Bruce Talcott nodded approvingly. He respected a man who could appreciate a good horse. "You picked a winner, Lantry. Trouble is he's only been ridden a few times. Better let me gentle him for you. Then I can deliver him to you in Durango."

"I need him right now," Lantry said. "Want to ride him to the Ashton place. Mind if I try him?"

Bruce roped the sorrel and tossed on a saddle. He stood back a bit dubiously as Lantry mounted.

The sorrel reared and came down twisting. Lantry made two mistakes. He spurred the horse and let the reins slacken. Down went the sorrel's head and up went his withers. Lantry was catapulted to a sprawl on the hard-packed floor of the corral.

Bruce stooped by him anxiously. After a quick examination he announced, "Sorry, Lantry. Looks like you got a broken arm."

A week later, with his arm in a sling, Lantry sat in the lobby of his Durango hotel. The arm was mending fast and he had no regrets. They'd kept him five days at the Talcott ranch, giving him every comfort and attention.

The only thing he'd missed was the inspection trip to Ashton's place on Disappointment Creek. Naturally he'd been unable to make that extra ride with a crippled arm. However he'd sent Charlie Sheep up there with instructions to count the cows.

Charlie had returned, reporting a count of two hundred and ninety-nine, all properly branded Flying N. One cow had died from a rattlesnake bite. A normal loss, they'd told him, and certainly one that couldn't be charged against the vigilance of Ashton.

After a few days of convalescence, Lantry had been furnished with a gentle horse for the ride back to Durango. "I'll bring the big sorrel in to you," Bruce had promised, "the next time I go to town."

Lantry was expecting it any day now.

At the moment he noticed an old man leading a string of burros up Main Street. The man had a small, blizzard-cut face and shaggy white hair. He tied his burros in front of the Grand Central and came limping into the lobby.

He spoke to the desk clerk. The clerk pointed to Lantry.

The old man approached Lantry's chair. "My name's Gus. Gus Irvine. I hear you been cowstakin' homesteaders. Did yuh ever try grubstakin' a prospector?"

Lantry looked up at him, faintly amused. "Are you a prospector?"

"Dern right I am. And some day I'll hit it rich. Here's a chance to git in on it, Mr. Lantry."

"What's your proposition?"

"You stake me to all the grub and dynamite I can load on three burros, and I give you a half interest in any strike I make in the next year."

"What'll you be looking for? Silver or gold?"

"Anything I can find," Gus said.

"Where will you prospect?"

"Up around Silverton, Ouray, Red Mountain, the Uncompahgres. Most anywhere. They's many a fortune in them hills, mister, jesta waitin' fer my pick."

Lantry was about to give a blunt no. Then the eagerness of the old man, burning like fire in his hollow eyes, stopped Lantry. One thing was evident; old Gus was zealous, sincere, confident, and would work hard. He'd pick and peck with an indefatigable energy for the next year, driven by his dream of riches.

Three burroloads of food and explosives wouldn't cost much. Only a few hundred dollars. It was like poking a white chip into a pot which, conceivably, could expand into a bonanza. Idle money lay in Lantry's bank box, crying for investment. Why not take this one small chance?

A self-deprecating smile curved Lantry's lips downward. "I'm a sucker. But everybody gets burned once. Maybe this is my turn. I'll grubstake you, Gus. But never again, so help me!"

"Thankee," Gus said. "And the quicker I load up, the quicker I kin git started."

"For my own protection," Lantry stipulated, "you'll have to sign a statement of the terms. I'll draw it up right now." He moved to a desk and wrote a contract, in ink, which bound Gus Irvine to the arrangement agreed upon. In consideration of three burroloads of supplies, the receipt of which was hereby acknowledged, Gus Irvine ceded to Jefferson D. Lantry a half interest in any mineral strike he might make within a year from the date of this instrument.

A wall calendar told Lantry that today was the thirty-first of July, 1881. He dated the agreement, then signed it. Gus affixed his own signature below. Since it was entirely for Lantry's protection, only one copy was made. "All it needs now," Lantry said, "is a witness."

As he looked around for one, a tall rangeman with wavy auburn hair entered the lobby.

"Hello, Lantry," Bruce Talcott greeted. "How's the arm? I just left that sorrel of yours at the livery barn."

"Thanks," Lantry said. "I won't let him spill me next time. By the way, what about witnessing this grubstake contract I just made?"

"Glad to oblige." Bruce signed the paper as a witness.

Lantry put it in his wallet. Then he gave Gus ten twenty-dollar bills. "That ought to load your burros. If it doesn't, come back for the balance."

"That orter do it, mister." Old Gus limped out to his burros, eager to pack them and be gone.

Lantry dismissed him from his mind. "What brings you to town?" he asked Bruce Talcott.

"The big celebration tomorrow. The whole country's coming in. This'll mean a lot to the Basin, Lantry."

Of course it would, Lantry agreed. The Denver and Rio Grande Railway had just completed its narrow-gauge track into Durango. And tomorrow, August 1, 1881, the first train would come chugging into town.

6

THAT FIRST TRAIN *did* come to Durango, on schedule, and the San Juan Basin boomed.

New settlers came, new stores, new saloons, new blood both good and bad. The hotels overflowed. The honky-tonks roared. Adventure lured, and vice thrived. A legion of restless young men, bitten by the cowboy bee, thronged into Durango.

As the cattle business zoomed toward its heyday Jeff Lantry took out brand after brand. He signed share contract after contract with men like Tom Gifford and Luke Carmody. Three hundred cows to the brand, no more, no less. By the time his entire stake was invested, he'd made twenty share deals with as many men.

His became a name to conjure with in the Basin. "The man of many brands," people called him. He owned no land, no equipment except two saddle horses and a calico mule, paid taxes only on livestock, and had no one on his payroll except a half-breed Piute named Charlie Sheep. His corral was a box at the bank. His ranch house was a room at the Grand Central. Each fall twenty small ranches delivered him half their weaning calves at the Durango stock pens. Lantry promptly shipped them to the Denver market.

The railroad had been running into Durango nearly four years when a train brought Marcella Blair. She alighted on the smoky depot platform and looked distastefully about her. One could see immediately that she was neither a soiled dove nor a hopeful romanticist. She looked Eastern, about twenty years old, and she stood out among the cinder-streaked passengers like a hothouse rose transplanted on a slag heap. Her dress was primly blue of a dark shade, the skirt sweeping decorously to the ground. Her jacket, just the span of a man's two hands at the waist, had a high collar banded in fur, and cupping a face unroughened by wind or sun. To the dozen or more men lounging on the platform her fairness was a thing to look at twice, and then again.

Ignoring them, and holding her skirts clear of the dust, Marcella marched straight into the depot. An agent was checking baggage there.

"Can you tell me," Marcella asked him, "how I can get out to a place called Disappointment Creek?"

He looked up and saw dark eyes which seemed both a little defiant and a little frightened. Also he became aware of shining black hair which escaped in curling tendrils from a velvet bonnet. As he gaped at her, Marcella repeated her question.

"Never heard of it," the agent said. Then on second thought he amended, "Wait a minute, miss. Seems to me it's a little crik that heads up around Lone Cone. Runs into the lower Dolores." He looked at her curiously. "What the heck'd you wanta go way out there for, miss?"

"Is there a stage?" she asked impatiently.

He chuckled. "A stage to Disappointment Crik? That's a good one. What the heck'd a stage wanta run out there for? Ain't hardly anybody lives there."

"Do you know a family named Ashton? The Gerald Ashtons?"

"Never heard of 'em."

"Thank you." She turned away.

"It's a two-day drive, miss," he called after her. "Two days in a buckboard. You'd have to stop over at Mancos the first night."

She went out and found a two-horse hack. "Take me to the best hotel, please."

What she saw as the hack rattled up Main Street didn't improve her impressions of Durango. On the right side of the street she saw shops and restaurants, mostly shabbily framed. On the left side were saloons and brothels. From them came the loud talk of men and the falsetto laughter of women. Marcella looked frigidly straight ahead. Dust lay thick everywhere, on the walks, on the beards of men, on the flanks of ponies standing cock-kneed at the racks. Someone threw an empty bottle into the street and a wheel of the hack crushed it. A disheveled man reeled down the walk with a painted woman clinging to his arm. No cleanliness, no decency anywhere, Marcella thought. Just the coarse, barbaric frontier town she'd expected. From her first sight of it Marcella Blair hated Durango.

"Grand Central Hotel," the hackman yelled.

He opened the door for her and then carried her bags in. Here she found a fairly clean lobby with bare floor and walls. Rocking chairs faced the street windows. In one of them sat a man more presentable than any she'd yet seen. In fact, he seemed rather good-looking and distinguished.

The clerk pushed a registry book toward Marcella. She signed:

Marcella Blair, Lima, Ohio.

The date at the top of the page was June 18, 1885. "I'll just be here one night," she said.

Back of her she heard a boy announce, "Your horse is ready, Mr. Lantry."

The distinguished-looking man got up and went out.

She noticed he was tall, muscular, and youngish, that his boots were polished and his clothes fit well. She saw him mount a big sorrel horse and lope off down the street.

"This way, miss." The clerk led Marcella up steps to a room.

She was down again almost immediately, asking, "Can you direct me to the newspaper office?"

"In the Windom Block," the clerk said. "Two blocks south, on this side of the street."

Marcella had no trouble finding it. A sallow, elderly man with a quill pen back of his ear sat reading proof there. "May I see Mrs. Romney?"

"She left town," the man said, "couple o' years ago."

"Isn't this the *Daily Record?*"

"Used to be. Now it's the *Durango Idea*. Anything we can do for you?"

The man had a kindly, sympathetic face, and it impelled Marcella to confide in him. "I'm trying to trace an older sister. Melissa Blair was her name. She came here four years ago and then dropped out of sight."

"You mean you haven't heard from her?"

"At first we did. She married a rancher named Gerald Ashton and he took her to a place called Disappointment Creek."

"What made you think Mrs. Romney might know about her?"

Marcella hesitated. When she explained, it was with a trace of bitterness. "In the spring of 1881 someone sent us a copy of the *Durango Daily Record*. Mrs. Romney had an article in it about the opportunities for young women out here. It didn't interest me. I was only sixteen at the time. But Melissa was twenty-one. Her engagement to an Ohio boy had just gone on the rocks, and she was feeling a bit high-headed about it. She wanted to get away. I think she wrote a letter or two to Mrs. Romney. Then she told us she was going to Durango."

"Didn't your family protest?"

"There was only my father. He tried to stop her, but it was no use. After Melissa had been gone a month we got a letter from her. It said she was working as a waitress in Durango."

The editor nodded. "Lots of nice girls did that. And later made first-class ranch wives."

"A week or two after that," Marcella said, "we heard again from Melissa. The letter was postmarked Dolores. It said she'd married a Gerald Ashton. They were on the way to his ranch on Disappointment Creek. Lissy hadn't seen it yet, but she said it ran three hundred cows branded Flying N."

"And then?"

"Silence. Not another word from her all these four years."

"Howcome your pa didn't come out here looking for her?"

"His health wouldn't permit. It wasn't long before he passed away. It left me all alone, and I worried a good deal about Melissa. At last I couldn't stand it any longer. I just *had* to know what's happened to her. So here I am."

"How may I help you, young lady?"

"You can tell me if you have a subscriber named Gerald Ashton."

"I don't."

Marcella looked at him desperately. "Then perhaps you can find out if the Ashtons still live on Disappointment Creek."

"That," the old editor said, "ought to be easy enough. Let me see if anyone from out that way is in town."

He went out on the walk and looked both ways along Main Street. A rider came trotting by. The editor hailed him. "Hi there, Mr. Consadine. Have you seen anyone in town from Dolores County?"

Mr. Consadine reined to a stop. As he faced the walk, Marcella had a good look at him through the window. He was a man of medium build, unusually personable, and rigged out like a prosperous cattleman. His saddle had silver trimmings. The man himself wore gauntlets, bat-winged *chaparejos,* and a cream-colored, undented sombrero. He had a pleasant, smooth-shaven face, light, close-cropped hair, and sky-blue eyes. "Haven't noticed anyone from up that way, Mr. Caffrey," he said genially. "Couple of Buck Shaw's men are in, though. There they are, over in front of the Esperanza."

Mr. Consadine rode on. He made rather a gallant figure, Marcella thought. But her main attention was on Mr. Caffrey, the editor. She saw him cross the street and speak to some cowboys at a saloon door.

Marcella waited, her fingers drumming impatiently on the desk. Then the editor came back, and his smile reassured her. "You don't need to fret any longer, miss. Just talked to some Y7 men. The Y7 ranges all through that country. And they say Gerry Ashton still lives on Disappointment Creek. He has a wife and a three-year-old boy."

The announcement both startled and relieved Marcella. Apparently she'd been an aunt for three years without knowing it. She inquired eagerly, "Do they know Mrs. Ashton's first name?"

"Sure. One of 'em says he stopped there to water his horse, not long ago. And he heard Ashton call her Melissa."

"Thank Heaven!" Marcella exclaimed. "I'll get out there as fast as I can." Then the mystery of it brought a furrow to her forehead. "But why didn't she answer my letters? You'd think she'd at least have told me about the baby."

"You putting up at the Grand Central, Miss Blair?"

"Yes."

"I'll inquire around town and see if there's anyone in from the Bridlebit. That's the nearest big ranch to your sister's place. They've got womenfolk there. If there's a Bridlebit rig in town, they could haul you out that far. The next day they'd send you on to the Ashtons'. Only other way'd be to hire a buckboard at the livery barn."

Marcella held out her hand. Perhaps Durango wasn't such a heathenish place after all. "Thank you, Mr. Caffrey. I'm so eager to see Melissa."

It was late evening. On the way back to her hotel Marcella stopped at a restaurant for supper. A man at the next table had his back to her. It was a straight, muscular back with sloping shoulders. The waitress who served him treated him like a customer of distinction. "There you are, Mr. Lantry. Medium rare with French fries. Can I get you anything else?"

Marcella recalled seeing him at the hotel. She'd been favorably impressed, just as she'd been with that rather dashing-looking Mr. Consadine. She hoped Melissa's Gerald Ashton would turn out to be a man of their type. Now she took a postcard from her purse and wrote a note to friends back in Ohio.

Arrived safely. Have located Melissa, and everything's all right. Am going out there tomorrow.

Marcella.

Twilight was deep when she went out on the street again. The post office, she was told, was on a side street just back of the bank. Marcella went there and mailed her card.

Walking back toward her hotel, she was careful to keep on the east side of Main Street. The few respectable women she saw were all keeping to the east walk. To do otherwise would be to lose caste in Durango.

Marcella was almost back to the hotel when a strangely

ominous hush came over the street. The atmosphere seemed suddenly electric. A man in front of Marcella stood on the curb gaping, holding his breath; he seemed to be petrified by something going on along the opposite walk.

Marcella couldn't help turning her head that way. She saw a man with crossed gun belts moving along the walk. He advanced in a half-crouch like a great hairy gorilla, his head thrust belligerently forward, his silhouette looming dark and ugly in the gloom of nightfall. Walking toward him, some thirty yards distant on the same walk, was a tall, erect man wearing a long black coat and a cavalryman's campaign hat.

Just as Marcella saw them, the man with crossed belts drew one of his guns. Two shots rang out. She saw smoke clouding fuzzily in front of each man. She couldn't tell which shot had come first. The man in the long black coat remained erect. Marcella saw a revolver in his hand. He stood there in grim dignity for a moment, then holstered the gun and turned into a saloon.

The other man lay sprawled on the walk. His arms were grotesquely outflung, and he didn't move. Horror froze Marcella. She saw customers emerge from a barroom and lean over him. Marcella heard one of them announce, "A bull's-eye! He's deader'n last year's grass."

The callousness of it, the sheer savagery, paralyzed Marcella. They were like animals, these Western men. Nothing was sacred to them, not even human life. A feeling of nausea swept over her. She felt degraded, just being a witness.

Then she lifted her skirts clear of the defiling dust of Durango and ran, literally ran, to the haven of her hotel.

7

MARCELLA HEARD A KNOCK on her room door just as she was retiring for the night. She put on a wrapper and opened the door. It was the friendly old editor of the local paper.

"You're in luck, Miss Blair," he announced. "I found out there's a buckboard in town from the Bridlebit. I talked to the man. He'll be glad to take you that far."

"My sister's place is near there?"

"It's a piece beyond the Bridlebit. They're right accommodating folks, the Talcotts are. They'll figure some way to get you on to the Ashtons'. The buckboard'll pick you up here at seven in the morning."

"You've been awfully kind," Marcella said. "Please tell the man I'll be ready."

She went to bed, impatient to be gone from Durango. Maybe it would be different out at Melissa's place. Somewhat less depressing than this atmosphere of saloon smells and sudden death. Melissa, she remembered, had always loved beauty. She'd have a flower garden, of course, and bright table covers, and framed prints on her walls. Artistic to her finger tips, Lissy was. Had she kept up her music? Did she have a piano out there? Marcella remembered her sister's sweet soprano voice. A hundred precious memories flooded back to her. Melissa singing lullabies to her as a child. Being five years older, Melissa had been half mother and half sister to Marcella. She remembered the dainty little aprons Melissa used to wear, keeping house for her father. There'd be the same gentle touch, of course, in any home she made.

And yet—why hadn't Lissy answered her letters? Why had she dissolved behind a four-year curtain of silence? Marcella slipped, at last, into troubled sleep.

She was up at six. June sunlight, painting rosy patterns on the window curtains, made the world seem brighter. By seven Marcella had had breakfast, packed her bags, and paid her bill.

The buckboard which drew up in front had a team of matched grays. It was a smart-looking outfit. The driver wore a flapping sombrero, a flannel shirt open at the throat, blue denims tucked into half boots, and a gun-weighted belt. When he came in Marcella saw that he was lean and tall, with reddish hair and lazy gray eyes, and that his face, while not handsome, gave an impression of good breeding.

He took off his sombrero and said in a soft, slow drawl, "You the lady wants to go out my way? I'm Bruce Talcott of the Bridlebit."

"If it won't inconvenience you?"

"No trouble at all. Glad to have company. We won't get any farther than Mancos tonight, of course. But you'll find a good hotel at Mancos."

Where had she seen him before? All at once she knew. She stood up, flushed and startled. He was dressed differently. But it was the same man. Last evening he'd worn an army hat and a long black coat.

"You needn't bother, after all," Marcella said coolly.

He stared in puzzlement. "You mean you don't want to go?"

"Not with *you*, Mr. Talcott. I saw you kill a man last night. You did, didn't you?"

"I *had* to," he explained. "There was no other way to—"

"There's another way for me," Marcella broke in decisively. She turned to the desk clerk. "Will you please send word to the livery stable that I want a rig and a reliable driver? Tell them I'm going to the Ashton ranch on Disappointment Creek and I want to get started immediately."

Bruce Talcott said quietly, "I'm sorry you feel that way. Good morning." He went out to his buckboard and drove away.

An hour later a rig considerably less sturdy than that buckboard rolled west out of Durango, taking the Mancos road. It was a rather rickety spring wagon with more rattle than spring. Its team was a snaky black bronco mismated with a mule. The driver, who called himself "Uncle Jack," was a white-haired old roustabout with tobacco juice staining his mustache.

However, Marcella could see that he was genial and harmless. "Best outfit I could patch up, miss," he explained, "on such short notice. Giddap." He flicked his whip. The snaky black wanted to run, and the mule wanted to plod. It skewed the doubletree and made the trace chains uneven. The wheels bumped over boulders. Marcella was jolted and bounced. "Can't we go a little slower?" she suggested.

"Never git there if we do, lady. It's more'n a hun'erd mile to where you're goin'. Lucky if we make Mancos tonight."

They passed grazing cattle.

"Them there's Luke Carmody's stuff. From up Lightner Crik. Got his start runnin' on shares fer Jeff Lantry, Luke did. That was four year ago. But Luke's on his own now. Got a right nice layout."

The road came to a hill and climbed steeply. Uncle Jack put up his whip and let the team walk.

"Never did believe in runnin' a team uphill, miss. I'm kinder like Major Talcott that way. Believe in treatin' hosses like people."

Marcella caught the name. "Talcott?" she echoed. She couldn't help wanting to know more about the man she'd just rebuffed.

"That's right. Major Talcott of the Bridlebit. Got a big cow-and-hoss ranch up on the west fork o' the Dolores. Gits all riled up, the major does, every time he sees a man mistreatin' a hoss. That's howcome he took a buggy whip to Cass Crawford."

"You mean Cass Crawford mistreated a horse?"

"Sure did. Right in front of the post office at Dolores.

He was beatin' that bronc over the head with a club when the major driv up. The major couldn't stand it. Hosses are like children to him. So he got out and took a buggy whip to Cass."

"What did Cass do?"

"He went to Durango and got drunk. Then he made his brag at every bar in town. He said if the major ever come in, he'd shoot him fulla bullets on sight."

Marcella shivered. "I saw it. Last night. The major came to town and they—"

"Nope," Uncle Jack corrected. "You got it wrong, miss. The major's got a boy named Bruce. They're as alike as two peas, 'cept Bruce is thirty years younger. Bruce figgered the old man was too slow to go gun fightin' with Cass Crawford. So he took on the job hisself. Put on his old man's long black coat and campaign hat, waited fer deep twilight and then walked straight at Cass Crawford. Cass thought he was the major. It looked like a cinch. The major's got a touch o' arthritis in his wrist and can't draw fast. So Cass let fly. And Bruce drilled him clean through the haid."

The team kept plodding up the hill. Marcella stared dully at the cedar sky line, her thoughts mixed and harassed. "I *had* to." That simple explanation from Bruce Talcott kept echoing. But it didn't satisfy her. He *didn't* have to. Surely there were civilized ways of settling these things.

"Why," she demanded, "didn't the Talcotts just have Cass Crawford arrested for making threats?"

Uncle Jack gave her a curious look. He freshened the quid in his cheek. "We ain't got a very big jail, miss. So we have to wait till a man does somethin' more'n talk loud at a bar before we slap him in there."

"But Bruce Talcott didn't *have* to kill him."

"Nope. He could've stayed at home and let Cass kill his

dad. Giddap."

They were at the top of the hill. Uncle Jack cracked his whip and started the team running down the other side. A wheel bounced over a rock, and Marcella almost lost her seat. "Won't hurt 'em none to lope downgrade, lady."

The descent steepened, roughened, the trail hairpinning around bend after bend. Rocks and deep ruts made the speed hazardous.

Uncle Jack yelled, "Take it easy, Blackie." He yanked the brake lever back to check the pace. But the black kept galloping on, skewing the trace chains, his forelegs even with the mule's nose. "Dern!" Uncle Jack exclaimed. "I told that Mex to put on a new brake shoe. Reckon he forgot it. This'n don't hold wuth a cent. Hi there, Blackie, slow up, dern yuh!"

They whirled around another hairpin on two wheels. And there, athwart the trail just ahead, lay a pine tree uprooted by last night's wind. Jack pulled desperately on his left rein to avoid a crash. The next Marcella knew she was pitched into space. She landed in a hillside bush. Every bone in her body, she thought for a moment, was broken.

When she crawled out, dazed, she saw the spring wagon lying on its side at the edge of the trail. Uncle Jack, muttering imprecations, was untracing the team. "Busted felloe," he announced. "Dern that Mex! Wouldn't't've happened if I'd had a good brake shoe. No help short o' Hesperus. That's only four mile from here. I'll ride the bronc, lady, and you kin ride the mule."

The prospect of riding a mule bareback, in her long skirts, appalled Marcella. But there seemed to be no help for it. She recovered her bags from the ditch. "How long," she asked dismally, "will this delay us?"

"No tellin'. We can't ride on three wheels, lady."

The sound of an oncoming team made them look up

the trail. Marcella saw two dappled grays, perfectly matched, hitched to a buckboard. They were trotting down the grade, well under control. Bruce Talcott reined them to a stop beside the wreck.

Again he took off his wide-brimmed sombrero and spoke in his slow, lazy drawl to Marcella. "Looks like you had some bad luck. Well, the offer's still open, Miss Blair."

"This time I accept gratefully," Marcella said. She met his eyes, flushing, and forced herself to add, "I'm sorry I was rude, Mr. Talcott."

"Think nothing of it. We'll send help back from Hesperus, Uncle Jack."

Bruce jumped to the ground and handed Marcella up to the buckboard seat. It was cushioned and comfortable, with a back to lean against. Bruce put her bags in among the ranch supplies he'd driven to town for. Then he climbed to a seat beside her and gathered up the reins. "Hope you're not bruised up any," he said anxiously.

"Oddly I'm not," Marcella assured him.

He drove expertly around the fallen pine and pushed the grays to a smart trot down the trail. Marcella turned to wave sympathetically at Uncle Jack.

Then she settled back comfortably. It was like changing from a freight train to a Pullman. Bruce Talcott's handling of the team fascinated her. The grays responded to the slightest twist of his gauntleted hand.

After a few miles they splashed through a ford at the La Plata River. Beyond lay the village of Hesperus. Bruce stopped to speak with a blacksmith there. After arranging for help to be sent to the stranded livery rig, he watered the grays and drove on.

"Do you know my sister?" Marcella asked. "Mrs. Ashton."

"Sure," Bruce said. "She's a right nice lady. Look, you can get a right good view of Red Mountain from here.

Those are the Uncompahgres up there." He pointed toward towering, snow-capped peaks to the north.

Marcella had an odd feeling he'd changed the subject. It disturbed her a little. She didn't pursue it. If he didn't want to talk about the Ashtons, she certainly wouldn't press him.

And she still wasn't sure about him. He sat on her left, which meant that the gun butt at his right hip almost touched her. That was the gun, she remembered, which had killed a man last night.

He talked mostly about horses. Durango had a race track, she learned. A big meet would be held there on the Fourth of July. "We got two entries," Bruce said chattily. "Trotters. Dad's partial to trotters. He'll drive in one event and I'll drive in the other."

The sun passed its zenith, and still an endless, mesa-fringed range loomed ahead. They climbed another long hill. Aspen grew at its summit, the tiny round leaves quivering. "We'll make Mancos before sundown," Bruce assured her.

They dropped into a broad fertile valley. Red roofs of a distant ranch made Marcella exclaim, "How lovely! What's that purple band around it?"

"Alfalfa," Bruce told her. "That's the Jallison place. We miss it three or four miles."

Just short of Mancos a small bunch of cattle blocked the road. A youngish rider with black curly hair was driving them. Bruce stopped his team, waiting for the trail to clear. "Hello, Tom," he greeted. "Your stuff's looking right good."

The man rode up to exchange salutations. "Tom, this is Miss Blair," Bruce said. "I'm taking her out to some folks of hers. Miss Blair, meet Tom Gifford."

Tom looped a leg around his saddle horn and rolled a cigarette. He had a solid, capable look. He wore a gun,

Marcella noticed, like all the other men around here. Bruce let his team stand there and rest awhile.

"Hear about the big strike, Bruce?" Tom Gifford asked.

"Durango's buzzing about it," Bruce said, "but I didn't pay much attention. Where was it?"

"Up above Ophir. An old rock-pecker named Gus Irvine made it. But he made it too late."

"Howcome?"

"They found him dead on a claim he'd staked out. Been dead a month, the coroner at Rico says. But he'd got the claim filed all right. And they say it's the richest strike since the Sunnyside Extension. Old Gus had tunneled smack into a ledge o' solid gold."

"What killed him?"

"Nothing but hard work and old age, the coroner says. He'd been at it all his life."

"Too bad he didn't live to cash in on it," Bruce said. "Well, we've got to be pushing on. See you at the races, Tom, if not sooner."

Tom Gifford raised his hat, and Marcella smiled a good-by. When the buckboard rolled on she looked back and saw him sitting his horse there. His hat was still off and he waved it to her. There was a certain homespun gallantry about him, she thought. Perhaps she'd meet him again. She found herself comparing him with Bruce Talcott. And with those two other rather interesting men she'd seen. What were their names? Lantry and Consadine. A composite of the four, she thought, might be Gerald Ashton. Maybe Melissa hadn't done so badly after all.

Ahead, just beyond Mancos, reared a rimrocked, cedar-covered mountain shaped like a battleship. "That's the Mesa Verde," Bruce told her. "Cliff dwellers used to live up there."

"Cliff dwellers?"

"An extinct race of Indians," Bruce explained. "They

settled up there about eighteen hundred years ago. Lived in caves under the rimrocks the first seven hundred years. Then they built rock apartments in those caves, with windows and galleries, and stayed on another five hundred years. I've been up there a few times. Guided a party of scientists up once. They got all excited about it. They want the government to make it a national park."

During the last mile into Mancos, Bruce told her more about the ancient cliff dwellers of the Mesa Verde. Evidently he'd absorbed a lot of information about their history and habits. Marcella wondered why.

When she asked him, Bruce said, "It's a sort of hobby of mine." A bit shyly he added, "Fact is I wrote my thesis about it. At the University of Tennessee."

It made Marcella reappraise him. What strange mixture of gunman and horse lover and history scholar had she met up with?

They were rolling into Mancos now. And Mancos, Marcella decided at once, was definitely an improvement over Durango. Great spreading cottonwoods shaded its street. Its gutters were crystal-clear irrigation ditches from the Mancos River. There were a few saloons but they didn't dominate the place. She saw no disreputable women. The hotel was adobe, looked cool and inviting.

Bruce ushered her into its lobby and left her there. "I got friends here I always stay with," he said. "I'll pick you up in the morning."

8

JEFFERSON LANTRY CANTERED HIS BIG SORREL, Mike, down Main Street in Durango. The news of the hour had brought a sardonic smile to his face. It was a smile at his own expense. Everybody was talking about that big gold strike up above Ophir. Gus Irvine's strike. The irony was that an old forgotten contract with Gus was still in Lantry's wallet. Always before he'd been lucky. But not now. "Lucky Lantry" didn't fit him any more.

"We just missed being millionaires, Mike, by the difference between one and four."

The date on the grubstake contract, he remembered, was July 31, 1881. But the agreement was only for one year. Which meant that it had expired on July 31, 1882.

And this was June of 1885.

Why couldn't that old coot have struck his bonanza three years ago?

Well, Lantry thought, a man couldn't have everything. All in all he'd done mighty well for himself in the Basin. Most of his share contracts had panned out profitably. He'd shipped many a carload of calves to the Denver market. He still owned six thousand head of cows, divided equally among twenty small ranches. He had money in the bank, plenty of it. He could do business with checks now. The original illicit stake had long ago passed out of his hands. Best of all, the Basin looked up to him. As a man of affairs he ranked with cattlemen like Buck Shaw, Jess Jallison, Sax Consadine, and Carey Talcott. And those fellows did it the hard way. They had to maintain houses and barns and corrals and irrigation ditches, and dig up big payrolls every month. Lantry prided himself on doing it the *easy* way. He still occupied that same room at the Grand Central. For four years it had been home and office to him, and from it he'd directed his vast network of affairs.

Right now he was looking for Charlie Sheep. He wanted to dispatch Charlie on an errand. Chances were he'd find the Indian at the Esperanza bar. "Ruby's Place," most people called it.

By contrast with its shabby competitors, the Esperanza was a palace. Lantry tied his sorrel at the rack there and went in. The glitter that met him made him smile reminiscently, as it often did. He remembered the first time he'd come in here, four years ago, and the girl with the gold nuggets for earrings. She didn't need to wear plain gold now. She could wear diamonds. She'd boasted she'd own the place some day. And now she did. She'd rebuilt it with a lavish hand; its massive mahogany bar with the silver footrail, its dazzling chandeliers, its handsomely fitted gambling-rooms and the silk and plush of its dance hall—all these had made it the show spot of Durango. There was no other like it, men said, between the Continental Divide and San Francisco.

Ruby wasn't in sight, at the moment. Neither was Charlie Sheep. It was too early for trade in mass, and only a few customers were at the bar. No girls at all, for Ruby never allowed her women in the barroom unless accompanied by male patrons. Lantry put his foot on the silver rail and ordered rye. He listened to the hum of talk. It was all about Gus Irvine's big strike above Ophir.

Charlie Sheep was probably back in the kitchen being fed. Or lolling in one of the small private rooms with a pitcher of beer. Ruby, Lantry knew, always pampered Charlie. She used every bait to make him hang around. It amused rather than irked Lantry. He'd be pretty stupid if he didn't know why Ruby did it. From the first she'd made a dead set for Jeff Lantry. She'd been perfectly frank about it, too. "You won't admit it, Jeff, but we're just alike. You and I. We've got the same drive—get ahead, get ahead. And aside from all that I'm nuts about you."

It failed to frighten Lantry. He was cocksure of his own armor against women. All women, good or bad. In a way he admired Ruby, even if she *had* made her start as a fancy girl. She was Success with a capital S, just as he was, himself. Beyond that he wasn't interested. He patronized this bar because it wasn't shabby and odoriferous, like the others, and here he could be sure of not being pawed by painted women. He'd never gambled a penny here, and he never would.

Nearly every day he needed Charlie Sheep for one errand or another. Ruby knew it, of course, and so by encouraging Charlie to hang around she promoted the frequent entrance of Lantry. Charlie, in time, had come to idolize her just as he idolized Lantry. He'd obey without question the slightest whim of either. He was like a shepherd dog, or a trained cow pony with two masters. Ruby Costello was his law because she was always feeding him. Jeff Lantry was his law because Lantry was an indulgent employer who'd once saved his neck.

Of that dual loyalty on Charlie's part Jeff Lantry was quite aware. No harm, he thought, could come of it.

He looked up now and saw Ruby entering through portieres at the rear. She was stunning, as always. Tall and stately under the fire-colored crown of her hair, she looked more like a fashionable hostess than a vice queen. Her black afternoon gown, just arrived from Paris, had neither ruffle nor ribbon. Ruby Costello didn't need them, any more than she needed to sway her hips or pad the full curves of her breasts. Men were sure to look at her when she made an entrance.

Men at the bar were looking at her now. Ruby waved to them, then passed on straight to Jeff Lantry.

"Have I kept you waiting, man of mine?" she asked facetiously.

He finished his drink. "Is Charlie around?"

She made a face. "So it's Charlie you want! Very well. Come along."

He followed her swishing skirts to a small room at the rear. Charlie Sheep sat at a table there with a steak dinner in front of him. The Indian bounded to his feet as Lantry entered.

"Never mind, Charlie. Go ahead and finish. Then take Mike to the livery barn." Lantry sat down opposite Charlie. "And tomorrow I want you to ride out to Verne Haggart's place on Bear Creek. Ask Haggart if he wants to renew his share deal for another year."

"I tell him." Charlie resumed wolfing his food.

Ruby Costello perched on an arm of Lantry's chair. "Did you hear about the big strike above Ophir?" she asked. Not that she was particularly interested. She just wanted to hold him here as long as possible.

Lantry grinned wryly. From his wallet he produced the old grubstake contract he'd made with Gus Irvine. *"Did* I? This is how near I came to being in on it."

Ruby took the paper from his hand, looked at it curiously. She saw at once, by its date, that the agreement had expired three years ago. Then she noticed the name of a witness signed at the bottom. Bruce Talcott.

The name reminded her of something. A loose string of unfinished business. A shadow crossed her face. It narrowed her eyes, and if Lantry had been alert he might have seen a gleam of cunning. But his attention at the moment was on Charlie Sheep. He had no faint notion of the hundred devious threads intertwined in the brain of Ruby Costello, or of the backstage role she'd been playing, these last four years, in the San Juan Basin.

"It might have made you rich, Jeff," she murmured, speaking more to herself than to Lantry.

"But now it's just a scrap of paper." Lantry laughed. "So I might as well tear it up."

He reached for the paper, but she held it back. Her smile was disarming. "No, Jeff, it's such a joke on you that I want to keep it for a souvenir. To show how you missed the boat. Perhaps I'll have it framed and hang it over the bar."

She slipped the old contract into her bodice and quickly

changed the subject. "Have you seen the new chorus over at the Coliseum, Jeff? I have a box for tonight."

He ignored the hint and stood up. "Now don't forget, Charlie. Verne Haggart. Tell him it's all right with me either way. If he doesn't want to renew for another year, I've got a man lined up to take over his cows."

"Me tell him," Charlie promised.

"So long, Ruby." Lantry left her abruptly and went out.

Ordinarily she would have followed, coaxing him to stay. But now other objectives had intruded to absorb her thoughts. She couldn't quite tie them together—yet. The name Bruce Talcott. And that multimillion-dollar strike of Gus Irvine.

She hurried to her dressing-room and closed the door there. Then she took the paper from her breast and gave it a shrewd study. The date, she decided, need be no obstacle. A single bent line would make a 1 into a 4.

Ruby went to her writing-desk and made that line in ink. It changed the date from July 31, 1881 to July 31, 1884.

This was only June, 1885. So, except for the testimony of a witness, the contract seemed to be still in force. It was only eleven months old, according to the date now on it. Presented in court, it would give Jeff Lantry a valid claim to one half of Gus Irvine's bonanza.

That much was clear to Ruby. Yet defeating it, she knew, would be the testimony of a witness, Bruce Talcott. She could easily foresee Bruce's reaction. "Yes," he would say, "I witnessed that grubstake contract. It was four years ago. I remember it because it was only a day before the first train came to Durango."

Ruby brooded over it through two cigarettes, balancing risks one against another. Eliminate Bruce Talcott, she reasoned, and this grubstake contract was money in the bank.

And Bruce Talcott, she remembered, needed to be eliminated anyway. Harry Listra had spoken to her twice about it. She always thought of him as Harry Listra, although nobody else in the Basin knew him by that name. Naturally no one dreamed that he was the leader and brains of the so-called Blue Mountains gang, and that Ruby Costello was his spy in Durango. Nor that for four years she'd collected a ten-percent commission on all loot accruing from her tips—an income which had enabled her to buy and remodel the Esperanza.

How stupid they were, Ruby often thought, for chasing a will-o'-the-wisp all these years! She knew, of course, that the Blue Mountains gang was really a myth. Actually the hide-out was eighty miles nearer to Durango, in the old cliff-dweller caves of the Mesa Verde. Fooling the sheriffs had been easy enough. A messenger merely took slit mail bags and empty wallets to the Blue Mountains, at intervals, and dropped them alongside canyon trails there. Posses, finding such evidence, had naturally concluded that the outlaws used that rugged and remote Utah wilderness as a mist to disappear in. Ruby and Harry Listra and Alf Fontana often laughed about it.

The only danger, Harry Listra had argued, was Bruce Talcott. And merely because Bruce had a hobby. The hobby of research into the history and lore of the Mesa Verde cliff dwellers. He'd already made several excursions up there, poking around. Get rid of him, Harry said.

And now that particular thread of intrigue wound itself around another one in the mind and plans of Ruby Costello. With Bruce Talcott out of the way, Jeff Lantry would be a rich man. He could cash in on a grubstake contract made with Gus Irvine. And Jeff Lantry would be, *must be,* in the end, her own. That was the single goal of Ruby's life. Never for a breath did she veer from it. Fortune meant nothing to her unless it came linked to Lantry. A mansion in New York, a villa in France, a yacht to sail the seas with —all these she must, and would if she played her cards right, share with Jefferson Lantry.

And Ruby knew Lantry. Murder was beneath him. She was sure of that. He was an alert opportunist, nothing more, nothing less. He wouldn't kill, neither would he conspire with killers and thieves. But he'd take his luck where he found it, any time, any place.

Suppose Bruce Talcott were found dead in the woods tomorrow!

Who would be suspected? The answer, to Ruby, was absurdly clear. Last night, she remembered, Bruce Talcott had killed a man named Cass Crawford. Crawford had friends. Tough friends. Bar rats, most of them, a type more likely to shoot from the dark than from the light. Any one of them might dry-gulch Talcott in retaliation for the killing of Crawford. That, if Talcott were found dead within the next day or two, would certainly be the popular conclusion.

The timing was perfect, Ruby decided. But only if it happened right away. Revenge motives soon cool off.

No one would for a moment suspect Lantry. Lantry was known as a warm friend of the Talcotts. And everyone knew, as Ruby did herself, that Jeff Lantry would never conspire to the murder of either a friend or an enemy.

But certainly he'd pick up a windfall if he found it in the middle of a road. Ruby could hand him back the grub-stake contract, admitting without a blush that she'd changed the date on it. But she'd claim to have changed it only after hearing about Bruce Talcott's death. "Too bad it happened, Jeff. But since it did, why not cash in on it?"

He'd see at once that the contract couldn't be disputed

when presented to authorities at Rico. The signatures were clearly genuine. It would look entirely orthodox and legal.

And he'd play it, Ruby predicted, exactly like a poker player who unexpectedly picks up four aces. Fraud? Yes, but from Lantry's standpoint there'd be no blood on it. He wouldn't be squeamish enough, or stupid enough, Ruby thought, to turn his back on a fortune.

And wouldn't it give her her first real hold on him? Of course it would! It wouldn't be so easy for him to brush her off, after that.

He wouldn't know she was guilty of murder. He'd know only that she shared the secret of his fraud.

But she must work fast. Where was Bruce Talcott right now? He was on the way home in a buckboard. She'd seen him drive out of town, alone, early this morning. It was a two-day drive to the Bridlebit. Which meant he'd lay over tonight in Mancos.

An agent of murder? Charlie Sheep, of course. Charlie was like a puppet; he'd obey any string she pulled. Especially when she told him it would bring riches to Jeff Lantry. Charlie was faithful, loyal, conscienceless, and dumb. He had an errand out that way tomorrow, an errand made to order for Ruby's purpose. And that Indian never missed with his rifle.

She returned to him just as he was finishing the steak supper. Her own conscience didn't bother Ruby. Too many men had been killed in holdups planned from her tips to Harry Listra.

"Look, Charlie. If you rode hard all night could you make the forks of the Dolores by noon tomorrow?"

The half-breed nodded, his mottled eyes worshiping her.

"Okay." Ruby lowered her voice to a low, brittle whisper. "Listen to what I tell you. Then load your rifle and ride."

9

THE MATCHED GRAYS TROTTED out of Mancos, headed for Dolores. It was early morning. Marcella looked fresh and rested.

"Tell me more about those cliff-dwelling Indians, Mr. Talcott. The ones who lived in caves on the Mesa Verde, a thousand years ago. Did they hunt on foot? Or did they ride horses?"

"They had no horses," Bruce said. "No sheep, no goats, no chickens, no burros. They did tame wild turkeys. The only domestic animals they had were dogs and turkeys. But I'm spurring my own hobby too hard, Miss Blair. Tell me about yourself. What did you do back in Ohio?"

"I put in a year as a student nurse," Marcella said.

After climbing out of the Mancos Valley the trail led through ridge pines. Soon it began dipping toward the Dolores. Occasionally they saw cattle. Bruce pointed out the various brands to Marcella. "That bar joining two circles is our stuff. The Bridlebit. That Circle K steer over there belongs to Jess Jallison. He's got the biggest ranch in the Basin, next to Buck Shaw. Buck's Y7 stuff hardly ever gets this far east. Those Bar X Box yearlings we passed a little piece back belong to Sax Consadine. Sax lives down on the New Mexico line, on lower Cherry Creek."

"What brand does Mr. Lantry have?" Marcella asked.

"Jeff Lantry?" Bruce chuckled. "Can't keep track of 'em. He's got a whole raft o' brands. Puts his stuff out on shares to homesteaders. Jess Jallison doesn't like it. Neither does Buck Shaw."

"Why?"

"They claim it overstocks the range, complicates the roundups, and encourages shoestring settlers. Dad and I don't look at it that way. This is a free country, so Lantry has a right to run his cows any way he wants to."

"What brand does my brother-in-law have? Gerald Ashton."

The question seemed to embarrass Bruce. He hesitated, then said, "Q4, I believe. Look, there's the Dolores River. You can see the sun shining on the riffles right through those pines."

Why, she wondered, did he always change the subject whenever she mentioned the Ashtons?

In a little while they rolled into the village of Dolores. Bruce pulled up in front of the general store. It was of unplastered adobe, as were the three saloons flanking it. To Marcella the place looked squalid and uninviting. "If you don't mind waiting a minute, I'll be right out." Bruce stepped down to the boardwalk and went into the store.

Marcella remained in the buckboard seat. Two or three small Mexican children, at play in the dusty street, eyed her curiously. No other life seemed to be abroad here, except a lean sheep dog lolling in the sun and a burro switching at flies. *Why*, Marcella wondered, *would anyone want to live in a place like this?*

Suddenly one of the saloon doors flew open, and a man came hurtling out. He landed in a lump in the gutter, and Marcella saw that he'd been thrown out by a bartender. "And don't come back in, you lousy bum!" the saloon man yelled. He disappeared inside.

For a minute the man in the gutter lay in a sodden heap. Then he picked himself up, stared blearily about, and staggered toward another saloon. He was ragged and unshaven, his face bloated hideously. Marcella shuddered. How could a human being get so low?

She saw him stumble. Then he reeled on a few paces and made his way, like a blind man groping, into the other barroom. *Revolting!* Marcella thought. She looked the other way.

Then Bruce Talcott emerged from the general store with a package. "Slim Borchard told me to bring him some forty-five shells," he explained. "Forgot to pick 'em up in Durango."

They were off again, the grays at a trot. Marcella hoped she'd never see Dolores again.

The trail led upriver. Wild flowers along the bank brightened Marcella. Primrose and clematis and columbine. A line of verse crossed her mind—*Though every prospect pleases, and only man is vile.*

The Bridlebit meadows were in sight when the shot came. Nothing could have been more sudden. One instant they were driving peacefully through the pines, and the next Marcella felt Bruce Talcott slump against her. The reins went slack in his hand and the grays, panicked by the shot, broke into a stampeding run toward the home corrals.

The bounce of the buckboard made Bruce slither still farther to the right. Marcella tried to support him and felt blood warming her hands. His vest was covered with it. Dizziness made her impotent, but only for a moment. Back at home she'd been a nurse, trained to care for helpless men.

The team was at a mad gallop. Marcella picked up the reins and pulled desperately. "Stop!" she cried. But the grays raced on.

Then she realized it was best to keep going. The Talcott ranch buildings loomed in the distance. The sooner she got Bruce there, the better the chance for saving his life. "Hurry!" Marcella shouted. She flapped the reins on the grays' flanks. The buckboard careened, all but overturned as it crashed over an irrigation lateral. Bruce's head and shoulders lay askew across Marcella's lap. Her left hand clutched his arm to keep him from falling off; her right held tightly to the reins. "Hurry!" she yelled again. Was she too late? Would he bleed to death? How far would they have to send for a doctor?

Cowboys in the barnyard saw her coming. It looked like a runaway, so they sprang to saddles and came racing toward her. But she was there almost before they got started. The grays of their own accord came to a snorting halt by the barn.

"Someone shot him!" Marcella announced frantically.

They volleyed questions. "Where?" "Who did it?" "What—"

She broke in on them. "Help me get him to bed. Then send for a doctor."

A minute later two ranch hands were carrying Bruce Talcott into the main house. Marcella followed them. "Bring a basin of hot water," Marcella directed instinctively. Everyone looked so helpless. An elderly man appeared, and she guessed he was Bruce's father. "Tear a sheet into twelve-inch strips," she said to him. "Iodine if you have it." Her own hysteria was gone now. Someone must take charge till a doctor came.

Almost before they'd laid Bruce on a bed she said crisply, "Strip him to the waist. Are you Major Talcott?" Carey Talcott, standing by, tight-lipped and pale, nodded. "Then make sure someone's gone for a doctor. I happen to be a nurse. I'll do what I can till he comes." She turned to two women servants, both Mexicans, who were trying to take off Bruce's shirt. "Not that way," Marcella said critically. "Let me."

Skillfully she removed the shirt and undershirt. The bullet, she discovered, had entered his back and emerged high on the left breast, well above the heart. The wound still gushed blood. While she waited for warm water and an antiseptic, Marcella stanched the flow with towels.

"Will he—" The question died on the major's lips. Marcella saw an agony of suspense in his eyes and answered quickly. "It shouldn't be fatal, Major. I'll do everything I can." She gave him a reassuring smile.

"Thank you," Carey Talcott said gratefully.

One of the men who'd carried Bruce in spoke up. "I hearn Doc Amory's over at Rico. He driv up from Durango to patch up some miner who—"

"Get him here at once," Marcella said. "Now everybody out but his father and these two women."

Warm water arrived, and Marcella bathed the wounds. She applied iodine, then wound strips of sheeting firmly around the patient's torso. Her movements were deft, sure, gentle. Bruce hadn't regained consciousness. Major Talcott produced a flask of brandy, but Marcella waved it away. "A stimulant like that might be dangerous right now."

Then she realized that someone ought to be chasing the would-be assassin. "It was two or three miles back," she said. "I think the shot came from a thicket near the trail. I didn't see the man. I've no idea which way he went."

Major Talcott stepped to the door and spoke quietly to some of his men who were waiting in the hall. "It was two or three miles back. Try to find the empty cartridge. Try to track him."

Minutes later Marcella heard a posse of ranch hands gallop away.

The door opened. A wheel chair bearing a frail and gray-haired lady was pushed in. Marcella smiled and said, "You are his mother? Please don't worry too much. I think he's going to be all right."

Nancy Talcott wheeled herself to the bedside. "Of course he is," she said. She took her son's hand and held it. Her eyes held tears, but her voice was brave. "The Talcotts are tough," she said to Marcella. "I was just your age when they brought his father in like this, one day back in Tennessee. There'd been a duel."

Marcella, flanked by Carey and Nancy Talcott, kept vigil all night by Bruce's bed. Twice he became conscious. Marcella let them give him a few drops of brandy. Nothing else, she said, till the doctor came. They begged her to get some rest herself, but she wouldn't. "There might be a change," she insisted, "and you wouldn't know what to do."

They knew by now that she was Marcella Blair, on the way to visit a married sister farther up the range.

"The sheriff will come from Durango?" Marcella asked.

"Not from Durango," the major said. "This is Dolores County. Our county seat is Rico, in the mining country east of here. The Rico sheriff will be along with the doctor."

Bruce was sleeping now. They talked in whispers.

"It's a miracle," Nancy Talcott said softly, "that you were with him when it happened. And you a trained nurse! How can we ever repay you?"

"Nonsense. He gave me a ride, after I'd been rude to him in Durango." Flushing, Marcella told them about Bruce's gun fight with Cass Crawford.

It was the first they'd heard about it. The major looked grim for a moment, then turned a tender gaze on his son. "Just like the boy," he muttered fondly, "to try to keep his old man out of trouble."

Then he was grim again, for now the motive for the sniping from ambush seemed clear. Some friend of Cass Crawford's must have done it. He'd be back in Durango by this time. The major hurried out to send word to the law officers of Durango.

In the morning a Mexican girl brought a tray in. Bruce was awake. Marcella fed him with a spoon.

It was nearly noon when the doctor came. With him was the Rico sheriff. Major Talcott conferred aside with the sheriff. The doctor gave brisk attention to the patient.

He was a small, oldish man with thin gray hair and a round face. His eyes, deep-set under bushy brows, had the weariness of many long forced rides by wheel and saddle. Marcella felt drawn to him at once, and she pitied him. She could see that he'd been mercilessly overworked, healing wounds in this land of violence and passion.

"The fresh bandages are ready, Doctor," Marcella said.

He looked gratefully at her. And at the clean, wide strips she'd prepared. "This is the temperature chart for the night," Marcella reported.

Her professional tone impressed him. He glanced at the precise record she'd made, then at the girl herself. "Am I dreaming?" Doctor Amory murmured. "Usually I find everything all bungled up, at these ranch shootings."

He took off the old bandages, noting the expertness with which they'd been applied. "Very good. You may bathe the patient, nurse. Never mind the iodine. I've something more suitable in my bag."

When the fresh bandages were on, the doctor turned to Carey Talcott. "He'd've bled to death, likely, if this nurse hadn't been here. As it is, he'll live to break many a bronco."

Marcella flushed. "Don't you believe him, Major. Young, healthy patients like your son have lots of resistance. You won't need me any more, I suppose."

"We need you to be our guest, young lady," Major Talcott said earnestly, "for as long as you'll stay. Your room is ready. Won't you, please—"

"If the patient doesn't need me," Marcella broke in, "I must be getting along. I really must. To my sister's ranch, I mean. Could you let someone drive me up there?"

"Of course," the major agreed with reluctance. "But you've been up all night. You need sleep."

"I'll catch up on sleep," Marcella insisted, "at Melissa's."

She saw Major Talcott exchange nervous glances with

his wife. He looked embarrassed and anxious. He started to say something, then checked himself. Again Marcella felt that odd restraint which had arisen every time she'd mentioned Melissa to Bruce Talcott.

It frightened her. "Is my sister ill?"

"Not at all," the major hastily assured her.

"And the baby?"

"Far as I know, the little boy's all right, too. Since you insist, I'll go order the buckboard." The major went out.

His invalid wife wheeled her chair closer to Marcella. "I haven't been able to go to see your sister," she said, "like a neighbor should. But she came to see me once last winter. She had the child with her. He's a sweet little thing. If there's anything we can do—"

Her voice trailed off, as though what she wanted to say might offend Marcella. It made Marcella more determined than ever to get started at once.

A buckboard drew up in front with a slim, towheaded cowboy at the reins. Marcella went out and found her bags in it. Major Talcott handed her up. Nancy Talcott wheeled her chair to the veranda to wave good-by.

"We'll never forget what you did for Bruce," the major said warmly. "Our home is yours, any time you'll come back."

Doctor Ed Amory came to the wheel and said wistfully, "You'd be a godsend to me in Durango, young lady."

At her questioning look he explained. "I have a big two-story house there. I live upstairs and use the first floor for a clinic and hospital. It's cluttered up with patients—everything from broken ribs to bullet poison. I keep a Mexican woman there, but she's an amateur. I need an office nurse. Need her desperately. Someone to run that clinic for me while I'm out on calls. If you could only—"

"But I can't," Marcella said firmly. "I'm just here for a short visit. I'll be going back to Ohio as soon as I've seen my sister."

Major Talcott presented the driver to Marcella. Slim Borchard was his name. "Take good care of her, Slim. If there's anything we can do—"

Again that note of mystery. "Please, let's get started," Marcella urged.

They were off at a trot. The buckboard crossed the meadow and plunged into piney woods to the north.

"Salt of the earth, the Talcotts are," Slim said. "I been workin' fer him five year. Give you the skin off his knuckles, the major would."

He kept up a running chatter, but Marcella barely heard him. Premonitions preyed on her. She remembered Melissa's last letter, posted four years ago at Dolores. It said she was married and on the way to her husband's ranch on Disappointment Creek. The name, somehow, hadn't seemed real to Marcella. It seemed more like a comic opera name, or a name in some symbolic book like *Pilgrim's Progress*. Like the Slough of Despond.

She'd hardly been able to believe that such a place existed. So she'd opened an atlas to the map of Colorado. And there she'd found it. *Disappointment Creek,* printed plainly along a tiny blue line near the southwestern corner of the state. Just as real as the words *Denver* and *Pueblo* and *Leadville*.

Marcella had only been sixteen then. She remembered tracing the tiny blue line downstream with her finger, noting that it emptied into a larger stream called the Dolores River. Dolores, she knew, meant "sorrows." Vaguely it had disturbed her then, and now it worried her more than ever. Disappointment Creek, that flowed into the River of Sorrows!

"Salt o' the earth," Slim Borchard repeated. "But he'll go bust some day, the major will. He'll go bust just as sure as them aspen leaves'll turn yeller in October."

"But why should he," Marcella wondered, "with such a fine big ranch?"

"Hosses, that's why. He keeps too many fancy hosses, miss. A ranch makes money on cows and loses it on hosses. Nobody loves a good hoss better'n I do. But except what yuh need fer a work string, they're a luxury. Many a time I told the major that. But he won't listen. A hoss eats four times as much grass as a cow. Didja know that? A cow'll graze a spell and then lay down and chew her cud. But a hoss keeps his head down allatime, agrazin' day and night."

"But you can always sell horses, can't you?"

"Not like you can sell cows. Cows are beef. But you can't eat a hoss. If he breaks a laig you shoot him. His skin ain't worth nothin'. Look on the livestock page of any newspaper. You'll see a price quoted for cattle, for hogs, for sheep—but not fer hosses. You go bust on hosses, miss, whenever you start usin' 'em fer pets, like the major does. I've knowed him to sell a carload o' steers and slap every dime right back into one race hoss. Worst kind of a hoss to go broke on is a race hoss. Top of all that, the major's so softhearted he won't prosecute rustlers. Not when they kill fer meat, I mean."

"For meat?" Marcella questioned.

"Yes'm. Say a man ain't got no stock of his own. His family's hungry. So he goes out and butchers another man's yearlin', skins it, and hangs the carcass up fer winter meat. That's rustlin'. You do that to one of Buck Shaw's yearlings and you get strung up. But if you do it to a Talcott yearling, you can get away with it. All the major asks is for the guy to bring him the crittur's hide and admit he butchered it fer beef. Then the major makes a note of it and says, 'If your luck changes, suh, you can pay me some day. If not, just forget it.'"

"I think that's just wonderful!" Marcella exclaimed. "He must be an awfully fine man."

"Sure," Slim agreed. "But don't you see what's bound to happen? Folks take advantage of it. Come spring roundup, there's plenty of Bridlebit beef missin'. And dern few hides to show fer it. Buck Shaw and Jess Jallison rode over once and raised hell. They told the major he just encourages petty rustlin'. And they're right. He does. When you argue with him he just says, 'I wouldn't feel right, suh, prosecutin' a man fer feedin' his hungry kids. Good day, suh.' " Slim made a gesture of exasperation.

Three hours brought them to a summit from which they could look down into a deep, narrow valley. It had a forbidding look, that dark, deserted valley. At the head of it reared a gigantic cone, its pointed peak thrusting upward into clouds.

"That there's Lone Cone," Slim said. "Disappointment Crik heads at the toe of it and runs west." He slammed on brakes and drove cautiously down a steep, twisting grade.

Not a house was in sight, down there. It was the loneliest country Marcella had ever seen.

The grade down seemed endless. The aspens fell away and then the pines. Scraggly oak replaced them. Marcella felt like she was dropping into a pit. A wilderness trap walled off from the world. Lone Cone towered over it, black and ugly, like a grim jailer.

The valley floor had only grass and scrubby patches of oak. The oaks were twisted and stunted. A depressing silence hung over the place. Marcella had never felt so isolated. She almost wished she were back in Durango.

The creek itself could have been stepped across. A twelve-inch pipe would have carried its flow. Slim turned his team down it. And here the trail was hardly more than a cowpath. Marcella looked for cattle. She didn't see any. Four years ago, she remembered, Gerald Ashton had had three hundred. She even remembered the brand mentioned in Melissa's letter. Flying N.

Slim Borchard kept driving downstream. Miles and minutes passed. The valley widened a little, but in the same proportion grew more barren. Even the scrub oak disappeared. The hills on either side now were treeless, brown, and forbidding.

The brownest thing in sight was an earth-roofed shanty just a little way ahead. An abandoned sheep camp, Marcella supposed.

She knew better only when Slim drove straight to it and stopped. "Here we are, miss," he announced.

A drab woman came out. She looked about fifty, Marcella thought. Her dress was a patchwork of old flour sacks. She was thin, haggard, hollow-eyed. A ragged child of about three clung to her skirt.

"Marcella!" the woman cried. She stood staring incredulously, for a moment, then rushed forward with her arms out.

Marcella jumped to the ground and ran into them. A lump in her throat choked her. It couldn't be true. This couldn't be her lovely sister, Lissy.

She was too stunned even to cry. She stood there, in a dumb daze, hugging Melissa. Melissa recovered first. "You shouldn't've come, Marcella." She made a brave effort to joke about it. "The Indians'll scalp you, away out here." Her laugh cracked. "Jackie, this is your Aunt Marcella."

Marcella stooped to put her arms around the little boy. He drew back shyly, unused to company. He was bare from the waist up, and his homemade pantaloons were too long. The small round face was berry-brown; and his legs and arms, Marcella saw, had the lean hardness of a wild animal's.

"Come right on in, Marcella." Melissa took her hand and led her into the shanty. "It's not much, I'm afraid. But Gerry's had bad luck. I'd've written you, but—"

She didn't need to say why. Pride, and nothing else,

must have kept Melissa Ashton from writing to her people.

The cabin had two rooms, one floored with pine boards and the other hard-packed earth. The walls were adobe, unplastered. The flat dirt roof sagged. One window had glass. It was scrubbed clean, Marcella noticed. The other windows were covered with oiled paper.

The front room had a double bed and a cot. The quilts were patchworks of deerskins. There was a homemade dresser with a photograph on it. "I'm sorry Gerry's not here." Melissa was talking half hysterically to cover up. "He went to a sawmill down near Dolores to see if he could get some work. Everything seems to have gone wrong lately—"

Marcella didn't hear the rest of it. She was staring at the photograph. It was of Gerald and Melissa Ashton taken on the day of their marriage, four years ago. The features of the man shocked Marcella. She recognized him at once.

Gerald Ashton was the drunken bum she'd seen kicked out of a saloon at Dolores.

10

SLIM BORCHARD HAD already brought in Marcella's bags. He re-entered now with some bulky packages and set them down. He took off his hat and said awkwardly, "Miz Talcott sent yuh some honey, ma'am. It's right nice alfalfa honey, ma'am. And some peach marmalade and a few other things. If they's anything else you need, she says fer you to—"

"Thank you, Slim. There's nothing else we need," Melissa said. Her chin was up. Marcella could see she was riding her pride stubbornly. "And please thank the Talcotts for everything, especially for bringing my sister here. But you must stay to supper before you go back, Slim."

The cowboy looked around the bareness of the room.

"I reckon I better get started right now, ma'am. It's a long, steep climb outa here. So long, folks."

He was gone. Marcella heard his team trotting up the valley.

The dam broke then. "I'm taking you away from here, Melissa. You and Jackie. Do you have a wagon?"

Melissa stared. "Take us away? And leave Gerry? We can't do that, child. Come, let's unpack your things."

And still Marcella couldn't cry. "I'll stay all night," she said. "Tomorrow we'll start for Durango. Even if we have to walk. When we get there we'll catch the first train to Ohio."

"And leave Gerry? You know I wouldn't do that, Marcella. He's Jackie's father."

Fury burst from Marcella. "I know who he is," she stormed. "And *what* he is. I saw him in Dolores. I hate him." Her voice rose to a pitch of bitterness. "I hate him and all this hard, heartless country that makes brutes out of men and crushes women. It's beastly. It kills. I saw it kill. It's a profane land, full of reeling drunks and bloody butchers. I won't let you stay here, Melissa."

Then the tears came. Marcella sat on the bed and sobbed convulsively. Lissy had been so beautiful only four years ago! And she was still only twenty-five.

Melissa sat down by Marcella and put an arm around her. "Maybe it *is* all that," she admitted. "But it's a land of loyalty, too. I have a husband. I married him with my eyes open. He's the father of my child. He tried to make a home for me. Unless he goes with me, I'll never leave it."

She got up to unpack Marcella's bags. When she opened the dresser drawers to put things into them, Marcella saw that the drawers were empty. "Haven't you any clothes yourself?" she asked wretchedly.

"I have my town dress." Melissa nodded toward a corner closet. "But I don't wear it very often."

Marcella got up and went to the closet. It was just a drape of canvas screening the room's corner. In it she found a hanging dress. It was threadbare. Marcella saw that it was the dress her sister had worn when she'd left Ohio four years ago.

Marcella turned on her fiercely. "I suppose you wore it when you called on Mrs. Talcott last winter. She told me you called."

"It wasn't really a call," Melissa said. "I just went to take them a cowhide we—"

She stopped in confusion. And Marcella remembered something Slim Borchard had said. "I see! Your precious Gerry butchered one of Major Talcott's yearlings. And to keep him from being prosecuted as a thief, you delivered the hide to the Talcotts."

"We'll pay them some day," Melissa protested. "We only did it to eat."

"You've no cattle of your own?"

"Not now. We did have, but—"

A childish voice piped up. "We got old Bess. And Nig and Brownie."

Bess, Marcella learned, was an ancient brindle milch cow. Nig and Brownie were a pair of decrepit nags sometimes hitched to the wreck of an old spring wagon. Except for a few chickens, these comprised the entire Ashton chattel.

Bit by bit the full and ghastly picture came out. Gerry, Melissa said, was English. The younger son of an impoverished Yorkshire family, he'd drifted to the American West to become a cowboy. For a year or so he'd worked on the big Jallison ranch near Mancos. Then he'd quit to file a homestead here on Disappointment. He'd met and married Melissa in Durango. The first year here hadn't been too bad. There'd been handicaps and hardships, but Gerry hadn't yet become an alcoholic. "We ran cows on shares for Jeff Lantry," Melissa said. "When the year was up we had a hundred calves, all our own. We branded them Q4. Then blackleg hit us. It took most of the calves. Gerry sort of gave up, then. He went to town—"

"He went to town and got drunk," Marcella finished scathingly, "and he's been that way ever since. Very well, I'll stay here till he staggers home. When he does I'll give him a piece of my mind. If he has a shred of decency left he'll get clear out of your life. Then I'll take you away from here forever."

Jeff Lantry rode his big sorrel down the Dolores trail. Charlie Sheep rode a length behind him, leading a calico mule. This was one of the regular inspection trips which Lantry made, quarterly, to all of his twenty brands.

But this time he must veer out of his way to call on the Talcotts. He'd always admired Major Talcott, and he liked Bruce equally well. The news about somebody dry-gulching Bruce had shocked Lantry. He assumed, like everyone else, that some friend of Cass Crawford was guilty of the sniping. Who else could it be? No one else had a motive. This afternoon he must stop by the Bridlebit and see how Bruce was coming along.

Some Eastern girl, they said, had been with Bruce when it happened. Lantry wondered why—and who she was.

High timber walled the trail on either side. They were approaching Dolores, and Lantry could already hear the river. It was about here, he recalled with a grim smile, that Charlie Sheep had once ducked into the woods to get rid of a stolen horse.

Something directly ahead made Lantry draw rein sharply. A man lay sprawled by the trail, face down. Lantry dismounted and went to him. He turned the man over. It was Gerald Ashton.

At first he thought Ashton was dead. Then a gash on

the man's head, and the fumes of liquor, brought him to another conclusion. It looked like Ashton had been on one of his habitual sprees last night in Dolores. Staggering up the trail he'd blacked out, here, lying in a stupor, perhaps, for hours. The wheel of some passing wagon might have struck his head. Or possibly the shod hoof of a horse. In the darkness no one had seen him. A heartbeat told Lantry he was still alive. He wouldn't live long, though, unless he got prompt and proper attention. Lantry's guess was that the skull was fractured.

"Stay here and watch him, Charlie." Lantry remounted and galloped on into Dolores.

The storekeeper there had a team and buckboard. Lantry borrowed the outfit. "I'll send it back from Durango," he promised.

He tied his sorrel to the endgate and drove back to Charlie Sheep.

"In with him, Charlie." They lifted the unconscious derelict into the buckboard bed.

"Him dead plenty soon," Charlie grunted.

"Maybe. And maybe not. Doc Ed Amory's a wizard with cases like this. We'll try to get him to Doctor Ed's clinic at Durango."

Lantry made the Indian take a bedroll from the pack mule and spread it in the buckboard. Ashton was put on it and made as secure as possible from joltings. Then Lantry climbed to the seat and drove rapidly southeast.

A few hours later he pulled up at Tom Gifford's place near Mancos. Tom was riding the saddle of a pedal grindstone, sharpening a sickle. "He's got a skinful of whisky and a broken head, Tom. Take a look."

Tom made a sympathetic examination of his old Circle K bunkmate. He bathed Gerry's head and bandaged the cut. Gerry didn't come to consciousness. "I think you're right, Lantry. Looks like a fractured skull from a lick by a wagon tire. Maybe Doc Amory could save him if you got him there quick enough."

"I'll push right along," Lantry said. "You better notify his wife. She's still up on Disappointment Creek, isn't she?"

Tom nodded. He saddled a horse and rode north. Lantry continued on southeast toward Durango.

He'd always been afraid Gerry Ashton would end up like this. Even three years ago Gerry hadn't been very steady or dependable. That was why Lantry hadn't renewed the share contract with him. Since then he hadn't seen the man at all. He'd heard of him occasionally, and that Gerry was going from bad to worse.

"Doctor Ed won't thank us for this, Charlie," Lantry said. "He's already overstocked with patients."

It was already dark. There were two divides to cross. It would be about dawn, Lantry knew, when they reached Durango.

Doctor Ed Amory got up in a grumpy mood that morning. He was tired. Every bone in his overworked body ached. And they weren't young bones any more. Hardly a week passed that he didn't have to make a fast, life-or-death drive to some distant ranch or mine or lumber mill. He was just back from the Bridlebit, where he'd spent a day attending Bruce Talcott.

Here in town his makeshift hospital was full. The patients, during his absence, had been inadequately attended. Some of them were in desperate condition. Many of them were feverish. One of them, a gun-fight casualty, had died during the night. And no help but a Mexican woman who meant well, but who simply didn't know how.

"Here comes one more, señor," she said as a buckboard pulled up in front.

"Damn!" said Doctor Ed.

Jeff Lantry and a Piute Indian came in with Gerald Ashton. "Looks like a cracked skull, Doc," Lantry reported.

"I wish someone would crack yours," Doctor Ed grumbled, "for piling him in here on me. All right, put him on that cot."

Lantry smiled. He knew that Doctor Ed often used a crust like that to cover up his softheartedness. Doctor Ed would be sure to give this derelict patient his most skillful attention.

"He was on a bender," Lantry explained, "up around Dolores. Passed out on the road, and a wagon ran over him."

Doctor Ed gave a quick examination. "Humph! Looks like it. Still got a breath o' life in him. I'll do what I can, Lantry."

Lantry started out. At the door he turned and said, "Send the bill to me, Doc. No use saddlin' another charity case on you. You got too many already."

Something about the door and porch, as he went out, seemed oddly familiar to Lantry. He couldn't remember having been here before. Not that it mattered. He went to the street and untied his sorrel from the buckboard's endgate. Charlie Sheep took the team off toward the livery barn. Lantry mounted and rode toward the Grand Central Hotel.

"We're suckers, Mike," he admitted with a quirk of his lips. "We don't owe that guy a thing."

Walking Mike down F toward Main Street, he tried to analyze why he'd offered to pay for Ashton's hospitalization. He hadn't meant to. The offer had been impulsive. Ashton wasn't working for him. Four years ago the man had been one of the original twenty share operators in Lantry's scheme of ranching. And the only one on whom Lantry had lost money. At the end of the year Lantry had bluntly declined to renew the contract. Ashton, he'd decided, wasn't dependable. Nor reasonably alert. He should have been home bleeding dewlaps instead of hanging around Dolores barrooms. That way he might have staved off the blackleg epidemic which had played havoc with the Flying N calf crop. At the end of that first year, Lantry had taken three hundred cows away from Ashton and turned them over to another man, Abel Dickshot of Cherry Creek, who'd done well with them. And since then Gerald Ashton had gone to hell fast.

I don't owe him a thing, Lantry told himself again.

Yet a picture kept tugging at a corner of his mind. That day three years ago when he'd taken the Flying N cows away from Gerry Ashton. The hovel of a cabin up there on Disappointment Creek. Ashton's wife standing in the doorway with a baby in her arms. The look in her eyes as she'd pleaded with Lantry to give her man one more chance.

Three years ago, it was. And subconsciously the scene had nagged at Jeff Lantry ever since. Maybe it was the kid, he thought. A boy, he'd heard, and three years old now. Born with two strikes on him, that kid was. And Lantry knew exactly what it meant. A crowded, underequipped orphanage was the only home his own childhood had ever known.

He dismounted at the hotel and went in.

The clerk said, "Back already, Mr. Lantry? Three gentlemen were in to see you yesterday. I told them you were out of town."

"Who were they?"

"Mr. Jallison, Mr. Shaw, and Mr. Consadine."

Lantry laughed. The idea of that trio being referred to as "gentlemen"! The term might fit Sax Consadine, who had certain social graces, but hardly the rip-roaring personality of Jess Jallison or a sun-baked sourdough like

Buck Shaw. Lantry could easily guess what they wanted. They'd accosted him individually, at various times, protesting against his range operations. But this was the first time they'd all three come at once.

"If they show up again, let me know." Jeff Lantry went up to his room, shaved, and went to bed.

Sax Consadine stood alone at the Esperanza bar. His left hand held a glass of brandy while his right was rolling dice on the bar. The dice were cubes of solid gold, too heavy to be practical for serious play. In fact Sax Consadine never gambled at all. Presumably he carried these golden dice merely as luck pieces, habitually rolling them whenever he had an idle moment. Just as some men carry two silver dollars and click them one against the other.

He was a blue-eyed man of medium build, graceful even in his silver-trimmed gauntlets and batwing chaps, always affable, and generally popular throughout the Basin. His ranch on Cherry Creek, astride the Colorado-New Mexico line, was well stocked and prosperous. Women liked him because of his manners and looks, and perhaps also because Sax Consadine wasn't "gun-heavy" like most of the Basin rangemen. At least not when he came to Durango. He always rode in with a carbine in his saddle scabbard, but never with a forty-five at his hip. He was a superb horseman, people said, and even a better rifleman.

Ruby Costello floated by. "Hello, Sax," she greeted casually. "Couldn't I interest you in a real game?" She made a face at the golden dice.

He rolled them again. "This way's cheaper, Ruby. I make mind bets and don't clean up on anybody but myself. And it's just as much fun."

"You're the poorest customer I've got, Sax. Unless it's Jeff Lantry. He won't play with me, either." She moved on to other patrons down the bar.

Two gun-slung cattlemen came in. They were Jess Jallison and Buck Shaw. "He's back in town, Sax," Jallison boomed. "I seen his sorrel tied in front of the hotel."

"So let's have it out with him," Buck Shaw suggested.

Sax Consadine gave the dice another roll. He put them in his pocket with a sigh. "You're handling it all wrong, Jess," he insisted. "Lantry's not the kind you can push around. Buck Shaw's got a better idea. Let's try it first."

"Sure," Shaw echoed. "I'll offer to buy him out."

He was a knobby, nail-hard man with bushy brows, a head shorter than the bulky Jallison. "I don't care what you do," Jallison roared, "long as you get him off my range. I'm tired of messin' with that jasper, him and his chain-ranch racket. They're stealin' me blind."

Jallison shook his enormous and shaggy head. Blackened by a stubble of beard, it seemed to grow directly out of his shoulders. The gun belt at his paunchy waist bristled with brass, and sagged low with the weight of a hogleg forty-five. "I'm tired of messin' with him," he repeated. "Let's go." He charged out, still wagging his head like a buffalo bull. Shaw and Consadine followed him with misgivings. "Let's not have any rough stuff. Easy does it," Sax counseled.

Ten minutes later Jeff Lantry was wakened by a knock. The hotel clerk called to him. "They're waiting in the lobby for you. The same three gentlemen. Mr. Jallison, Mr. Shaw, and Mr. Consadine."

Lantry got up and took his time about dressing. Let them wait. He did not put on his gun. Nothing would happen, he thought, except a bulldozing harangue from Jess Jallison. Buck Shaw, of course, shared Jallison's viewpoint completely. But he wouldn't get tough about it. Neither would Consadine.

When Lantry found them in the lobby, Sax was seated and rolling a cigarette. He alone of the three looked amiable. Jallison was standing, his head thrust forward bellicosely. But it was Buck Shaw who spoke first.

"Look, Lantry," Shaw began, "I'm offerin' to buy you out at top market price. I'll take every brand you got and slap my own Y7 on 'em. Name any fair figure you want. That way there'll be no more trouble."

Lantry gave him a level smile. "What trouble is there now?"

"No use goin' into all that again," Buck retorted. "You're cowstaking twenty shoestring outfits, and they're a pain in the neck. I'll buy your six thousand cows at thirty-five per head. What do yuh say?"

"I say no." Lantry's tone was final. "Anything else on your mind?"

A bellow came from Jallison, but Sax Consadine cut him òff. "My turn now," the Bar X Box man said placatingly. "Okay, Jeff. So you won't sell your cows. Then keep 'em. Only run 'em like I run mine, and like Jess runs his, and like Buck runs his. Buy you a big ranch spread somewhere. With meadows and water rights and everything. An honest-to-goodness layout. Then hire yourself a crew and be an orthodox cowman."

"Sure," Shaw chimed in. "That's the ticket. Get rid of all these sharecroppin' nesters of yours and get yerself a real ranch."

"I hadn't heard of any for sale," Lantry said.

Shaw's eyes narrowed knowingly. "It won't be long, though. What about the Talcott layout? Just what you need, Lantry. Talcott's horse-poor and busted. Everybody knows that. The banks'll be clampin' down on him any day now. When he goes under, bid in the Bridlebit. Then you could—"

"The answer is still no," Lantry said curtly. "Major Talcott's a friend of mine. I like the way he minds his own business. I'd like you a lot better, Buck Shaw, if you'd do the same."

Shaw turned to Consadine with a gesture of futility. "We're wasting our time, Sax. No use tryin' to pound any sense into this guy's head. Let's amble."

Shaw and Consadine left the hotel. But Jallison stood his ground. He brought a notebook from his pocket and consulted a memorandum. "I been keepin' tabs on some of those share deals of yourn, Lantry. Here's an item. Abel Dickshot. He's right on the edge of my range. You furnished him three hun'erd cows."

Lantry looked at him curiously. "That's right. What of it?"

"At the end of a year," Jallison boomed, "he delivered you a hun'erd and forty calves. I know, because I saw 'em shipped from Durango. He kept a hun'erd and forty for himself. That made two hun'erd eighty calves outa three hun'erd cows in one year. A ninety-three-percent crop! Don't make me laugh, Lantry."

Lantry flushed. That calf crop of Dickshot's *had* looked rather big. "Well?" he challenged.

"He couldn't've got that many calves," Jallison charged, "unless he wide-looped some of mine. And if Dickshot did it, plenty more o' your pets been doin' the same thing. Stealin' me blind. When you accept those rustled calves, Lantry, it makes *you* a thief, too. How much longer you think I'm gonna—"

A piston stopped him. The piston was Lantry's right fist. It shot straight from the shoulder to Jallison's jaw. The Circle K man, all two hundred and forty pounds of him, toppled backward and down. He hit the lobby floor with a thump.

When he came to his knees he was rabid and clawing for his gun. Lantry snatched it from his hand, broke it at the hinge. He emptied the brass from it and then handed the unloaded gun back to Jallison. "Better not try loading it again," he warned. Resentment still boiled in Lantry.

Jallison got to his feet and for half a minute he made the rafters ring. He shouted, ranted, roared. His barrage of maledictions carried to the street walk, and people stopped there, looking in. The hotel clerk had stooped discreetly behind his counter. Lantry stood watching the man, half smiling but alert. He'd have to throw another punch if Jallison took another shell from his belt.

The big rancher didn't. He became suddenly aware that onlookers were peering in from the street. His bellows subsided. He pitched his voice low, and Lantry remembered his reputation for being deadly only when he was quiet.

"I'll give you thirty days," Jallison said softly.

"Thirty days to do what?"

"To get out of this Basin. Sell out and get out. I'll be back in town a month from today," Jallison said. "If you're here I'll kill you on sight."

"I'll be here," Lantry promised.

"You'll be dead," Jallison said, his voice trembling with fury but low-pitched. He went out, and Lantry watched him stalk to a saloon across the way.

Lantry went up to his room and buckled on his gun belt. He'd better keep ready from now on. Jallison had promised him thirty days before forcing a fight. But it might come sooner.

How stupid it was, Lantry thought. For four years he'd shared this range with Jallison and Shaw and Consadine. And now, out of a clear sky, a gun fight. Why? Because he'd taken a punch at Jallison's jaw.

But why had he thrown the punch? Then he remembered. It was because Jallison had called him a thief. Ridiculous! If Abel Dickshot had wide-looped a few slick-ears, it was the first Lantry knew about it. Certainly he wouldn't connive at anything like that. And just as certainly he wasn't going to let anybody call him a thief.

A thief? Lantry looked up, happened to see his reflection in the mirror. Something he saw in his own eyes disconcerted him, gave him a sense of inner discomfort that he couldn't shake off. Why was he so jumpy at being called a thief?

Was it because he really was one?

Jeff Lantry was a realist. He forced himself to look frankly into his own mirrored eyes. What about the two hundred thousand dollars he'd dug up in the woods? Did that make him a thief? Was it a subconscious conscience which had impelled his punch at Jallison?

Lantry shrugged it off. Of course not. He hadn't stolen that money. He'd just found it in the woods. It was a break, a chance to get ahead. He'd have been a dope not to grab it.

I'm getting to be an old woman! Lantry thought. He'd brush it from his mind and never think of it again. What he needed right now was a drink.

He went out and crossed to Ruby's Place, the Esperanza. It was full of customers, and Lantry's entrance silenced a buzz of talk. He knew that Jallison's ultimatum was all over town by now. Lantry must sell out and get out, within a month, or shoot it out with Jallison.

At the head of the bar stood Sax Consadine. He was rolling his golden dice. Sax grinned amiably and said, "No hard feelings, Jeff, I hope. I told Jess he'd better not try pushing you around. Join me?"

Lantry nodded. He stepped up and ordered rye.

And Sax Consadine kept rolling his cubes of gold. He was rolling them, now, with his *left* hand.

From the far end of the bar Ruby saw him. Her eyes narrowed. When Harry Listra rolled those dice with his *right* hand, it meant nothing at all. When he rolled them with his *left,* it meant much. But only to Ruby Costello.

11

TO RUBY THE SIGNAL SAID, "Meet me at the usual place right away."

She never thought of him as Sax Consadine, always as Harry Listra. Her response now was prompt, simple, inconspicuous. To the bartender she said, "I'll have an absinthe frappé, Pablo."

Pablo served her. He wasn't in on it himself. Only Harry Listra knew. When he saw her sipping it, it told him she'd caught his message. He put the dice away.

Ruby, in a few minutes, went back to her private apartment at the rear. Anita, her maid, was there. "Send for my horse, Anita. I feel like a canter up the river."

As she slipped into her riding-habit, Ruby wondered what Harry had on his mind. They made it a rule never to speak to each other at the bar except within the hearing of other customers. And then, of course, only as hostess to patron. All important business must be transacted well beyond the ears of Durango.

Sometimes Harry wanted to let her know that members of the gang were asaddle and near town, ready to hold up any lush victims she might tell them about. Or sometimes he merely wanted to pay her a ten-percent commission on loot from her last tip. Perhaps this time he wanted to discuss the hazard of Bruce Talcott. Perhaps he'd guessed that she herself had inspired the recent dry-gulching of Talcott. Or maybe he thought that some roving member of their crowd had taken it upon himself to eliminate the Bridlebit man. Harry Listra would never know, of course, about Ruby's own personal angle in the motive—that she'd wanted to win a fortune for an outsider named Jeff Lantry and at the same time win Lantry for herself.

The grubstake fortune was lost now. It was spilled milk,

and no use crying over it. Ruby Costello was a gambler who knew when she'd lost a throw. Because Bruce Talcott, they said, would recover. Being alive, he'd deny having witnessed any grubstake contract in 1884. The fact of forgery would be out then, and the whole plan wrecked.

And so, with a grimace of regret, Ruby had given it up. She'd have to find some other way to entrap Jeff Lantry.

She put on a black derby riding-hat with a silver hatpin spiking it to her rose-red hair. In this, and in her long black riding-habit, she went out a side door and found her saddled mare waiting. Often she took rides up the river trail, and her sortie today caused only the usual interest. Cantering north out Main Street, she looked like a cut from a magazine advertising a horse show. At the top of the street she forded the Animas and rode on through the ghost town of Animas City.

Just beyond it, and a little way into a side canyon, grew a thick clump of cottonwoods. Ruby dismounted there, sat on a stump, and waited. Soon she heard a loping horse. The man the Basin knew as Sax Consadine drew up beside her.

He didn't dismount. "Who took that shot at young Talcott?" he asked her abruptly.

"How would I know?" Ruby evaded. Since the thing had been bungled, there was nothing to be gained by telling him.

He shrugged. "Okay. Let's forget Talcott. He'll be laid up for months and so there's no danger of him poking around up on the Mesa Verde this season. Now listen, Ruby. Keep your ears open for any bar talk about a girl that's out here to see the Gerry Ashtons."

"What do you want to know about her?"

"I want to know if she's a relative of Ashton, or of Ashton's wife. She was with Bruce Talcott when he was shot. Then she went on to the Ashton homestead on Disappointment Creek."

"Why is she dangerous?"

"Have you forgotten? That quarterly remittance, of course. Maybe she knows about it. Maybe that's why she's out here."

Ruby bit her lip. She was a little irked about the Ashton remittance business because, although only a minor coup of Harry's, it was one she'd never been paid a commission on. It was a thing Harry had been able to manage without her advice or help.

"She doesn't know about it, Harry. If she knew she'd have told the sheriff the minute she hit town."

Harry, still in the saddle, rolled a cigarette. "Look, Ruby. All she could possibly know is that a check for a hundred pounds has left London quarterly, for the last four years, addressed to Gerald Ashton in care of General Delivery, Farmington, New Mexico. She probably doesn't even know that unless she's kin to Gerry himself. Before she could talk to Gerry, he was run over by a wagon and knocked cuckoo. Somebody brought him in to the hospital. The Ashton women'll probably be along to take care of him. Doc Amory's operating on him today, I hear. Maybe he'll come out of it and maybe he won't. But if this girl's only some kid sister of Ashton's wife, everything ought to be all right."

Ruby turned it over in her mind. It was a sharp mind, sharper even than Harry Listra's. "You overlook something, Harry. Suppose the postmaster at Farmington hears about the accident to Ashton. He probably will, because it's in the papers. And suppose Ashton's laid up six months with a broken head. You don't dare let Alf Fontana cash any more of those checks."

Harry nodded. "I'll tell Alf to lay low. And if you hear any bar talk about it, let me know." He wheeled his horse and left her without even raising his hat. There'd never been anything remotely like romance between Harry and Ruby. No one knew that better than Ruby herself. Harry Listra, if he dared, would cut her throat.

But he didn't dare. Ruby had taken the necessary precautions to insure that he wouldn't. The complete story of his life lay in a Denver bank box, to be opened if anything ever happened to Ruby Costello.

Harry, she thought now, had been stupid to mess around with such chicken feed as the Ashton remittance. True, he'd collected a hundred pounds per quarter for four years. But considering the risk, it wasn't worth it. Why couldn't he stick to nice, safe holdups in lonely canyons?

Harry's background was known to Ruby in all its devious details, and often his daring shocked her. She knew the bold ruse, for instance, which had given Harry his start as a San Juan Basin cattleman.

A fugitive from a Texas murder, Harry Listra had arrived in the Basin with nothing but an idea. An idea based on a fact—the fact that a cow won't cross a frozen river. A horse will. But a cow won't.

And so some seven years ago Harry Listra had made a practice of driving bred cows south across the wide San Juan River, in northern New Mexico, just before the winter freeze. The ice came and penned the cows on the south side. Sometimes their Colorado owners found them there. Sometimes they didn't. Those that weren't found were marooned till spring, by the frozen river, and had calves. Many of the calves were weanable before the spring thaw. These Harry cut out and kept for himself. He'd needed men to help him, and that crew had become the nucleus, in later years, of the mythical Blue Mountains gang of outlaws.

Using the calves gleaned from his ice trick, Harry Listra, as Sax Consadine, had started his big Bar X Box spread

on Cherry Creek. Its present crew were those of the outlaw gang whose faces weren't known to law officers. The
rest of the gang lived in a Mesa Verde hide-out, riding on
raids at the beck and call of Harry Listra.

All of these threads recurred to Ruby as she mounted
her mare and rode back toward Durango. She remembered
the day she herself had first arrived from Texas. A job at
the Esperanza dance hall where she'd come face to face
with a customer, Harry Listra. Only everyone was calling
him Sax Consadine.

She'd known him in San Antone. And so to Ruby it had
offered a perfect opportunity for blackmail. Trapped,
Harry had offered to set her up as the gang's town spy and
give her ten percent on whatever loot accrued from her
tips. It had been highly profitable. With her winnings
she'd become the vice queen of Durango.

Now she remembered the stagecoach holdup four years
ago when Harry, slitting open a mail sack, had found a
letter postmarked London and addressed to a Circle K
puncher named Ashton. It was from some British barrister
informing Gerald Ashton that the family estate had re-
couped moderately, enough to provide him with a remittance of a hundred pounds per quarter. If Gerald
would acknowledge receipt of this notice, and inform the
solicitors of his permanent address, a draft would be sent
quarterly.

And so Harry had imported an old Texas associate
named Alf Fontana. Fontana wasn't a gunman. He wasn't
even a horseman. But he was an artful forger and confidence man. Gerald Ashton by that time had quit the Circle K to file a homestead far to the north on Disappointment Creek. It hadn't been too difficult to get a sample
of his handwriting. Fontana had practiced it till he could
produce perfect imitations. The rest was easy. A letter to
London directing them to send the draft each quarter to

Gerald K. Ashton, General Delivery, Farmington, New Mexico. Since then, Fontana had presented himself there once every three months to pick up the check and forge an endorsement.

The present hazard, Ruby reflected, was that Ashton was now in a Durango hospital, only forty-odd miles from Farmington. There'd been an item in the Durango weekly about it. If the Farmington postmaster saw it, it wouldn't be safe for Fontana to call for the next check. Or if Ashton died, his wife would notify her husband's kin in England.

Where would that leave Harry Listra? Harry would still be in the clear, Ruby concluded. Fraud would be exposed, but only on the part of Alf Fontana. And Fontana belonged to the undercover section of the gang which hid out on the Mesa Verde. Harry would lose nothing except a continuation of the checks from England.

Ruby cantered down Main Street toward the Esperanza. Men on the west walk waved to her, called to her jocosely. But the east walk of the street ignored her, and this, as always, embittered Ruby Costello. Three prim housewives shopping along the respectable walk turned their backs as she passed. The snobs! Always drawing the caste line. Forever snubbing her because she was a saloon woman. Ruby hated them. And yet she knew it was a line she could never cross. At least not here in Durango. But wait till she'd dropped her net over Jeff Lantry. She could laugh at them then. Some day she'd make Jeff Lantry take her to New York, to Paris, to Vienna—far beyond the horizon of these backwoods prissies. Many of them had set their caps for Lantry, and he hadn't even looked at them. Some day they'd see him get on a train, leaving Durango forever, with Ruby Costello.

Again Lantry rode west along the Mancos trail. Charlie Sheep was with him, leading the calico pack mule. A forty-five was on Lantry's hip, in case he should meet Jess Jallison. After a two-day rest, he was resuming his circuit of inspection.

He topped a rise and saw a buckboard climbing the grade toward him. It was a two-seated rig, and he recognized Tom Gifford as the driver. Tom didn't own an outfit like that. He must have borrowed it from the Talcotts. Yes, those matched grays were a Bridlebit team.

A girl was on the front seat with Tom. A young, dark-haired girl whose fairness clearly hadn't been long exposed to the suns and winds of the Basin. That drab woman on the back seat was Melissa Ashton. She had a small boy in her lap, apparently sleeping. The rig, headed toward Durango, came on up the hill and stopped when Lantry drew abreast of it.

"How is he, Mr. Lantry?" The question came with a desperate anxiety from Melissa.

"Doctor Ed operated yesterday," Lantry told her. "It was a bad skull fracture. Ed had to take out a splintered bone. He says Gerry'll be laid up a long time. Five or six months, maybe. With good luck and good care he's got a chance."

Melissa questioned him eagerly, and it was a minute before she remembered to introduce her sister. "Marcella, this is Mr. Lantry. We owe him so much for taking poor Gerry into town."

"It was kind of you." Marcella said it with reserve. Her face had a rebellious look, Lantry thought, like she was here under pressure. He got the idea that she gave her brother-in-law an extremely low rating and was doubtful if his salvage was worth while. Her prettiness, Lantry saw at once, had completely captivated Tom Gifford.

Obviously they'd started for Durango immediately upon being notified by Tom of Ashton's accident. They must have used their dilapidated spring wagon as far as the

Bridlebit, Tom riding at the wheel. And there Tom had borrowed this smart rig from Carey Talcott.

Bruce, Melissa reported, was getting along fine.

"But he wouldn't be," Tom put in warmly, "if it hadn't been for Miss Blair. She's a nurse and she knew right what to do." His eyes and his tone, however, indicated that he looked upon Marcella more as a goddess than a nurse.

It amused Lantry as he rode on. Men always amused him when they fell for a pretty face. It wouldn't do Tom any good, Lantry was sure. That girl looked like she detested this range and everything on it. Chances were she'd catch the first train back East. For Tom's sake, Lantry rather hoped she would. He liked Tom. And a tenderfoot wife would be a millstone around Tom's neck.

Nothing like that, Lantry assured himself, would ever clutter up his own life. He spurred the sorrel and loped on toward Mancos.

On the street at Mancos he came face to face with Jess Jallison. Jallison was in short sleeves and beltless. He wasn't wearing a gun. The big Circle K man accosted Lantry with a deadly calmness.

"I'm not heeling myself for a month, Lantry. Then I'll belt on a forty-five and ride to Durango. I want to be fair. You'll need that long to sell out and leave the Basin."

"I'm not selling out, Jallison."

"In that case," the rancher said quietly, "be ready to trade slugs when I see you in Durango."

12

THE CIRCUIT OF INSPECTION took Lantry a week. Arriving back in Durango, his first stop was at Doctor Ed's hospital.

Again something strange and intangible disturbed him as he passed through the picket gate there.

Inside, the big downstairs room looked different. Lantry

hardly knew it. The floor was scrubbed, the cots were neatly arranged, and the windows had white curtains.

A dozen patients were there. Lantry saw Gerry Ashton on a cot at the rear. He seemed to be sleeping. A girl in starched white was bending over a Mexican child at the front. She was feeding the child with a spoon. "Your fever is all gone now, Manuelito. They'll be taking you home tomorrow." Her voice was sweet and soothing. As she turned toward the next cot she collided with Jeff Lantry.

Lantry grinned. "So you're still here?"

Her eyes were suddenly bitter. "What else can I do?" A harsh frustration replaced the gentleness of her voice. "My sister won't leave *him*." She gestured disdainfully toward Gerry Ashton. "And I *can't* leave Melissa."

Lantry looked at her curiously. "Do you want to?" he asked.

"Do I want to leave Lissy? Of course not. I came to take her away from this—" She broke off. It was clear that words were inadequate to measure her contempt for Durango.

"How is he?" Lantry inquired.

"He'll be here for months. But he'll live to get drunk again. And again and again. He'll live to take her back to that horrible hovel."

"You mean Disappointment Creek? It's a pretty good grass country, Miss Blair."

Her eyes hardened. "It's good only for rattlesnakes and lizards. It's a graveyard for everything decent and beautiful. Can't you see what it did to Melissa? It's ugly and hateful, and I hope I never see it again."

Someone came in, and Lantry turned to face Doctor Amory. The old doctor looked cheerful and unharassed. He slapped Lantry on the back. "There've been changes around here," he beamed. "How do you like it? Used to be something of a crow's nest, this place. Now look at it." Doctor Ed surveyed the room proudly. "Just like this upstairs, Lantry. I got a housekeeper, now. Mrs. Ashton. That's what I've needed all along. An office nurse and a housekeeper."

Marcella drifted away to attend one of the patients. Lantry was about to leave, himself, when he remembered he'd offered to pay Gerry Ashton's medical expenses. He took two twenties from his wallet and gave them to Doctor Ed. "Whatever more it comes to," he said gruffly, "let me know, and I'll take care of it."

He left abruptly and went out to his horse. Just as he swung to the saddle Marcella Blair came outside. She stood at his stirrup and looked up at him with something like embarrassment.

"I suppose you think I'm terribly bitter, Mr. Lantry. But you don't understand. Melissa was so beautiful when she left home. Finding her in that awful place was— It was like finding her dead."

Lantry smiled soberly. "I can see it would be," he admitted.

"And please don't think we're ungrateful. Doctor Ed told us you offered to pay the bill. I saw you pass him some money just now." An odd look came to her face. "Do you know what it made me think of?"

Lantry shifted uncomfortably in his saddle. He didn't answer.

"It made me think," Marcella said, "of Luke ten: thirty-five." She smiled, and it was the first time Lantry had noticed how really lovely she was. Then she hurried back into the house.

He rode toward the hotel with her last phrase echoing. *Luke ten: thirty-five.* What the hell did she mean by that? It sounded like a verse from Scriptures. What the hell would that have to do with him, Jeff Lantry?

It nagged at him and made him curious. He must look it up. But where? If there was such a thing as a Bible around the Grand Central Hotel he'd never seen it. Certainly he hadn't seen the inside of one himself since early childhood. They'd kept one, he remembered vaguely, at the orphanage.

On an impulse Lantry reined the sorrel uphill again and turned to the right on Second Avenue. He stopped at the little Episcopal church there. Lantry had scarcely been aware of its existence. Yesterday he would have laughed if anyone had suggested his stopping here.

He went in and found a gaunt, elderly man in a threadbare black coat. Lantry didn't know his name. He asked bluntly, "What does it say in Luke ten: thirty-five?" The rector looked at him curiously, and Lantry felt his face burning.

Then the man picked up a leather-bound book. He opened it, thumbed a few pages, and said, "It's in a story about a traveler who picked up a wounded man by the road and took him to an inn. In the thirty-fifth verse it says, 'When he departed, he took out two pence, and gave them to the host, and said unto him, Take care of him; and whatsoever thou spendest more, when I come again, I will repay thee.'"

Lantry gaped. "Is that all?"

"That's all. What more would you want, young man?"

"Thanks." Lantry went out to his horse. His lips took a grim down curve as he spurred the sorrel toward Main Street. "She thinks I'm a damned saint, Mike." He laughed, but the laugh had a crack in it. A false note. A loose and intangible string was floating in his mind. He couldn't quite pin it down. It gave him an uncomfortable, guilty feeling inside, and it seemed to have nothing whatever to do with Gerry Ashton or Marcella Blair.

It was a feeling which had preyed on him, subconsciously, since the day he'd carried Gerald Ashton into Doctor Ed's house.

All at once he remembered. Amy Driscoll's boarding-house four years ago. The day they'd lynched Frank Foster. It was the *same* house, there at the corner of Second and F. Doctor Ed had taken it over for a residence, an office, and a hospital. Lantry's face flamed. Once he'd swindled his way into that house to steal from a dead man—and today a girl with starry eyes had likened him, in that very house, to a damned hero!

"Hell!" Lantry muttered. He reined Mike savagely to a stop in front of the hotel.

Dismounting, he started automatically across the street toward the Esperanza. He had no purpose except to find Sheep, who was probably hanging out there as usual, and tell Charlie to put up the horse.

But after a step or two Lantry stopped. He turned back into the hotel lobby. "Send over to the Esperanza," he directed the clerk, "and see if Charlie Sheep's there. If he is, have him take my horse to the barn."

As he went up to his room, Lantry wondered at himself. At his motive, rather. Why hadn't he gone to find Charlie? On the other hand, why should he? If he wanted a drink, he could get one right here. Lantry took a bottle from his closet shelf and poured himself a stiff one. His eye fell on a brassbound trunk. It was empty now, except for a sheaf of contracts. Once it had been packed with Frank Foster's loot. Lantry kicked it moodily. He closed the closet door and sat down, sucking at his liquor. He felt unreasonably cheapened and depressed. And angry at his own mawkish-ness. For he knew now exactly why he hadn't crossed to the Esperanza. If he'd gone, he'd've gotten mixed up with that red-haired harpy over there. She was so different from Marcella Blair. They were two opposite atmospheres, two opposite worlds—two opposite sides of the street.

A man just couldn't go from a girl like Marcella to the likes of Ruby Costello.

Ruby was at the bar when a messenger from the hotel came in. Was Charlie Sheep around? Yes, there he was drinking free beer in a booth. "Mr. Lantry wants his horse put up," the messenger said. He went out, followed by Charlie.

Ruby was irked. Why hadn't Jeff come himself? She'd been lonely for him. She'd been counting the days until he'd be back from his circuit of inspection. She wanted particularly to see him right now. She knew, of course, about the ultimatum from Jess Jallison. In less than three weeks Jallison would come in, gunning for Lantry. She must advise and coach the man she loved. Not that she doubted his ability to best Jallison. The unearned reputation Lantry had won, four years ago in a gun fight on the Pine River trail, still clung to him. Most of Durango thought he was fast on the draw, in a class with Tom Gifford, and Ruby fully shared that confidence. But she must make sure that Jeff took no chances. She had a plan for improving the chances. Adopting it, Jeff could hardly miss a massive target like Jess Jallison.

But today Lantry didn't appear at the Esperanza.

A day later he again sent for Charlie Sheep by messenger. It both annoyed and puzzled Ruby. Why was Lantry avoiding her?

She looked out and saw him ride past along Main Street. "Hello, Jeff," she called. He seemed not to hear her and rode on. She saw him turn up F Street toward Second Avenue. What would he be doing up there?

Lantry found Doctor Ed in the downstairs ward. Marcella wasn't there.

"She's been working too hard," the doctor said. "I made her take the afternoon off."

Lantry concealed his disappointment. "How's Ashton?" he asked.

"As well as could be hoped. He's semiconscious most of

the time. You can't expect him to come out of a thing like that very fast. I took out a piece of skull the size of a half dollar."

"What about his liquor appetite? Will he still have it?"

"Chances are he will. The first normal day he has, he'll be yelling for it like a Comanche Indian. But we won't let him have any. That's a promise I made to Melissa."

Lantry went out and rode back to Main Street. Halfway up the block he saw a man and a girl window-shopping. Tom Gifford and Marcella Blair. A furrow formed between Lantry's eyes. So Tom was still hanging around town. Maybe Tom wasn't so dumb, after all. Lantry dismounted and tied Mike to a rack. He heard a ripple of laughter from Marcella. She needed to laugh. She'd had nothing but shocks since landing here in the Basin.

Before he could reach them, Tom and Marcella had turned in at the drugstore. Passing, Lantry saw them perching on stools for sodas. Three would be a crowd, he thought, and went moodily on home.

June turned into July. An atmosphere of suspense grew in Durango. Everybody knew about Jess Jallison's challenge to Jeff Lantry. Lantry had been given thirty days to sell out and get out. And he wasn't getting. The month would expire on the twentieth. Jallison wasn't a man to back down. Neither was Lantry.

Names to conjure with, those two. And time was running out. They'd meet head on, on the day of decision, like two freight trains driving toward a crash on the same track. Men at the bars talked of nothing else. Girls in the bawdy parlors whispered in nervous falsettos.

Maybe they'd meet before the deadline. At the racing events on the Fourth of July. That was always a big day in Durango. The entire Basin usually came in. Surely Jess

Jallison would come with the rest.

But Jallison didn't show up for the races. And the event lacked its customary luster this year because the Talcotts weren't there. The major had been scheduled in one trotting race, and Bruce in another. But Bruce was out of action, recovering from a rifle wound. And Carey Talcott wouldn't leave his son's bedside.

With the Talcott entries canceled, the races were rather tame. Lantry rode up to see only the last event. The track was between Fifth and Sixth Avenues, near H Street, just four blocks up the hill from the Grand Central Hotel. A brass band was blaring forth when Lantry arrived. He sat his saddle, watching the horses take post. This was a stock-saddle running race. Tom Gifford, he noted, was in it. Too bad he wasn't in time to place a bet on Tom.

His eyes wandered to the grandstand. Then to boxes in the foreground. Gay parasols were there, and escorts in their spangled best. Lantry blinked when he saw Marcella Blair. Her parasol hid the man she was with. Then, riding to another angle of view, Lantry saw that he was Sax Consadine.

So Tom had a rival! Lantry smiled. But the smile lacked mirth. Not that he had anything against Sax Consadine. Sax was a solid citizen with polished manners and a silver-trimmed saddle, to say nothing of ten thousand cows. Was it just a date? Or was Sax really interested in Marcella? Absorbed over it, Lantry forgot to watch the race at all. It was finished before he knew it. He heard people shouting Gifford's name. So Tom had won. Sax Consadine was doing pretty well today, too. Lantry felt strangely isolated and lonely. He saw Tom ride up to Consadine's box, saw Marcella lean forward to congratulate him. Everybody seemed to be having a good time except Jeff Lantry.

A morning later he called at Doctor Ed's to inquire about Gerry Ashton. At least he assured himself he went for that purpose. He found the doctor and Marcella on either side of Ashton's cot, pleading with him to be quiet. Gerry had reached the difficult stage of his convalescence. He was begging for whisky.

"One little one won't hurt me!"

"It won't help you either," Marcella said. She turned and saw Lantry, shook her head, and motioned for him to leave the room.

Lantry went out on the porch and waited. It was a long time before Marcella came out. She didn't mention Gerry Ashton. Her eyes were stern and disapproving. "It's so stupid!" she said. "Why do you do it?"

Lantry stared. "Do what?"

She looked down at the gun in his holster. "Mr. Consadine told me. Yesterday at the races. Then I asked Tom Gifford and he admitted it's true. Why," she demanded severely, "don't you grow up?"

"Grow up? What do you mean?"

"You've made a date for the twentieth, haven't you? To kill a man or be killed yourself?" Her tone was scathing.

"I didn't make the date," Lantry said. "The other man made it."

She made a gesture of impatience. "You're like cavemen. Waiting to beat each other over the heads with spiked clubs. And I can't even make the sheriff listen to me!"

His eyes widened. "You've been to the sheriff?"

"Why shouldn't I? This is the nineteenth century. We're not savages, Mr. Lantry. But the sheriff just shrugs it off. He says unless you file a complaint against Mr. Jallison, there's nothing he can do."

Resentment flushed Lantry. "What do you want? Should I run like a coyote? Or should I hide behind the sheriff like a child clinging to its mother's skirts? Suppose you look after your own troubles and let me look after mine."

"Very well, I will." Her chin was up. "Good day, Mr.

Lantry." She turned and went back in to Doctor Ed.

Lantry walked stiffly down to Main Street and crossed to the Esperanza. It was the first time he'd been there in two weeks. Sax Consadine was at the bar rolling his golden dice. Lantry joined him, ordered a highball.

"How's your gun arm, Jeff?" Sax grinned. "Got it all limbered up for Jallison?"

Lantry didn't answer. At the far end of the bar he saw Ruby Costello. Pablo was putting an absinthe frappé in front of her. Ruby raised it to her lips. Consadine, at Lantry's elbow, shifted the dice from his right to his left hand. He continued to roll them on the bar, chatting amiably all the while.

Lantry tossed down his liquor and went out.

From the hotel lobby, half an hour later, he saw Ruby Costello riding her sidesaddled mare north toward Animas City. She often took rides like that, and always she looked stunning in her trailing black habit. Lantry assumed she did it to advertise herself and her palace of chance.

In a little while he noticed Sax Consadine riding in the same direction. It seemed natural enough. Sax had cattle in all corners of the range.

Morning greeted Durango with the news of another bold raid. A stage had been held up by masked men on the toll road to Silverton. Outlaws had made off with a mine payroll and the wallets of all passengers. The sheriff had already hit the trail with a posse. Another coup by the Blue Mountains boys, people said.

They were sure of it when, days later, the posse straggled wearily back into town. The outlaws, as usual, had vanished into thin air. But empty wallets had been found, and a slit payroll bag, in a lonely canyon of the Blue Mountains. Utah authorities, the sheriff said, had taken up the hunt from there.

Men shrugged and went about their routine affairs. It was just another small explosion amid the sound and fury of Durango.

13

LANTRY KEPT AWAY from Doctor Ed's house. Marcella's rebuke still stung, and the less he saw of her the better. After all she was only a tenderfoot idealist with no faint idea of the raw, rugged realities of the Basin. She shouldn't have come here in the first place.

He'd close the door of his mind on her. With that firm resolution, Lantry resumed dropping in at the Esperanza almost daily. Sometimes he went there to find Charlie Sheep, and sometimes just for a quick one with friends around town. Ruby Costello cornered him whenever she could. It was like a game, and Lantry rather enjoyed it. He was vain enough not to mind being hunted.

Once, near the middle of July, she inveigled him to a private room for a glass of champagne.

She had a purpose. "Time's running out, Jeff. What are you going to do about Jallison?"

"Nothing."

"Don't be silly. In just five days he'll be in town with a loaded gun."

"So will I."

"But you must plan it, Jeff. Listen. He'll come in early. You stay out of sight till late in the day."

"Why should I do that?"

"He'll go from bar to bar looking for you. He'll take a drink at each bar. After about eight jiggers, he'll be gun-slow. His draw won't be either quick or sure."

Lantry looked at her with a feeling of disgust. He'd always known she was cold-blooded. "You want me to wait till he's drunk and then murder him! No thanks, Ruby."

He left his champagne untasted and went forward to the barroom. Ruby followed, biting her lip. "But I didn't mean it that way, Jeff."

A youngish, sunburned stranger at the bar accosted him. "Are you Jeff Lantry? My name's Pettibone. Dave Pettibone from Chama. I got a homestead over that way. And I lease a school section adjoinin'."

"Yes?"

"What about staking me to some cows? A calf-crop share deal, like you always make. I'd take right good care of 'em. Look me up at the Pagosa Springs bank."

Lantry rather liked the cut of him. The man looked solid and capable.

"I'll keep you in mind, Pettibone. Maybe one of my men won't want to renew when we ship calves in October. Or I might want to get rid of one of 'em. In that case, if your references are all right, I'll take you on."

"Thanks," Pettibone said. "I'll be ready, any time you say."

Lantry made a note of his name and went out.

He kept away from Ruby's Place all the rest of the week. Neither did Doctor Ed's house see him. He didn't like Ruby because she was evil, and he avoided Marcella because she was an impractical prude.

Main Street saw him daily, going to and from the restaurants and shops. Usually he ate at the Chuck Wagon, Durango's largest eating-place and directly across from the Esperanza. Men whispered as he passed, eying him speculatively, as they might eye a race-track entry. Soon, they knew, he'd make a Roman holiday for Durango. This was a sporting town where the best man won, whether it be a rock-drilling contest or a battle with guns. In neither case would there be any interference. When man met man, in the rugged individualism of Durango, other men stood aside.

Late in the morning of the nineteenth Tom Gifford tied his horse in front of the Grand Central. He found Lantry in the lobby.

"Hello, Jeff. How you feelin'?"

"Fine, Tom. How's everything on the Mancos?"

"Just fine," Tom said. "Cowstuff's puttin' on tallow, and the grama's beginnin' to cure." He sat down and rolled a cigarette uneasily. They were old friends, these two. But old friends, often, are harder to advise than new.

"Look, Jeff," Tom blurted out, fixing his gaze on the gun at Lantry's hip. "Just between you an' me, did you ever shoot at anything bigger'n a jack rabbit?"

Lantry grinned. "I potted at a coyote one time."

"And missed, I'll bet. See here, Jeff, you haven't got a Chinaboy's chance with Jallison, and you know it. He was born with a gun in his hand. Been throwin' lead all his life."

"What do you want me to do? Back out? Catch a train for Denver and take a room at the Y.M.C.A.?"

Tom was tongue-tied. His code forbade him to suggest any form of retreat. There was really nothing he could say or do.

Lantry grinned. "No use me trying to fool you, Tom. As a gunman I'm just a bluff. But you're the only one knows it. Everybody else thinks I helped you shoot it out with those two killers on the Pine River trail, that time. It gave me a rep. The only thing I ever did to back it up was to ride around with a gun on my hip, these last four years."

Those were the facts, known only to Gifford and Lantry.

"It'll be suicide," Tom said bluntly.

"Maybe. So what? Let's step over to the Oasis and I'll buy you a drink."

When Tom shook his head, Lantry remembered that the cowboy was a total abstainer. "I was on my way," Tom said, "to see how Gerry Ashton's makin' it. Want to come along?"

Lantry was about to decline. Then it occurred to him that this could easily be the last full day of his life. It wouldn't hurt to see Marcella just once again. "Okay, Tom. You talked me into it."

The sorrel was tied at the hotel hitchrack. They mounted and rode stirrup to stirrup down to F Street, then up the hill to Doctor Ed's.

Both Doctor Ed and Marcella were in the main ward. Gerry Ashton was asleep. "Oh, hello, Tom!" Marcella said brightly. "We've missed you." She turned to Lantry with reserve. "Good morning, Mr. Lantry."

Ashton's case, they learned, was progressing favorably. The hazards from now on, Doctor Ed said, would be mental and temperamental rather than physical. "We have to watch him," the doctor confided. "Soon as he gets strong enough, he might try sneaking out for a drink."

Footsteps were coming down the stairs. From the hall doorway a cheery voice announced, "Come and get it, folks."

It was Melissa Ashton calling them to the midday meal. Lantry blinked at the change in her. The crushed look, all the drabness, was gone from her. Her face was smooth, her eyes bright, and she wore a neat house frock with a yellow apron. She was almost as pretty, Lantry thought, as Marcella.

"Mr. Lantry!" She gave him both of her hands. "And Tom Gifford. It's so good to see you."

"Set two more plates, Melissa," Doctor Ed insisted. "It's high time we're having guests. Come along, you fellows."

He took their arms and led them toward the door. Melissa lifted her skirts and dashed upstairs to set the extra plates.

Climbing those stairs brought back uneasy memories to

Lantry. They depressed him and painted a dull flush on his face. The last time he'd passed up these steps his purpose had been to prowl for the loot of a lynched felon. He remembered the slippery guile with which he'd intruded upon the boardinghouse woman, Amy Driscoll.

"You haven't seen our happy home, have you, boys?" Doctor Ed chattered as they came to the top of the stairs. "We've remodeled it some. Dining-room's up front. That room at the back is Marcella's."

The room at the back, Lantry recalled, had been Frank Foster's. The man who'd swung from a pine tree that cold dawn, four years ago. Did Marcella know it? He hoped not.

They found Melissa in the front room with a chubby little boy. He was starched and scrubbed, an amazing transformation from the wilderness waif Lantry remembered. "This is Jackie," Melissa said proudly. "He likes Durango."

Doctor Ed picked the child up with a grandfatherly affection and set him in a high chair. Marcella seated Tom next to herself. Lantry, across from them, again felt a sense of isolation. To cover it he asked Doctor Ed how long they'd have to keep Gerry Ashton here.

"Six months," Doctor Ed answered.

"Why six?" Lantry questioned. "Why not four or eight?"

"He's sick in two ways," Amory said. "He's got a broken head. Also he's an alcoholic." His frankness brought no reaction from Melissa and Marcella. Lantry sensed that they'd discussed it often before.

"What's that got to do with six months?" Lantry asked curiously.

Doctor Ed looked grimly at Melissa. "Shall I tell him about that other case I had one time? Up at Leadville?"

"I don't see why not, Doctor," Melissa said. "It was Mr. Lantry who brought Gerry here." She turned to Lantry with a grateful smile. "We can never thank you enough," she said.

"One time up at Leadville," Doctor Ed related, "there was an alcoholic. He was a no-good bum. He couldn't handle his liquor and he couldn't leave it alone. They had to throw him out of the bars. He went lower and lower, mooching drinks by day, sleeping in the gutters by night. One night he had a burning thirst, and no one would stand him a treat. So he smashed the window of a liquor shop and stole a quart. They put him in jail for six months."

"So what?" Lantry queried.

"It cured him," Doctor Ed said simply. "Six months of enforced abstinence was just what he needed. He hasn't taken a drink since. He's got gray hairs now, and a good job, and a nice family."

The old doctor beamed at Melissa and then at little Jackie. Melissa got up suddenly and went to the kitchen for more biscuits. And Lantry knew, now, why Doctor Ed took such a personal interest in Gerald Ashton's case. The man in the Leadville story had been Ed Amory himself.

When Marcella said good-by to Lantry, she referred to the Jallison matter only indirectly. "I take back one thing I said, Mr. Lantry. This country isn't *all* savage and brutal, like I thought. The exception is Doctor Ed."

"He's pretty much of a guy," Lantry admitted.

"He told us that story the first night we came here. It did wonders for Melissa. She's been walking on air ever since. He tells her the six months will be up in December. He says his Christmas present to her will be her own husband, physically and morally sound. Do you think it could really happen?"

Lantry shrugged noncommittally. "If it happened once it could happen again. I better be running along now."

"Come back and see how it—" Marcella stopped quite

suddenly, and he saw a lurking dread in her eyes. He wouldn't be able to come back, perhaps. She was thinking of tomorrow, when he must trade bullets with Jess Jallison.

"Oh, I'll be around every now and then," Lantry said carelessly. He went out to the hitchrack where Tom Gifford was waiting. They rode down to Main, where Tom turned left and Lantry turned right.

The hotel lobby, when Lantry entered it, had never seemed so desolate and bare.

In the morning he bathed, shaved meticulously, and put on his newest clothes. The shirt he chose was soft, creamy silk, open at the throat. He took particular care with his fingernails. The hotel boy had already polished his boots. They were half boots, and Lantry tucked his trouser cuffs neatly into them. He tried the action of his gun and put in six shells. With the gun at his hip he went to the Chuck Wagon for breakfast.

Where had he better let Jallison find him? Not in the hotel lobby. Unwary guests might be around. Nor on the street, where a stray bullet could easily hit some shopper.

It had best be at a bar. Bar customers would expect the encounter and keep out of the way. Which bar? Jallison would naturally look for him at Ruby's Place. Since the thing must happen, Lantry wanted to get it over with as soon as possible.

At nine in the morning he crossed to the Esperanza. He took his stand at the deep end of the bar and ordered rye. Pablo set it out. Lantry paid for it but didn't touch it. His wits must be clear, his hand steady. Only a few customers were around this early. Ruby herself was probably asleep.

Other customers came in. When they saw Lantry, most of them backed out. The few who remained took their drinks to wall booths. No one wanted to be between Lantry and the entrance. He had the entire bar to himself.

Nine-thirty. Charlie Sheep sidled in and slid into a booth near the front. Pablo took him a schooner of beer. Charlie didn't pay for it. He never paid for anything at Ruby's.

Ten o'clock and Ruby herself came in. She wore trailing black, even to black jet earrings and a high black comb in her hair. Lantry grinned. "Not in mourning for me already, are you, Ruby?"

She came to him and put an anxious hand on his arm. "Oh, Jeff! You shouldn't have come so early. Why don't you—"

He brushed her away. "It's my party," he said gruffly.

Pablo mopped the bar, his broad brown face beaded with sweat. Men in the booths whispered, in subdued suspense, casting cautious glances toward Lantry. Talk sifted in from the sidewalk, and it was all about Jess Jallison.

"Jeff Lantry can handle him, all right."

"I dunno. He's fast, Jallison is. Me, I'm keepin' outa there."

Ten-thirty. Lantry heard a horse lope up the street. The rider dismounted at the Esperanza rack. An ominous hush told Lantry it was Jallison.

When Jallison pushed the swinging screen inward, he looked like a mountain. Huge and black-stubbled he loomed there, his great head bulging from his shoulders, his bulky waist crossbelted, his leathered hips weighted with two guns.

Lantry had never known him to wear two guns before. *How many shots does he want at me, anyway?* He himself stood with his holster away from the bar. His right arm hung loosely. He mustn't rush things. The play was Jallison's. All he could do was defend himself, and let blood fall where it would.

Jallison took five slow, heavy steps toward him. He stood

at mid-bar. His voice came dangerously quiet. "I see you're still in town, Lantry."

"Where else would I be?" Lantry challenged. "I'm in business here."

"This is the showdown," Jallison warned.

"Looks like it," Lantry said.

"It's you or me," Jallison said, and went for his guns.

His own draw, Lantry realized, was awkward and slow. Why didn't the man kill him? Then he saw Jallison pitch forward, his face convulsed, his arms outflung. Something had whizzed down the room. Its hilt showed between Jallison's shoulder blades as he fell.

A knife! A boot knife, expertly thrown.

Jallison landed in a sprawl, directly at Lantry's feet. For a moment he was on all fours, swaying. Then he flattened and lay still. Lantry looked at a booth beyond him and saw Charlie Sheep.

Other customers leaped upon Charlie and pinioned him. Someone yelled for the sheriff. They all knew that Sheep, to save his master's life, had hurled the knife.

The fact sickened Lantry. He leaned weakly against the bar. He looked into Pablo's eyes and saw suspicion there. Men crowded in from the walk, took in the scene at a glance. There lay a dead man, knifed in the back. There stood Lantry with a cold gun. And there, struggling in the grasp of outraged bystanders, was Lantry's man, Sheep.

Had Lantry put Sheep up to it? A dozen pair of suspicious eyes asked the question.

Lantry knew he hadn't. But how could he prove it to Durango?

14

"WE GOT HIM, SHERIFF," a customer yelled. A sallow, tired man with a brass star had come in.

Sheriff Lund stood staring at Jallison on the floor. Then his pale, washed-out eyes lifted to meet Lantry's. Lantry nodded, motioning toward Charlie Sheep. "That's right, Sheriff. He did it. I'm sorry as hell about it."

The Indian had stopped struggling. He stood limp and stolid in the grasp of his captors. Lund questioned Pablo and a few of the patrons. The victim, they said, had been on the point of shooting it out with Lantry when Charlie Sheep had knifed him from the rear.

Lund looked at Lantry and asked in a dull monotone, "He worked for you as a guide and bodyguard, didn't he, Jeff?"

"He's been my guide and wrangler for four years," Lantry said stiffly. "I don't need a bodyguard."

Lund took charge of Charlie Sheep. "Pablo, watch the body till the coroner gets here. Jeff, you better come along, and we'll talk this over."

The sheriff marched out with his prisoner, and Lantry followed. He felt bitterly humiliated, walking down Main Street at Lund's elbow. The Indian came along docilely enough. Durango stared at them, from saloon doors, from wagon seats, from the sidewalks. The story was spreading furiously.

At B Street Lund turned two blocks up the hill to Third Avenue. Then south to a vacant area at the end of Third. Here, isolated from the town, stood a squat, flat-roofed jail. There was only one cell. At the moment it was empty. Lund gave Charlie Sheep a shove into it and locked the door.

He went outside, hunkered on his spurred heels there, and looked up at Lantry. "I've known you a long time, Jeff. So I know dang well you didn't put him up to it. Other folks might think different." Lund took a deep bite from a tobacco plug and chewed vigorously.

"I can't help what they think," Lantry said. "I knew

Charlie was dumb. But I didn't think he was *that* dumb."

"Dumb," Lund agreed. "That's it, Jeff. He's like an animal. A watchdog. He thinks the world and all of you. So when it looked like you was gonna be gunned up, he tossed the knife. No one told him to. It was just animal instinct."

A sharp thought stung Lantry. *No one told him to?* What about Ruby Costello? She, too, thought the world and all of Jeff Lantry. She was treacherous, conscienceless, a cold schemer. Her cap had long been set for Lantry, and he'd been amusedly aware of it from the first. She was boldly conceited, conceited enough to think she'd get him some day. She'd have every motive to coach Charlie Sheep in any act designed to save Lantry's life.

Lantry went into the jail and spoke through the bars. "Who told you to do it, Charlie?"

"No one tell me," Charlie said.

"Was it Ruby?"

The half-breed shook his head stubbornly. "No one tell me. Him fast gunman, Jallison. Me no want him kill you."

It was all Lantry could get out of him. He went outside to Lund and said wearily, "If you want me I'll be at the hotel."

Lund looked up at him with a grimace. Tobacco juice stained his mustache. "I wish to hell I could chuck this here job, Jeff. Been tryin' to resign fer the last year. Know anybody wants this badge? What about Tom Gifford? He'd be a good man fer it."

"I guess Tom'd rather stick to ranching," Lantry said. He knew what was in Lund's mind. Durango would boil over about this knifing. Man-to-man gun fights were taken in stride. But a knife in the back was something else.

"He deserves hangin'," Lund admitted, thumbing over his shoulder toward the bars of Charlie's cell. "But not from a tree. I reckon I'd better sit up all night with him, Jeff."

"If you need any help," Lantry said, "let me know."

He walked back to the hotel. Passing the corner of Second and F, he glimpsed a face at a window. This was Doctor Ed's house, and the face was Marcella's. Pain and horror were etched on it. Lantry realized that the whole ugly story must have reached even to this quiet house of mercy. He compressed his lips grimly and walked on.

All afternoon men rode into Durango. Cattle hands, most of them. Lantry looked from the lobby and saw half the Circle K crew lope by. Jallison's outfit. Loyal to Jallison, all of them. They wouldn't be likely to take this lying down. Neither would Buck Shaw's crew from Dove Creek. For years those orthodox cowmen, and every man on their payrolls, had shared a prejudice against the chain-brand interloper, Jeff Lantry.

Main Street was milling by sundown. Men stood in knots, gesticulating, debating. It was clear that two theories were clashing head on. One, that Charlie Sheep had acted on his own with the instinct of a dumb watchdog; the other, that his master had coached him in the act.

When Lantry went out to supper, half the town slapped him on the back and expressed warm confidence. The other half stood apart, muttering, armed to the teeth and staring coldly.

The irony was that no one could ever prove it, one way or the other.

Lantry went to bed early.

It was about midnight when two shots from the street awakened him. He sat up in the dark, with an odd feeling that it had all happened before. Then he remembered his first night in this room. The night of April 11, 1881.

He went to his window and looked out. Yes, there it was,

the same scene. Men on the march. Masked men. Boots thumping the boardwalks as they trooped in a common direction. The direction was south, toward the jail.

Lantry thought of old Sheriff Lund, on guard alone there. He'd have more than he could handle. Dressing hurriedly, Lantry buckled on his gun. That half-breed Piute, however guilty, was entitled to a trial in court. He'd been Lantry's man. Ignorant and misguided, he'd been, none the less, loyal. Fury burned in Lantry. If he could help it, they wouldn't drag Charlie out of that jail.

He went out the back way. Avoiding Main Street, he hurried two blocks uphill to Third Avenue. The houses there were shuttered and dark. Lantry raced south along the gravel walk. Lund, alone at the jail, would be helpless against that mob.

Part of the mob had already assembled when Lantry arrived. Others were trooping up A and B Streets from Main. Lantry pressed through them, saw a square silhouette with barred windows. In front of it stood Lund. Lund had a shotgun. Lantry took a stand at his elbow.

"Need a deputy, Sheriff?"

"You're sworn in," Lund said. "Temporary duty, y'understand. Just for tonight."

He raised his voice and spoke to the crowd. "Listen, men. The guy in there's guilty. Nobody claims he ain't. But you're no court. Neither am I. We'll let a judge say when they hang him."

The crowd swelled. A sullen roar came from it. Those in front were masked. By their *chaparejos* Lantry could tell that they were mainly range hands. "Okay, Lund," a voice said. "You done your duty. We'll all vote fer you agin next time. Right now you kin stand outa the way."

Lund didn't move. Neither did Lantry. In the darkness Lantry didn't see a man circle the jail. The man had a singletree in his hand. He climbed the rear wall of the jail with it and lay flat on the roof.

The mob in front surged forward a little. Lund raised his shotgun. Lantry drew his forty-five.

Then something crashed on his head. It was a singletree wielded by a man on the roof. Lantry buckled; as his knees hit the ground the forty-five flew from his hand. Lund whirled just in time to see an arm reach over the jail eave and strike again. The singletree stunned Lund. As he went down, the mob swarmed over him like stampeding steers.

Lantry, sprawling underfoot and half-dazed, heard the jail door crash. Men poured inside. A dozen pistol shots rang out. Another volley. Then another. They weren't wasting rope on Charlie Sheep. He was being fired on through the cell bars. The vigilantes swarmed out again. They moved away. The night swallowed them.

Lantry stood up, rubbing a lump on his head. He helped Sheriff Lund to his feet. "They've gone, Sheriff. You did everything you could."

They went inside and found Charlie Sheep dead, bullet-riddled on the cell floor.

The lump on his head kept Lantry in his room all the next day. Doctor Ed Amory came to the hotel for a look at him. "Nothing serious," he announced. "You'll be up and around tomorrow."

"Okay," Lantry said. He took out his wallet. "While you're here, better let me pay Gerry Ashton's bill to date. How much is it?"

"It's all paid," Doctor Ed said.

"Who paid it?"

The doctor's eyes twinkled. "You paid part of it," he said. "Melissa pays me a little more of it every time she looks hopeful and happy. Jackie pays a little on it every time he curls up in my lap. Marcella pays some on it by working for less than she's worth. The big payoff will come, of course, from Gerry himself. By December, if my medicine's any good, he'll be a man again."

When Lantry went out, a day later, he found Durango still divided into two camps. Those who suspected him of conspiring in a treachery and those who didn't. Buck Shaw came in from Dove Creek, flanked by three of the toughest-looking cowhands Lantry had ever seen. They were the same trio, he remembered, he'd met that day four years ago in a Dolores saloon. The three from whom Charlie Sheep, on a stolen buckskin horse, had taken panicky flight.

Later Lantry saw Shaw and his gunnies consorting with Jallison men. The entire crowd went into a huddle down by the river. Rumors flew that they were taking up Jallison's feud right where Jallison had left off.

It was Sax Consadine who told Lantry about it. "They wanted me in on it, Jeff," Sax said. "But I'd rather stay neutral. Frankly I think they're right on the basic count. The way you do business spoils the range. Some of your share people wide-loop slick-ears. Your whole scheme is an encouragement to nesters. I wish you'd quit it, Jeff. But I'm a man of peace. I don't believe in these tough ultimatums."

"Like Jallison's? Giving me thirty days to sell out?"

"Buck Shaw's gonna give you a little better break than that," Sax confided. "He admits thirty days isn't long enough. He says he wants to be fair. All he asks is that when you ship your calves in October, like you always do, you ship your cows, too. And that you don't bring any more into the Basin."

A day later Buck Shaw called gravely at Lantry's hotel. He made exactly that demand. He wasn't tough about it. Today he wasn't even wearing a gun.

"And if I don't?" Lantry questioned. "What then?"

"If you don't, you'll have not one but thirty gun fights

on your hands." Buck Shaw leaned closer and spoke earnestly. "Listen, Lantry. Jess Jallison was popular with his crew. They liked him. They think he was murdered at your bidding. I don't know whether he was or not. That's not the point. Jallison's crew, and most of my own, think he was. They're itching to fill you full of slugs. The only reason they haven't is because I called them off. I asked them to give you till fall shipping-time to clear out. There's sense in that. Your calves won't be weanable, and therefore not shippable, till fall. If you ship them in October, and your cows with them, and never come back, okay. If you don't, you're a dead pigeon."

"I'll run my own business," Lantry said.

Buck Shaw shrugged. "That's as long as I can hold them off. Fall shipping-time. After that, it's your funeral." He went out, climbed to his saddle, and loped away.

Before the end of the week, Sheriff Lund resigned his office.

Lantry had just heard the news when someone knocked at his room door. He opened it, and there stood Major Carey Talcott. The major looked older, thinner, grayer. "Come in," Lantry said warmly. "How's Bruce?"

"Can't stop but a minute," the major said. "Bruce is coming along fine. Just want to know if you'll take supper with me tonight, Lantry. Seven o'clock at the Chuck Wagon Café."

"I sure will, Major. Thanks."

"See you at seven, then. Got an appointment at the bank right now. Have to rush along. So long, suh."

The major left abruptly. *Probably wants to give me some friendly advice,* Lantry thought. *About Buck Shaw and the Jallison outfit.*

It puzzled Lantry a little. Major Talcott was a forthright man. If he wanted to give advice, he wouldn't need to make a supper date for it. *Maybe,* Lantry reconsidered, *he wants to borrow some money.* There were rumors about a heavy debt hanging over the Bridlebit, due to extravagant investments in racing stock.

At seven o'clock, the true answer jolted Lantry.

The Chuck Wagon, in spite of its homely name, was the most spacious and best-appointed restaurant in Durango. Arriving there at seven, Lantry found that Major Talcott had chartered it for the evening. A long curved table, shaped like a horseshoe, filled the room. Sixty guests were seated at it, banquet-style. Major Talcott was presiding. The single vacant chair was at his right.

Jefferson Lantry was escorted to it. His face flamed when he saw who was present. The east side of Main Street was there. The leading merchants, the professional men, all the better element of Durango. Ladies from Third Avenue were there. Lantry saw the round gray face of Ed Amory, with Melissa Ashton sitting next to him.

The wine glasses were full. Major Talcott stood up, a commanding figure in his double-breasted white vest and black frock coat. "To our special guest of the evening, ladies and gentlemen. One whom we all hold in the highest esteem—Mr. Jeff Lantry."

All present drained their glasses. Everybody smiled and waved at Lantry. He sat down in confusion.

A running chatter started, lasting through six courses, and not a word was said about the Jallison incident. Lantry knew, by then, that this was just the major's way of showing his colors. It was his vote of confidence in Jeff Lantry.

It made Lantry feel humble, sitting through it. He could hardly feel proud, because deep inside he knew he didn't deserve it. What would they think, he wondered, if they knew about Frank Foster? If they knew he'd stripped a dead man of his loot to get ahead, get ahead—

Looking along the table he missed one face. Melissa was

there, and Doctor Ed, but not Marcella. Certainly Marcella had been invited. The major would be especially fond of her because she'd saved his son's life. Her absence now looked pointed, as though she might not share this generous confidence. He knew what she thought of Durango. That it was cruel, savage, barbaric, a cockpit of unbridled passions. How much worse she'd think it now—after the treacherous knifing of Jallison and the shooting of Charlie Sheep!

Over the coffee Lantry heard talk of Tom Gifford. A voice asked, "Will Tom accept?"

Another voice: "You mean the sheriff job? Hope so. The citizens' committee went to Mancos and offered it to him. He claims he doesn't want to leave his ranch. But Luke Carmody offered to look after his stock for a season or two."

"Let's keep after him. We sure need Tom on that job."

That was the nearest reference made to the recent crime wave in Durango.

Lantry went home feeling that it had been the biggest night of his life—or would have been, had Marcella been there.

But the next day he saw her go into a Main Street drugstore. Doctor Ed often sent her to have prescriptions filled.

Lantry followed her in, raised his hat. "It's a warm day, Miss Blair. What about an ice-cream soda?"

She smiled and perched on a stool at the counter. "Thank you. I'll take strawberry. And it happens I wanted to see you, Mr. Lantry."

He took the next stool. "You could have seen me last night," he suggested.

"No, because it was my turn to take care of the ward. You ride the circuit of your ranches now and then, don't you? Do you ever get down around Farmington?"

"Yes. That's not far off my loop. Why?"

"The Farmington postmaster sent us a card. He said he read in the paper about Gerald Ashton being laid up at our hospital. An item of mail was there for Gerry and did we want him to forward it? We did, and it came yesterday."

"Anything important?"

"Miraculously important, Mr. Lantry. A legal envelope postmarked London. In it was a draft on an English bank for a hundred pounds."

"A windfall!" Lantry applauded. "Good for Gerry. He told me once he was English, but that his family had either died off or gone broke."

"Evidently they made a comeback," Marcella said. "This is the envelope the check came in." She brought it from her purse and gave it to Lantry. "The strange thing is— why should they address it to Farmington? Gerry says he never gave them an address like that. The last address he gave them was five years ago, when he was a cowboy on the Jallison ranch at Mancos."

Lantry nodded. "What do you want me to do?"

"The next time you're in Farmington, please talk to the postmaster. You might ask him if any other mail ever came there for Gerald Ashton. And if he has any idea how that address could have been established."

"Will do," Lantry promised. They finished the sodas and went out to the front walk. They stood there for a while, talking earnestly about Gerald Ashton.

From the Esperanza doorway across the street, Ruby Costello saw them. The tête-à-tête over there looked intimate and personal. Ruby's eyes narrowed to slits of resentment. Was that why Jeff hadn't come around lately?

More than a few whispers had reached Ruby about the pretty young nurse at Doctor Ed's. Very little went on in Durango that Ruby didn't hear about. She knew that Sax Consadine had escorted the girl to the Fourth of July races, and that Tom Gifford had taken a shine in the same direction. And now Jeff Lantry!

Lantry, the cynic, the self-sufficient, who pretended to scorn women! Falling for a starched white uniform and a pretty face! He wouldn't get away with it, if Ruby could help it. Or if he did, he'd pay for it. She, Ruby Costello, had staked the first claim there.

She saw the pair stroll slowly south to F Street and turn uphill toward Doctor Ed's. So he was taking her home. Ruby watched impatiently for Lantry to come back. He didn't. So he was staying for lunch. Ruby turned back to her bar, ordered a double Scotch. She was in a mood to throttle Marcella Blair.

15

LANTRY LOST NO TIME riding to Farmington. It was only a short way across the state line in New Mexico. He showed the envelope to the postmaster there. "How long has Gerald Ashton been getting mail here?"

"Four years," the postmaster said. "He gets a letter just like that regular, every three months. I noticed because of the fancy engraved envelope coming all the way from England. Ashton always called for it a few days after it came. But this time he couldn't, naturally, him being laid up in a hospital."

"Describe Ashton," Lantry demanded.

"He's about your height and build. Brown eyes, as I remember. Clean-shaven, dresses like a cowpoke. Dark hair and—"

"Ashton," Lantry broke in, "has yellow hair and blue eyes. You've been handing out mail to the wrong guy. What kind of a horse did he ride?"

"First one, then another. Once I noticed a Bridlebit on the left hip. You mean to say—"

"I mean don't hand out any more Ashton mail till Ashton himself shows up, properly identified."

The Bridlebit brand, Lantry thought as he rode home, meant nothing at all. For years Major Talcott had been selling horses on bills of sale. No doubt he'd also lost a few to rustlers. As a matter of fact this sorrel gelding on which Lantry himself was mounted had a Bridlebit brand.

Some outlaw must have impersonated Ashton, collecting a hundred pounds per quarter for perhaps four years. It burned Lantry. He thought of Melissa living in stark poverty all that time, in a homestead hovel.

Back in Durango he went into a huddle with Doctor Ed, Melissa, and Marcella. "Why," Doctor Ed wondered, "did the impostor miss collecting this last check?"

"He was afraid to," Lantry guessed. "If the postmaster had read about Gerry being laid up in Durango, he'd know the guy calling for the mail couldn't be Gerry. What about shooting a letter to those London lawyers?"

"I'll get one off right away," Doctor Ed promised.

"Can you think of anyone," Marcella questioned, "who fits the man's description?"

Lantry grinned cryptically. "Nobody nearer than myself. The postmaster says he's about my height and build, brown eyes, dark hair, clean-shaven, and rigs himself out like a cowpoke. I'll keep my eyes open next time I ride around the range."

When he went out on his September inspection circuit, Lantry rode alone. Although he really needed a man to replace Charlie Sheep, an obstinate pride kept him from hiring one for this trip. It would look like he was fortifying himself with a bodyguard. They'd think he was afraid of meeting Circle K men on the trails. So he'd show his defiance by riding alone. As for camp help, he wouldn't need it if he stayed all night with his various share ranchers.

This September inspection was always the most important of the year. It was the last he could make before shipping-time in October.

It was Lantry's fall routine to go to Denver on the first of October and be on hand there when the calf shipments arrived. That way he could watch the market, time the shipments, check the weighings, and pick up his checks directly from the commission people. The main thing was to avoid freight jams on the D & RG narrow-gauge. The tiny cattle cars held about thirty calves each, and the little engines could only pull about fifteen cars at a time up Cumbres Pass from Chama. Which meant that the shipments couldn't go all at once. From Denver Lantry could write or wire one man to ship on the fifth, another to ship on the seventh, and so on until the entire calf crop was rolling.

This year he planned to vary that routine in one detail. He would ship to Kansas City instead of to Denver. Kaycee was a bigger market, and he ought to get better pound prices. Missouri Valley feeders were beginning to bid actively for calves there, to fatten over winter on corn. The railroads would have to shift the cattle from narrow-gauge to standard cars at Pueblo, but that didn't matter. And for Lantry himself the trip to and from Kansas City should be comfortable enough, because sleeping-car service had now become nationwide. They'd even installed a sleeper on the narrow-gauge night train from Durango over Cumbres Pass.

At his first stop Lantry found everything all right. A normal calf crop with the calves fat and about ready to wean. "You'll get your shipping-instructions from Kansas City this year," he told the man.

"Who shall I turn the cows over to, Mr. Lantry? Or shall I keep 'em another year myself?"

"I'll let you know about that," Lantry said, "when I

send you the shipping-orders." That way he could keep his men on edge. By keeping them in suspense about next year, till the last minute, he gave them a motive to make the best possible showing *this* year.

His standard contract called for the share man to deliver all three hundred cows and half the calves to the Durango stock pens. There the calves were cut directly into cattle cars and shipped. It made a convenient and efficacious way of weaning. The man then either took the cows back home, or turned them over to his successor.

Lantry rode on to Abel Dickshot's place on Cherry Creek. He made a stern inspection there, because Jess Jallison had boldly accused Dickshot of having produced, last year, an impossibly large calf crop. Ninety-three percent. Not impossible, Lantry knew, but definitely improbable. Dickshot's place lay squarely between the Consadine and Jallison ranches. Conceivably the man might have wide-looped a few slick-ears from his neighbors.

This year everything seemed to be all right. The tally showed two hundred and two cows with calves by side, and ninety-eight dry cows. Perfectly normal.

Yet two things disturbed Lantry. He saw nine c in a C cows, each with a calf by side, grazing in a near-by swale. The c in a C was ninety miles north, near Telluride. Its riders probably didn't know these nine cows had strayed this far south. Possibly Dickshot had an eye on them. The night before shipping-day, he might cut the nine calves out and push them along in the drive to Durango.

He wouldn't dare cut them out now. If he did he'd either have to brand them or pen them in a corral. In the first case they'd run straight back to their mothers with telltale brands which could convict Dickshot. In the second case the mothers would close in on Dickshot's corral and bawl there, possibly attracting attention from passers-by.

Lantry spiked the whole thing by saying, "I'll drop a

card to the c in a C and tell 'em I saw some of their stuff down here."

Dickshot looked chagrined. His eyes avoided Lantry's.

Lantry stayed to lunch with him. Dickshot's wife served generous helpings of fresh beef. "One of my own yearlings from last year's crop," Dickshot said.

But was it? A rancher usually doesn't dress one of his own beeves before frost. Lantry took a look in the meat dugout. A fresh quarter was hanging there. He asked to see the hide. Dickshot showed him a yearling hide with the Dickshot brand on it. But the hide wasn't as fresh as the beef.

"I shan't renew your contract," Lantry said brusquely, and rode away.

So Jallison had been right about Dickshot! And not unnaturally Jallison had assumed that many of the other Lantry contract ranches were doing the same thing. Rustling all the meat they could eat and picking off a few slick-ears for shipment.

At all the other homesteads on his circuit, however, Lantry found everything as it should be. "I'll send shipping-instructions from Kaycee," he announced at every call.

Late September found him circling back toward Durango. On the last day out he met two Circle K men on the road. Their stares were bitterly hostile. One of them said, "This is your last season here, Lantry."

The other one said, "If it wasn't fer Buck Shaw, we'd of shot you fulla holes already."

Lantry smiled. "I'll remember to thank Buck," he said, and rode on.

The Circle K outfit was carrying on, he'd been told, pending settlement of Jallison's estate. Next year, they said, the big ranch would be either sold or leased.

Riding up Main Street in Durango, Lantry passed the

Esperanza. Ruby waved to him from its doorway. He ignored her and rode on to the hotel.

"Back again, Mr. Lantry?" the clerk greeted. "Hear the news? We got a new sheriff. Tom Gifford."

"Good," Lantry said.

The clerk grinned. "Tom always said he wouldn't take that job. But he's got a good reason now. It'll give him more sparkin'-time in town."

The inference was too broad to be missed. So Marcella Blair was the magnet which had reconciled Tom to a job in Durango! Lantry went thoughtfully up to his room. He sat on the bed and brooded through three cigarettes.

Then he shined his boots, dressed in his best, and went calling at Doctor Ed's.

Ruby Costello watched sullenly from her gambling-hall window. This made the third time she'd seen Jeff Lantry take that girl into the drugstore for treats. He hadn't been inside her own place since the knifing of Jallison.

Something told her he'd *never* come again. She'd lost him. And he in turn had lost his head over that nurse girl. Ruby went to her bar, seething.

The ghost of a plan came to her. A way to strike back at Lantry. A way to strip him of his last penny and make a bum out of him. At first it was only a filmy outline in Ruby's mind. She'd have to build it up and make it take shape. Lantry, she'd heard, was shipping to Kansas City this year. He wasn't known there. That fact, plus certain well-known threats made by the Circle K crew to Lantry, was all Ruby had to go on at the moment.

If her scheme worked, she'd need to know every intimate detail about Lantry's shipping-program this fall.

At the far end of the bar stood a be-chapped and gun-slung cowboy named Bud Channing. He was one of Sax Consadine's riders. In fact, Bud was of that section of the so-called Blue Mountains gang whose records were un-known to the law, and who could come at will into Du-rango.

Ruby moved down the bar to Bud's elbow. She whis-pered a precise instruction. Bud blinked, asked a few questions, and went out.

He found Lantry, an hour later, in the hotel lobby. "Hired anybody to take Charlie Sheep's place, Mr. Lan-try?"

"Not yet," Lantry said.

"What about me?"

"I thought you were riding for the Bar X Box, Chan-ning."

"I was. But I ain't now. I'd make you a first-class wrangler, Mr. Lantry."

The man looked capable. And reasonably intelligent. He could ride and pack and make camp and he knew cat-tle. Certainly he'd be an improvement over Charlie Sheep.

And Lantry had a weakness for being waited on. It was a complex dating from his underprivileged childhood at the orphanage. That was why he'd kept Charlie Sheep so long. Having someone constantly at his beck and call gave him a vicarious sense of dignity. A successful man didn't run his own errands. No one could accuse him of hiring this man for a bodyguard. Hadn't he just ridden a com-plete circle of the range alone?

"I'll take you on," Lantry agreed. "For the shipping-season, anyway. I'll be in Kansas City all through October and November. You can hang around the Durango stock pens and check the tally of calves as each bunch is carred."

"*Bueno*. Anything you want me to do right now?"

"Yes. Take my horse to the livery barn. And while you're down that way stop in at the depot. Ask them to make me sleeping-car reservations all the way through to Kaycee. I want to leave here on the evening of October second."

"Anything else?"

"You can mail these letters as you pass the post office."

Bud Channing took two letters and went out. They were to a banker at Pagosa Springs and a merchant at Chama, inquiring as to the reputation and responsibility of a young homesteader named Dave Pettibone. Lantry needed a man to replace Abel Dickshot. Pettibone, he remembered, had applied for a share deal. If replies to these inquiries were favorable, Pettibone would get the contract.

A day later Dave Pettibone rode into Durango and looked up Lantry.

"What about it?" he asked eagerly.

"I'm checking up on you," Lantry said. "Ought to hear by tomorrow. Can you stay over a day or two?"

"Sorry," Pettibone said. "Got to get back to the ranch. Mowed a patch of third-crop alfalfa yesterday. If I don't stack it tomorrow, it'll bleach."

Lantry nodded approvingly. He liked a man who put the harvesting of a crop above everything else. "I think it's all right, Pettibone. Just a matter of form, these check-ups. Tell you what. Can you be at the Chama depot when the eastbound passenger goes through the evening of the second?"

"Sure. My place is right near Chama."

"Good. The train puts on a pusher engine there to make the Cumbres Pass grade. Takes 'em about ten minutes. I'll get off and give you the final answer. And tell you just when to pick up your three hundred cows. Right now they're being handled by a fellow named Dickshot."

"Fine, Mr. Lantry. I'll see you on the depot platform at Chama."

That evening Bud Channing reported to Ruby at the Esperanza.

"He leaves on the second, Ruby. Got himself a sleeper

berth to Pueblo. And he wired a Kaycee hotel for a reservation."

"What hotel?"

Bud consulted a note. "The Coates House."

"Know anything else?"

"Sure. He's got a date to meet a guy named Pettibone on the Chama platform while they put on a pusher there. This Pettibone's gonna take over—"

"Never mind that," Ruby broke in. Her eyes flashed. Here was just the break she needed. It filled a missing link in her scheme. Today was September thirtieth. They'd have to work fast. "Get out to the Bar X Box, Bud, quick as you can ride. Tell Sax I want him. And right away."

By nine in the morning golden dice were rolling on the Esperanza bar. Sax Consadine rolled them with his left hand. And Ruby, at the far end of the bar, ordered an absinthe frappé.

Sax waited twenty minutes, then went out to his horse. He rode at a running walk north across the Animas ford and on through the ghost town of Animas City.

Ruby was waiting in the cottonwood grove. She sat on a log there, the toe of her riding-boot tapping impatiently.

"What's up?" Sax demanded.

"The biggest tip I ever slipped you. Jeff Lantry!" Her eyes were slits of fire, her voice brittle and charged with venom. "We can strip him to his last dime, even to the shirt off his back."

Sax had never seen her so eager, so bitter, so vindictive. "Lantry? I thought you were sweet on that guy." He grinned. "Threw you over, did he?"

She ignored his jibe, and her words flew at him like a volley of arrows. "Get Alf Fontana. And four strong-armers. Be at Chama when the train goes through tomorrow evening. Lantry will get off that train, but he won't get back on. Take him to the Mesa Verde caves."

The Bar X Box man gaped. "Ransom? Not on your life! It's a sucker's racket, and I wouldn't touch it with a ten-foot pole."

"Don't be stupid, Harry. Can't you see? Alf Fontana will get back on that train, in the dark, in Lantry's clothes, with Lantry's wallet, with Lantry's berth, with Lantry's reservation at a Kansas City hotel. Alf will be Lantry until the last carload of cattle is bought and paid for. And until the last cent has been checked out of Lantry's bank in Durango."

"Hell!" exclaimed Harry Listra. The boldness of it rocked him on his heels.

"That's not half of it!" Ruby exulted. "We not only take Lantry's cattle and money, we take his reputation, his pride, his Mr. Bigness. When he doesn't come back, when he writes his share people to ship every cow and calf, and checks out every dollar in his bank here, what will Durango think?"

Harry saw it, now. The full acid of her vengeance. Durango would conclude that Jeff Lantry was *afraid* to come back. That the Jallison-Shaw threats had borne fruit. They'd ordered him to sell out and stay out—or fight. And on a showdown, he didn't have the nerve to fight. All the San Juan Basin would explain it that way. No one would seem to be missing. It would seem only that a coward had run away.

"He won't know you or I have anything to do with it," Ruby pointed out. "All he'll ever see is the inside of a cave, and he'll think it's the Blue Mountains of Utah."

Harry smiled. "And then, after we clean him out, we put a slug through him."

"No," Ruby said firmly. "After Alf Fontana cleans him out, and brings you the money, and you pay me my ten percent, you bring Lantry, blindfolded, back to Durango."

"Are you crazy? What for?"

"You drop him, picked clean, in the street in front of the Esperanza. A busted, bearded, starved bum. I'll go out and be sweet to him. I'll take him in, feed him, give him a drink. I'll be his good angel, Lady Bountiful. If he's grateful, I'll cry on his shoulder. If he isn't, I'll laugh in his face."

16

THE TRAIN WAS READY TO PULL OUT. It was late afternoon of October second. The depot platform, at the foot of C Street in Durango, was crowded. Doctor Ed Amory, Sheriff Tom Gifford, and Marcella Blair were there to say good-by to Jeff Lantry.

Lantry's bags were packed for a two-months' absence. He called Bud Channing and gave him last-minute instructions. "Remember, Bud, I'll write or wire each share man just when to ship. You meet each herd at the Durango stock pens and check the number of calves against the tally list I gave you. Understand?"

"Sure," Bud said.

"And everybody gets a renewal," Lantry added, "except Abel Dickshot. A man named Pettibone'll take over the Dickshot cows."

Tom Gifford drew Lantry aside. "Maybe I can cool the Circle K crowd off a little, Jeff, by the time you get back."

Doctor Ed joined them. His thumb dug at Lantry's ribs. "Don't stay away too long, Jeff, or else Tom here'll beat your time with Marcella."

Tom flamed to the ears. Lantry grinned. He patted his pockets to make sure he had everything. Yes, it was all there. His tickets, his wallet, his checkbook, his stock record, his hotel reservation, and his letter of introduction from the Durango bank to the Clay-Robbins Live Stock Commission Company of Kansas City.

Marcella stepped up and gave him one item more. She

hadn't heard Doctor Ed's quip. "Will you match this for me, Jeff? They don't have it at the stores here." She gave Lantry a strip of yellow silk. "I'm making a party frock for Lissy and I need four yards. Try the department stores at Kansas City."

"I'll send it along," Lantry promised.

The conductor shouted, "All aboard!"

A porter took Lantry's bags up the sleeping-car steps. There was only one sleeper. Jeff Lantry followed. As the chain of narrow cars pulled out he stood in the rear vestibule waving at his friends.

"Don't go dude on us," Tom yelled.

"Don't forget that sample," Marcella called. "Four yards."

"I won't," Lantry promised.

He went to his berth, propped his feet on the opposite seat, and relaxed. It was nearly sundown now. Lantry looked idly from the window as the tiny train crawled out of the Animas Valley and into the San Juan foothills. A drummer in the berth ahead turned to borrow a match. When the news butch came along Lantry bought an apple. By the time he'd finished eating it they were stopped at Pagosa Junction.

He closed his eyes, dozed awhile. When he opened them it was dark outside. The porter was already making up berths.

The next stop would be Chama. Ten minutes to put on a pusher there. Plenty long enough to say yes to Dave Pettibone. Responses to inquiries about Pettibone had been entirely favorable.

The conductor came along and looked at Lantry's transportation. "Change to the Missouri Pacific at Pueblo," he said. He gave Lantry back a punched ticket and a berth stub.

Lantry stretched his arms, yawned. He decided to turn

in just as soon as they left Chama.

"Chama!" the brakeman yelled.

Lantry went out to the rear vestibule. The train whistled, slowed to a stop. Lantry stepped down on a cinder platform. A few people were there, some getting on, some getting off. There was a single cow-town street with a row of stores on the other side of it. A man stepped out of the gloom. "Are you Jeff Lantry?"

"I am."

"Dave Pettibone's bronc pitched him a little while ago. Sprained his ankle. A doctor's tapin' it up at my place right across the street. Dave says he was supposed to meet you. Want to see him?"

"Right across the street? Sure." Lantry followed the man across to the row of stores.

He was led through a door. Too late he saw it was only an empty warehouse. Something heavy hit him on the head. Lantry sagged to the floor, totally unconscious.

It took the five men about three minutes to strip him naked. One of them, Alf Fontana, put on Lantry's clothes. They were the clothes a prosperous stockman would wear on a trip to market. Fontana pulled Lantry's wide-brimmed cattleman's hat low over his eyes and crossed to the depot platform. Taking tickets from his pocket, he found by a stub that Lantry had berth number 8. The pusher engine was on now. Ascending to the sleeper's rear vestibule, Alf Fontana calmly rolled a cigarette.

Except for height, general build, and coloring, he knew he didn't look at all like Lantry. His face was fuller and his features blunter than Lantry's. Darkness was in his favor. He was wearing Lantry's tailored corduroys. As the train moved out he pulled Lantry's hatbrim lower over his eyes.

A minute later he strolled up the dim aisle of the sleeper.

As he passèd it, he spotted berth 8. The porter was making down number 6. Alf Fontana brushed by him and went on to the men's smoking-room at the front. There he sat down on the leather bench. He stuck the berth stub conspicuously in the outer band of his hat, let his chin sag on his chest so that the hatbrim completely shielded his face, and pretended to doze.

He heard the labored puffing of two engines as the train crawled up the Cumbres grade. Fontana let an hour slip by. Then he went quickly back to berth 8. It was made up now. He got into it, behind its green curtains, and drew a breath of relief. He was safe at least until morning.

There was a berth light. Before undressing, Fontana made an inventory of Lantry's pockets. A wallet, a stock record, a letter of introduction, a checkbook, a ticket to Kansas City via the D & RG and the Missouri Pacific—and a scrap of yellow silk.

The scrap of silk puzzled Fontana. But the other items made up just what he needed. In Kansas City he'd be Jefferson D. Lantry of Durango. There were risks, but think of the stake! The entire estate, cash and chattel, of Jeff Lantry!

The checkbook showed Lantry's present cash balance at the First National Bank of Durango. The figure brought a gleam of elation to Alf's eyes. He looked again at the memo of a hotel reservation in Kansas City. The Coates House. Nothing to do now but practice Lantry's writing. Harry and Ruby had provided him with samples of it, and on that score Alf Fontana had no misgivings at all. As a career forger and confidence man, he was made for the part. Now he turned out the light, undressed, and crawled under the blankets. The train rumbled on.

Reviewing the coup, it seemed to him that the only crude thing about it was the way they'd had to get rid of Dave Pettibone. Two masked men from Harry's gang had held Pettibone up on the way to Chama. After taking his horse and wallet they'd belted him over the head. It would look, Alf hoped, like a routine road job of passing outlaws. No reason for Pettibone to connect it with his appointment to meet Lantry at the Chama depot. He'd probably write Lantry a note of apology for not showing up.

Everything else had been executed with finesse. Jeff Lantry was expected at Kansas City, and there Lantry would seem to arrive.

Alf smiled in the dark. A million times better, this racket, than the penny-ante grift Harry had originally imported him for. Forging endorsements on checks to an English remittance man. Chicken feed. That was all blown up now, and in its place this blue-chip play for the fortune of Jeff Lantry.

Alf Fontana slept. The train crossed the Continental Divide, the San Luiz Valley, and the Sangre de Cristo.

When Alf wakened it was broad day outside. He heard the porter unmaking berths. Alf kept in his own as long as possible. Not till the porter shook his curtain and said, "We're comin' into Pueblo, suh," did he start dressing.

A morning stubble, he decided, would help his deception. So he wouldn't shave till he was on the other train. One of Lantry's bags, a fat Gladstone, was in the berth with him. By reaching out and feeling under the berth Alf could touch the other bag. It was a flat suitcase. Lantry had always been a fancy dresser. There'd be plenty of smart duds to sport about Kaycee in. But until he got off this train he must wear only the suit and hat in which Lantry had come aboard at Durango.

Alf had them on when he slipped out of the berth. He hurried up to the smoking-room. It was crowded, and so he continued on forward to the chair coaches. Some drummer who'd got on at Durango might know Lantry. Alf killed time by buying a paper and reading it in a day coach. The paper helped screen his face. Not till a brakeman called Pueblo did he return to the sleeper.

The confusion of disembarking made the rest easy. The porter took Lantry's bags out to the depot platform. Fontana followed with his hatbrim pulled low. He tipped with a silver dollar, picked up the bags, and disappeared into the station crowd.

An hour later he'd established himself on another train, in a standard Pullman of the Missouri Pacific. Fontana stretched out and relaxed. He didn't need the hat now. No one this far from Durango would know Jeff Lantry. He took out a sample of Lantry's handwriting and studied it. Later, whenever the train stopped at a station, he made practice copies on the back of a timetable.

He'd have it pat before long. Already he had it well enough to sign *Jefferson D. Lantry, Durango,* on the Coates House register.

While Alf Fontana rode cushions, Jeff Lantry rode the hard bed of a wagon. A blindfold covered his eyes. He was tied hand and foot. A sack was over his head with a hole to breathe through, just in case the blindfold slipped. And as a triple precaution a tarp was stretched over the wagon bed. His captors were taking no chances.

This was his second night out from Chama. Lantry guessed vaguely that the general direction was west, but he couldn't be sure.

From the wagon seat came voices. Two men seemed to be there. Lantry heard a third and a fourth riding at the wheel on horseback. Through the daylight hours of yesterday they'd stopped at a deserted shack where there'd been a strong sheep smell. They'd fed Lantry there.

Now he heard a man say, "Whatsa idea takin' him allaway to the Blue Mountains? Why not plant him under sod right here?"

"Orders from the boss," another man said. "And shut up, Jonesy. He might be listenin'."

So they were taking him to Utah! This was the Blue Mountains gang, Lantry concluded. The clothes he wore weren't his own. What did they hope to gain by it? What more did they want than his wallet?

Day came, and they camped in a deep arroyo. Lantry was fed, but the blind wasn't taken from his eyes.

Night, and the wagon moved on again. Lantry felt it ford a wide, swift river. He wondered if it was the Pine, the Animas, or the La Plata.

Night after night they moved on. On the fifth night Lantry heard a man say, "Better circle Dove Creek, Bart. Somebody might see us."

Dove Creek wasn't far from the Utah line. To Lantry it meant that they were almost to the Blue Mountains.

It didn't occur to him that the wagon had been circling for the last two nights, merely to make the destination seem eighty miles more distant than it really was.

On the sixth night Lantry could tell they were climbing a steep grade. The team frequently had to stop. "Chock the wheel," a man said at every rest. They were ascending, Lantry concluded, high into the Blue Mountains of Utah.

Late that night he was removed from the wagon and put astride a horse. His hands were still tied, and the blind was still over his eyes. The wagon turned back. Captive and captors proceeded by saddle. Lantry, riding a led horse, sensed that it was a steep, narrow ledge trail.

When day came they kept on. This high and deep in the wilderness no one was likely to meet them. Lantry heard a dislodged stone fall over a cliff and go crashing into an abyss far below. Later the ground leveled off, and he could smell cedars.

Then a descent. Probably into some mountain-locked canyon. Lantry listened for water but heard none. A dry canyon, he concluded.

They stopped, took him from the horse, and led him afoot up a narrow footpath which seemed to hug the wall of a cliff. "Here we are, brother," a man said.

He removed the blind from Lantry's eyes. Lantry blinked. He was in a deep, wide cavern with a smoke-black roof.

A dozen men were lounging about. There were a table, bunks, and an open fire. Smoke from the fire curled up to the rock ceiling.

"Make yourself at home, brother. You'll be here a long time."

Lantry wondered why. It couldn't logically be ransom. He had no kinsman or friend close enough, or wealthy enough, to pay for his release.

These men were all armed. A blistered crew they were, derisive, just now, rather than hostile. With one exception Lantry had never seen any of them before. The exception was Jonesy, who was the decoy Lantry recognized as having approached him on the Chama platform. A man with a rifle stood guard at the cave's entrance. Looking out, Lantry could see nothing but a blank sheer wall on the opposite side of the canyon. The canyon was narrow, boxed, deep. The view told him nothing. Any mountain range could have cave-pocked cliffs like this one.

"Keep back of the fire," a horse-faced man said. His voice identified him as Bart. "Take one step beyond it, and we fatten you with lead. Show him where the grub is, Toby."

Toby, a swarthy Latin of huge girth, seemed to be the head cook. He took Lantry to a pile of grub boxes at the back of the cave. "When you are hungry, señor, you will feed yourself."

Lantry fed himself and then sat on a box to appraise his captors. He listened to their talk, picked up a few names.

Bart and Cody and Maxie and Dalhart. Maxie seemed to be in charge. Dalhart, with a knife scar from lips to ear, looked the most vicious of the lot. Cody wore cowboy chaps and walked with a limp. Several of them, including the cook, Toby, seemed fairly amiable. Jonesy and Dalhart sat on a cot playing cards.

The crudeness of the camp puzzled Lantry. It didn't look at all permanent. He couldn't imagine a successful gang of outlaws holing up in this cavern summer and winter.

A hint of the answer came when Maxie left and disappeared down the ledge trail which hugged the canyon wall. When he came back an hour later he wore a different jacket and had taken off his spurs. It told Lantry that they had other quarters close by. Probably down on the cedared floor of the canyon.

He noted a label on a grub box. *Moab Mercantile Company, Moab, Utah.* So they did their trading at Moab.

One of the men was sulking a little. Lantry heard him complain to Dalhart. Dalhart rebuked him. "Pipe down, Hooper. We stick right here till everything's clear, like we allers do."

Night came. A cot was assigned to Lantry. His ankles and wrists burned where the cords had held them. He'd slept only fitfully in the jolting wagon. Tonight he slept like the dead.

Next day was the same. Lantry waited on himself, was ignored as long as he kept in the rear half of the cave. The cave was a hundred feet wide and nearly as deep. From scraps of talk he concluded that all these men were underlings. The real leader of the gang wasn't here. Sometimes Lantry heard that leader referred to as "Harry," but more often merely by the pronoun "he."

"He says we gotta keep him fer a pet." Dalhart's thumb jerked toward the prisoner. "He says if we gun him, the lid's off. And don't ast so dang many questions, Hooper."

"Kin we go downstairs, come dark?" Jonesy asked. "I like to froze last night."

"We can if we get the all-clear signal," Maxie said.

Evidently they got it, for soon after dark Lantry was blindfolded and led out of the cave. The route went downward, hairpinned in a series of reverses before Lantry felt solid earth underfoot. Then a ten-minute walk with underbrush scraping his elbows.

They took him into a building of some kind where he heard a fire crackle. "Put him to bed, Toby."

When the blindfold came off a minute later, Lantry found himself in a tiny, dark room. By touching them he could tell that the walls were unbarked pine logs. There was a cot with blankets. *"Buenas noches, señor."* Toby went out, and Lantry heard the snap of a lock.

This, he concluded, was the permanent quarters. Maybe a ranch layout among the cedars of the canyon floor, with a water supply and a corral for horses. Apparently the outlaws kept in the cave only for a day or so after a raid, repairing to this more comfortable retreat as soon as all risk of pursuit was over. The cave would be more easily defended, and less easily discovered, than this house. Looking down from a rimrock above, pursuers, if any, might glimpse a cabin among the cedars. But the dark mouth of a cave in a sheer cliff would seem to be only one of many similar ravages made by prehistoric high water.

More and more the motive of his duress puzzled Lantry. Who was "Harry"? And why did "he" insist that Lantry be "kept for a pet"? Most of all, why would the "lid be off" if they gunned him?

The desk clerk at the Coates House, Kansas City's most elegant hostelry, was suavely cordial. "Certainly we have a reservation for you, Mr. Lantry." He dipped a quill pen in ink and passed it to Alf Fontana. With a convincing flourish Alf signed:

Jefferson D. Lantry, Durango, Colorado.

The clerk tapped a bell. "Boy, take Mr. Lantry's bags to 217."

In his room Alf Fontana spent the rest of the day practicing handwriting. He was vain of his art. By nighttime his imitations of Lantry's hand had reached perfection.

In his baggage he found garments habitually worn by Lantry on trips to Denver. A plaid sport coat, a double-breasted vest, an Ascot tie which matched pearl-gray gloves and a center-creased felt hat.

But for the time being Fontana decided not to use them. He'd look more like a cattleman if he kept to the corduroys and boots and high-crowned sombrero in which Lantry had left Durango.

He had them on next morning when he caught a Twelfth Street cable car to the West Bottoms. The car rattled down a long inclined viaduct, threaded its way among implement factories and odoriferous packing-houses, turning at last south on Genesee Street to a sprawling domed building which looked like a courthouse, but which actually was the Kansas City Live Stock Exchange.

Vast acres of cattle pens reached out from this building. Fontana heard a thousand bawling steers, a medley of shouts and whipcracks from drovers. Already this place had become the second largest cattle market on earth.

Fontana strode confidently into the Exchange Building. Numerous livestock commission companies had offices there. He turned in at a door marked *Clay-Robbins & Company.*

Minutes later he was seated across a desk from a jolly little man with sideburns. Mr. Robbins was reading his letter of introduction from the First National Bank of Durango.

He turned beaming to Alf Fontana. "Delighted to serve you, Mr. Lantry. They say you've always shipped to Denver, until this year. Glad you're giving Kaycee a break, for a change. When will your stuff be in?"

"I'll start it rollin' right away, Mr. Robbins. Take a coupla months, maybe, to get it all here. Ten cars every day or so."

Mr. Robbins wasn't at all bowled over. He'd often dealt with cattle kings of the west, big operators all the way from Texas to Montana. "Your home-town bank says you've been quite successful, Mr. Lantry. Have a cigar."

Alf declined and rolled a cigarette. He imagined Lantry would have done that. "If I have," he said, "it's because I've stuck rigidly to *young* stock. Started out four years ago with six thousand two-coming-three-year-old cows. Those cows are now seven years old. If I keep them too long, they'll be canners. No money in canners, Mr. Robbins. So this fall I plan to ship *both* my cows and calves. Next spring I can start all over again with three-year-olds."

Robbins puffed his cigar, nodding approval. "You're quite right, Mr. Lantry. The peak of a cow's production comes between the ages of three and seven. At seven years of age the cow still rates as beef; but at eleven she becomes a canner."

"Which means," Alf explained, "that this fall I'll ship every hoof I've got. Six thousand seven-year-old cows, two thousand weaning calves, and a hundred-odd bulls. I'll try not to have them stack up on you too deep, Mr. Robbins."

Back in his room at the Coates House, Alf began penning letters on the hotel's stationery. To each of Lantry's twenty share ranchers he wrote a precise shipping-direction. He'd decided to ship everything, the letters said, in order to start fresh again next season with young breeders. The first ranch was directed to ship on the tenth, the second on the twelfth, the third on the fourteenth, and so on until shipments were completed.

The writing was a convincing imitation of Lantry's. Convincing, too, because it would seem that Lantry's real motive was fear. To the world of Durango, he'd seem to be capitulating to an ultimatum laid down by the Jallison and Shaw crews. Sell out and get out! Lantry, they'd say, was doing just that.

Fontana wrote four other letters. One to the Durango bank confirming his program. One to the general freight agent of the D & RG Railroad at Denver, asking that the right number of empties be spotted at the Durango shipping-pens on the proper days. One to the Colorado State Brand Inspector giving notice of his shipping-intentions, so that an inspector could check brands at loading as required by law. And one to Bud Channing at Durango, enclosing a summary of the shipping-instructions.

Alf Fontana mailed all the letters simultaneously. Then he went to a bank and opened an account in the name of Jefferson D. Lantry. His initial deposit was two hundred dollars, of which a hundred was in cash and a hundred was in a check drawn on Lantry's account at Durango. As a reference he gave the Clay-Robbins Live Stock Commission Company.

"I'm shipping in some cattle," he told the cashier. "When they're sold, I'll instruct Mr. Robbins to deposit the proceeds to my credit here."

"Happy to have your account, Mr. Lantry."

Sauntering back to the hotel Alf delved through his pockets for a match. His hand came out with a scrap of yellow silk. Now what the devil, he wondered for the tenth time, had Jeff Lantry been doing with that?

17

DURANGO, A WEEK LATER, was abuzz with talk about Jeff Lantry. Men stood in groups, at the bars and on the walks, and most of the comment was derisive.

"I thought Jeff had more guts than that."

"Reckon he figgered he'd sooner be a live coward than a dead hero."

"Didn't have no Injun to toss a knife fer him, this time, so he skinned out. Betcha my saddle agin yourn, Jim, that we never see him again."

Jim pulled at his lip thoughtfully. "I dunno, Zeke. It kinda makes sense, if you look at it right. More money in young cows than in old ones. Sellin' out seven-year-olds in the fall to buy heifers in the spring ain't such a bad idear."

Jim was in the minority. They were at the Esperanza bar, and he appealed to the hostess there. "What's your slant on it, Ruby?"

"You mean about Lantry selling out? I think he's just plain yellow. Have one on the house, boys." Ruby floated to another group down the bar.

At the First National Bank, officials went into a huddle. Again there was divided opinion. Some said it was a smart business move on Lantry's part, others thought it was a case of cold feet. But no one had the faintest suspicion that the shipping-directions hadn't been penned by Lantry himself.

Another matter came up. "Major Talcott's coming in today. He'll want another extension."

The cashier looked gravely uncomfortable. He liked Carey Talcott. But business was business. "Frankly," he sighed, "I'm afraid we've carried the major too long already."

Across the street, Doctor Ed Amory stood chatting with

Sheriff Tom Gifford. They saw the frock-coated figure of Major Talcott dismount at the bank and go in.

Doctor Ed said, "I'm afraid they'll say thumbs down."

Tom nodded. "He's in pretty bad shape after losing that big contract to deliver cavalry horses to the army. Since the army stopped fightin' Indians, they don't need so many horse troops. But the major didn't see it comin'. He's horse-poor and mortgaged to the ears."

"Heard from Jeff?" Doctor Ed asked.

"Just a postcard," Tom said, "asking me to keep an eye on Bud Channing and give him any advice he needs."

"Weren't you surprised, Tom, to hear he's selling out?"

A shadow crossed Tom's face. He'd been more than surprised. He'd been hurt, too, because his friend Jeff hadn't discussed it with him. "It might be," he offered, "that the Kaycee commission people talked him into it. Warned him about not hangin' on to cows till they got to canner age. One thing you can paste in your hat, Doctor Ed. Jeff didn't do it because he's afraid. He's got nerve to burn. All the guns in the Basin couldn't bluff him out unless he had a good reason of his own."

At Doctor Ed's hospital on Second Avenue, Marcella Blair stood on the front porch looking restlessly down the street. She had every reason to be cheerful, but wasn't. Her star patient, Gerry Ashton, was mending fast. Right now he was sitting up in bed, reading a magazine. It was a week now since he'd begged them for liquor. His redemption had brought bloom to the cheeks of his wife Melissa, changing her from a dowdy drudge into a bright and buoyant young matron. With a fresh start, plus a hundred pounds per quarter from London, the Gerry Ashtons should do well from now on.

Yet Marcella was uneasy and dissatisfied this morning. She saw Melissa coming uphill from the post office, ran to meet her at the gate.

"Anything for me, Lissy?"

"Not a thing, Marcella."

"Did you try the express office?"

Melissa nodded. Then she smiled teasingly. "Men aren't very dependable, Marcella, when you send them shopping for dress goods. You'll find that out after you're married."

"The shops probably didn't have it," Marcella said. "Or maybe he'll bring it when he comes back."

"But he's not coming back. Didn't you hear? At least he won't be back till spring. He's selling out, Marcella."

"I don't believe it," Marcella said.

"Why?"

"Because he wouldn't be afraid of those—" Marcella stopped, biting her lip.

Her sister gave her a chiding look. "Of all the perverse women!" she exclaimed. "Until now you've been ranting about how uncivilized he was to stay here and fight it out with guns. And now, when he very quietly and sensibly avoids fighting it out with guns, you get all het up."

"I'm not het up. And I haven't been ranting," Marcella denied coldly. "I don't care in the least what he does. I *did* think, though, that he'd have the courtesy to do a simple errand." She went irritably back to her patients.

Melissa remained on the porch, thinking, wondering, listening. Was her sister really serious about Jeff Lantry? And would Lantry ever come back? A medley of sound came to her over the air waves of Durango. Most of it came from the D & RG terminal down at C Street and Railroad Avenue. Switch engines scooting back and forth. The clang of car couplings. A plaintive bawling from calves and cows. They were shipping out Lantry's cattle.

Bud Channing sat on the shipping-pen fence, whittling. He saw the last of the Abel Dickshot bunch shoved into cars. Three hundred cows, six bulls, and a few more than a hundred calves. Bud made a check in his tally book. So much for Abel Dickshot. Day after tomorrow the next bunch would be trailing into Durango.

Bud slouched up Main Street, stopping when he saw Sax Consadine's horse tied in front of the Esperanza. He went in and found Sax rolling his golden dice. Sax bought him a drink.

"Hear your boss is selling out, Bud."

"Every hoof and horn," Bud said.

A jeer came from one of Buck Shaw's men down the bar. "Knows what's good fer him, that jasper does."

Sax gave a sigh. "Kinda sorry to hear about it. I always liked Lantry." He changed the dice to his left hand and rolled them again.

An hour later he was facing Ruby Costello in the grove above the old Animas City ghost town. "It's high, wide, and handsome, Ruby. The cattle are rolling east, now. In two months the cash'll roll back west, straight into our laps."

"Any chance of a slip?" Ruby sat on a log, tapping her boot nervously with her riding-crop.

"Not unless somebody from Durango happens to make a trip to Kaycee and runs into Alf there. You always got to take chances on any big play."

"How will Alf cash in?"

"Easy. When each shipment is sold, the commission company'll hand Alf a check made out to Lantry. Alf will slap it in a bank. Little by little he'll check out Lantry's account here in Durango, depositing it in Kaycee banks. He'll use a dozen banks so any one account won't get too big. When everything's sold, he tells 'em he's gonna take a trip around Missouri and Iowa breeding-farms to pick up heifers to start with again next year. He'll draw out all his money and take it with him. Only he doesn't buy any heifers. He brings the dough straight to me."

"What," Ruby worried, "is to keep him from skipping out?"

"I sent Trigger Smith to Kaycee to watch him," Harry Listra explained. "He'll keep an eye and a gun on Alf, just in case."

"Don't forget my ten percent, Harry."

"You'll get it."

Her straight gaze warned him. "You know what happens, Harry, if I'm found dead some cold morning."

He nodded grimly. "Sure. It blows the lid off. You got all the dope on me in a Denver bank box. But two can play that way, Ruby. So just in case you might do a little double-crossin' yourself, I've put all the dope on *you* in a bank box. To be opened, you understand, only in the event I die with my boots on."

"*What* dope on me?" she demanded. "I had nothing to do with that Texas killing."

He grinned derisively. "No, but you've had plenty to do with Colorado killings. You passed out plenty of tips to the Blue Mountains boys. Some of those tips paid off in slugs. And you collected ten percent every time."

"But nobody can prove it."

"Can't they? Don't forget you made a mistake once, Ruby, before we had everything down to a system. You sent me a tip in writing. By messenger. About a stage job. The stage driver was killed. Your written tip is pinned to the dope in my bank box, baby."

She flushed. There was nothing she could do about it. Nor could she blame Harry Listra. He was merely practicing a safeguard she'd devised herself.

"So you're safe as long as I don't die with my boots on," Harry said. "And vice versa. And now about Lantry. Sure you want him turned loose? It'd be a lot simpler to rub him out."

"No," Ruby insisted stubbornly. "Keep him alive. Clean him out, then dump him in the dust of Durango."

Snow came to the San Juan Basin. And still the cattle of Jeff Lantry arrived from four directions, bunch by bunch, to be prodded into cars at Durango.

Early in November the management of the Grand Central Hotel received a letter from Kansas City. It seemed to be from their oldest tenant, Jeff Lantry. It enclosed a check for his room rent to date. He wouldn't need the room any more. Would the hotel kindly turn his things over to Bud Channing, who would store them?

Bud Channing found a few odds and ends of clothing in the room. Also there was a small, brassbound trunk. He packed the trunk and put it in storage. The entire town knew it by nightfall. Here seemed to be conclusive evidence that Lantry wouldn't be back before spring, if ever.

The house of Doctor Ed Amory heard nothing from him at all.

Doctor Ed stopped by to see Tom Gifford. Tom was just back from Rico, seat of the neighboring county of Dolores. "I saw a notice posted on the courthouse door there," Tom said. "It sets a date for a public auction on the Talcott stuff, hoof, hide, and acre."

The news saddened Doctor Ed. But he'd been expecting it. "How's the major taking it, Tom?"

"Chin up, as always. Bruce takes it the same way. They're thoroughbreds, those people. Bruce is up and around now. He'll be riding to town any day."

"What's the latest from Jeff Lantry?"

"Still in Kaycee. I got another card from him. Sent his regards to you. Said remember him to the Ashtons and Marcella. Said he plans to spend the winter in Missouri and buy heifers in the spring."

"You know what I think, Tom?" The old doctor's eyes

narrowed shrewdly. "I think he's mixed up in some big deal there. Like he's speculating in Kaycee realty, or the grain exchange, or something."

"Why?"

"Because I found out he's transferring his entire Durango account to Kansas City banks."

Tom whistled. "That's real money, Doctor Ed. Jeff had four years' profit salted away here. Wonder what he's up to?"

Doctor Ed shrugged. "It's *his* money. If he wants to shoot the moon with it, it's none of our business. Why haven't you been up to see us lately, Tom? Sax Consadine's been shining around almost every day. What's the idea giving him a clear track with Marcella?"

"I been pretty busy," Tom evaded.

But he was too transparent to fool Ed Amory. The doctor went his way convinced that Tom had already spoken his piece to Marcella and that she'd turned him down. Sax Consadine, on the other hand, seemed to be gaining ground. Was Jeff Lantry the reason for it? Marcella might be hurt because Lantry had dropped so suddenly out of her life.

Which is none of my business, Doctor Ed brooded, *except that I'd hate to see Sax get her on the rebound.*

Was there another foil in sight? Yes, Bruce Talcott was up and around. He'd make a good match for Marcella. Doctor Ed resolved to have Bruce to dinner the first time he came into town.

The November snow melted, and early December found the ground bare.

Sax Consadine rolled his golden dice, saw Ruby respond by ordering an absinthe frappé, and then met her at the upriver grove.

"Alf's back," he announced jubilantly. "The total take

was four hundred thousand. Here's your ten percent."

He handed her a package. Ruby opened it and counted four hundred bills of a hundred dollars each.

She patted the money fondly. Forty thousand dollars! By far the biggest commission she'd ever earned. She stowed it in her saddlebag, inquiring, "Where's Lantry?"

"The boys are bringing him in," Harry said. "Tonight. Ask him where he's been and he'll tell you the Blue Mountains."

The night was cold and dry. Saloon row was normally boisterous till midnight. Then trade fell away, and by two o'clock the sidewalks were nearly deserted. All respectable elements of Durango were asleep. At four only a few of the saloons were doing business. The Oasis had a sprinkling of customers. A few more lingered at the Esperanza.

Ruby Costello stood at her bar arrayed in her most dazzling gown. It was jet-black with a plunging neckline. Her brilliant hair was coiled high on her head against the backdrop of a diamond-studded comb. It wasn't unusual for her to be up this late. Night was her element. And this was the night she'd been waiting for.

Pablo brought her a vermouth. Ruby stood sipping it, attentive to each sound from outside. It was about five o'clock, and still winter-dark, when she heard a buckboard clatter up the street.

"Wonder who'd be coming in at this hour?" she murmured to Pablo, and drifted to the door.

The walks were deserted. Nothing was in sight but a buckboard which stopped directly in front. A man was pushed over its endgate. He hit the frozen ground with a thump and lay perfectly still there. The buckboard rattled on, turned a corner, and disappeared.

"Pablo!" Ruby called. "Come quickly. I'm afraid someone's hurt."

Pablo joined her, and they went out into the street. The man who lay there was ragged, bearded, and unconscious. He seemed to be a tramp or some down-and-out desert rat. Pablo rolled him over, smelled liquor on him. "He is very drunk," he reported.

"The poor fellow!" Ruby murmured. "Bring him inside, Pablo. If we don't the next wagon will run over him."

Pablo dragged the man into the Esperanza barroom. He put him on a couch there. The several customers of the place came up curiously. They saw scars and bruises on the derelict's face. "Looks like someone beat him up," a man suggested, "and then slipped him a Mickey."

Another guest peered closer. "Hell!" he exclaimed. "Damned if he doesn't look like Jeff Lantry!"

"Jeff Lantry!" Ruby echoed. "But that's impossible. Jeff's in Kansas City."

Pablo brought cold water and swabbed the victim's face. In a little while he opened his eyes. They were brown eyes, dull and haggard now.

Ruby looked into them and gasped, "But you are right! He *is* Jeff." She dropped to her knees by Lantry and took his head in her arms.

She cooed over him, cried over him, and her tears were convincing.

"Call the doctor!" she commanded. "Call the sheriff! Did you see who was in that wagon, Pablo? They must be caught and punished. Oh, Jeff!"

Lantry was too groggy to say anything. The scene was only a blur to him. At last he begged faintly for water. Ruby held it to his lips.

After a while new faces grew in the mist about him. One of them seemed to be Doctor Ed. Another was Tom Gifford.

Doctor Ed made a quick examination. "Nothing wrong with him," he reported. "Been drugged, that's all. More in your department than mine, Tom."

"I'll take him to my room," Tom said. "Can you stand up, Jeff?"

They got him to his feet. With two men supporting him, Lantry was led outside. Ruby Costello followed, her hand tremulously on Lantry's arm. "If there's anything you need, Jeff, dear, please let me know. *Anything*."

"Where've you been, Jeff?" Tom demanded.

"Blue Mountains," Lantry muttered thickly. "Utah. Get 'em, Tom."

Tom's room was just around the corner on G Street. They got Lantry there and put him on the bed. Ruby tried to follow them in. But Doctor Ed pushed her out gently. "We can handle him," he said, and closed the door.

It wasn't turning out quite the way she'd planned. Durango had excluded her, as it always excluded her when she came on this wrong side of the street. The wrong side for her but not the wrong side for Jeff Lantry. If Ed Amory had slammed the door on her, instead of closing it gently, he couldn't have more pointedly shut her out.

Bitterness simmered in Ruby as she recrossed to the Esperanza. But she couldn't be cheated now. Lantry was cleaned out to his last dollar. She'd made a bum of him. She could look down at him, now, not up. Either way she had him. If he came to her she'd coddle him, back him, refinance him, set him on his feet again—and win him. If he didn't, she could laugh in his face.

Outside the street was coming alive. Footsteps, excited voices. News always traveled fast in Durango. Ruby heard prancing horses. A posse was assembling. The sensational return of Jeff Lantry was already on a hundred lips. Ruby's bar began filling up.

She stood at the deep end of it, sipped a vermouth and listened to a babel of comment.

"Didn't go to Kaycee, after all."

"Kidnaped at Chama."

"Somebody slickered him. Cleaned him out."

"The Blue Mountains boys done it. Held him in Utah somewhere while they they picked him like a pigeon."

It was nothing that Ruby didn't already know. But she kept her ears open for new angles.

More customers crowded in with the latest details.

"Where's Gifford?"

"He's already got a posse started to the Blue Mountains. They'll join up with Utah deputies at Moab."

"Why Moab?"

"Because the hide-out can't be far from there. It's just on the other side of the Blues. Jeff says their grub boxes showed they buy their canned stuff at Moab."

More of it. Questions and answers. "Did Tom go with 'em?"

"No, Tom's busy sendin' telegrams to Kaycee. Somebody impersonated Jeff there, looks like. It's too late to nab him, I'll bet, or else they wouldn't't've turned Jeff loose. I'll take mine neat, Pablo."

"Did Jeff recognize anybody?"

"Nope. The big shot of the outfit wasn't there at all. Some jigger named Harry."

Then the blow fell. It jolted Ruby Costello and brought her a sense of defeat. A lean, sunken-cheeked man at the head of the bar was talking. He was Adam Alton, Durango's leading attorney.

"Nonsense!" Alton was protesting. "Lantry hasn't lost a dollar. All he's out 's a little skin off his neck and two months of his life."

"How do yuh figger it, Ad?" a voice demanded. "Tom says they got away with every cow and calf, and then checked out his balance in the banks."

"When banks cash forged checks," the lawyer explained pedantically, "they have to reimburse the victimized depositor. It was their mistake, so they have to make it good."

"You mean the banks get socked, 'stead of Lantry?"

"No. Banks carry insurance against loss by robbery and fraud. The insurance company gets socked, 'stead of either the banks or Lantry."

The crowd gaped. Ruby saw her plot crumbling. She hadn't considered banking laws or the safeguards of insurance.

Someone asked, "What about that Clay-Robbins Commission Company of Kaycee? Don't they get socked, too?"

"No," the lawyer said. "The commission company sold Lantry's cattle, wrote checks payable to Lantry, and deposited them to his credit in Kansas City banks. When the impostor forged checks to draw the money out, he was defrauding the banks only. But those banks, like our own here, are also insured. So in the end all the loss stacks up against some big bankers' indemnity corporation in New York." Attorney Alton drained his liquor glass and went out.

Ruby stared dully after him. What had she gained? True, she'd collected her ten percent. But here was Lantry, high, dry, and still rich. Her leash had slipped. He didn't need to be coddled or consoled. He was still on the other side of the street.

18

DOCTOR ED KEPT LANTRY in bed for a day and night. Rest and good food speedily revived him. He remained in Tom's room on G Street, where only a few selected visitors were admitted to see him. Cashier Crump from the bank. The bank's attorney. Tom himself was in and out. He showed Lantry answers to telegrams sent to Kansas City. They made the pattern of the fraud fairly clear.

"Looks like your man Bud Channing was in on it," Tom

guessed. "He took off coupla days ago. Nobody can find him. Reckon it was Bud tipped 'em about your stop at Chama."

Everyone was sympathetic. Even Buck Shaw of the Y7 dropped in. He looked a bit sheepish as he offered a hand to Lantry. "I wanted you to sell out," the Dove Creek man admitted, "but I didn't want it to be this way. Any help you need to round up that Blue Mountains outfit, just call on the Y7. We'll be in there ashootin'."

"It was our mistake," Banker Crump said sadly. "But we're fully covered. It'll take a few months to straighten things out, but in the end you won't lose a penny."

Lantry's spirits rebounded. "Maybe nobody'll lose anything," he said hopefully. "When we raid that hide-out we oughta find the money there. I'll know the place when I see it."

He was impatient to join the chase. But first he wanted to see Marcella Blair.

In the morning sunlight he walked up to the hospital on Second Avenue. Three rocking chairs were on its porch. Gerald Ashton, smoking a cigarette and looking fit, sat between Marcella and Melissa.

"Jeff!" They all called to him in a breath!

He went to them, grinning. "Sorry I couldn't match that silk for you," he said gaily to Marcella. "But they didn't have any over in the Blue Mountains. Gerry, you old son-of-a-gun, you look ready for a roundup right now."

"A saddle'll feel good," Gerry said. "They've coddled me long enough around here." His cheeks showed a ruddy color, and his eyes were clear.

Marcella shook hands a bit shyly. "We heard all about it, Jeff. We thought you'd—"

As she broke off lamely, Gerry winked at his wife. "She thought you'd run out on her, Lantry. But Sax and Tom, between them, kept her from being too lonesome."

It was Melissa who made a fuss over Lantry. She brought another rocker for him, then made him tell the story all over.

"Nothing to it," Lantry said, "except I was shanghaied to Utah. Which reminds me, Gerry. That gang's got a slick forger with it. Must be the same slicker who cashed your checks from London."

"We've received the second one now," Melissa said happily. "So we feel rich, don't we, Gerry?"

"Hold on a minute," Lantry put in. "You're overlooking a bet. That guy intercepted those London checks every quarter for four years. So you're still short sixteen of them. According to banking law, the bank has to make good. Just like in my case. Why don't you make it come clean?"

Ashton looked a little embarrassed. "So they told us," he admitted. "But the man cashed the checks at a little two-by-four bank in Farmington. It's not insured, like big banks are. The bank cashed 'em in good faith. It thought it was doing me a favor. So I—"

Melissa finished for him. "He means he doesn't think it's fair to penalize that struggling little bank at Farmington. So he won't put in a claim against it."

Gerry flushed. "It wouldn't be quite—" He groped for a word, and his British ancestry found one. "What I mean is, it wouldn't be cricket."

Lantry stared at him. He could hardly believe it. Was Gerry crazy? The idea of letting sixteen hundred pounds go by the boards! He started a protest, then checked himself. He saw Melissa looking at her husband not with rebuke, but with pride. Her hand reached out to Gerry's and gave it a squeeze.

It gave Lantry an odd feeling of inferiority. And it angered him a little. It was sheer nonsense, of course, a stupid distortion of ethics. That blithely British sense of fair play would never get Gerry anywhere. Cricket! You couldn't get ahead that way. If banks made a mistake, they had to pay for it.

"You'll stay to lunch with us, Jeff?" Marcella invited.

Suddenly he didn't want to. Something nagged at Lantry now, and depressed him, as it always did at this house. Always it made him see himself in that upstairs room, sneaking a map out of Frank Foster's hatband. Two hundred thousand dollars stolen from a bank.

And now banks, through an insurer, would pay it back to him doubled. Cricket?

Lantry evaded Gerry's calm, blue-eyed smile. He felt shamed. But it was an angry, rebellious shame. "Thanks, Marcella," he said abruptly. "But Tom's waiting for me. We've got to be joining up with that posse in the Blue Mountains. I'll be seeing you."

He left them and walked rapidly down the hill.

Three horses were tied in front of Tom's place. One was his own sorrel, Mike. Another was Tom Gifford's. The third was a roan racer with a Bridlebit brand on the hip.

"Look who's here," Tom greeted as Lantry entered.

It was Bruce Talcott. "On my legs again," Bruce grinned, "and rarin' to ride." His face took serious lines. "I've been thinkin'. Describe that cave again, Lantry. The one they took you to the first day."

Lantry described it in detail.

The eyes of Bruce Talcott narrowed. "A smoke-blackened roof!" he brooded. "Hell's bells! Know what it means? They've been making suckers out of us for years, those guys."

"What do you mean?" Tom prompted.

"I mean I wrote a thesis at college, one time. All about the prehistoric cliff dwellers of the American Southwest. They lived in caves for seven hundred years. Then they cut those caves up into rock apartments for the next five hundred years. Time they'd built fires in those caves for twelve centuries, they'd smoked up the ceilings. Black as the ace of spades, those ceilings are. It says so right in my thesis."

They gaped at him. "So what?" Tom demanded.

"So this—cave dwellers did *not* live in the Utah Blue Mountains. But they *did live* in canyons of the Mesa Verde in La Plata County, Colorado. That's where we'll find your outlaws, Tom. They've been right under our noses all these years."

Lantry nodded with conviction. That Moab, Utah, label on a grub box had been meant to fool him. Just like empty purses and slit mail bags left in the Blue Mountains.

"So what are we waiting for?" Bruce finished. "Get some men and broncs, Tom, and we'll ride."

As Gifford started out to round up deputies, a thought made Lantry call him back. "We'd better not advertise this in Durango," he suggested. "We've always thought they keep a spy here in town. The spy might send a warning."

Bruce said, "Lantry's right. I'll pick up Slim Borchard of the Bridlebit. He rode in with me. Then the four of us can pick up a few of the Circle K crew as we go by. Break out some ammunition, Tom."

By noon four heavily armed men were riding west out of Durango. Lantry, Talcott, Gifford, and Borchard. Slim Borchard grimaced wryly. "Mesa Verde, huh? Shucks, that hump o' cedars rises right up outa Mancos. You could stand on the rimrock and see your ranch, Tom. You could almost toss a pebble down on the Circle K. Them Jallison waddies'll be rarin' to go."

"I explored up there a few times," Bruce told them, "when I was a kid. There's a mess of deep box canyons through it, crisscrossing every which way. Might take us a week to find the right one."

"It smells like cedar," Lantry said. "Log house in the canyon bed and a big cave high up in the wall."

Sundown brought them to the Circle K. Jallison's old crew was still running the place, pending a settlement of the estate. They'd already heard the sensation about Lantry. And like Buck Shaw, they were no longer hostile. Tod Newcombe, the foreman, offered his hand. "We figgered you was skeered of us, Lantry. I see you ain't. After we shoot it out with them outlaws we'll talk things over."

He assembled men, horses, and pack mules. The mules were loaded with bedrolls, grub, and ammunition. The posse was twenty strong when, at dawn, they took a steep, narrow trail up the Mesa Verde slope.

"They take you in this way, Lantry?" Slim Borchard asked.

"How would I know? I was blindfolded coming in and out. I can identify the cave when I see it. And the inside of a cabin."

"Anybody think to bring along some grain sacks?" an optimist asked. He was one of the Circle K men.

"What for?"

"To fetch the money back in. Four hundred thousand! Gee! And me workin' fer twenty bucks a month all my life!"

The ledgy narrowness of the trail made them proceed single file. Bruce Talcott rode point with a ready rifle. The outlaws might have a sentinel at the top of the trail. Every scabbard had a rifle or carbine in it. Gifford, second in line, called back, "Everybody pick a rock when they start cutting loose."

Later Lantry heard two of the Circle K's talking about Bruce. "This here'll be his last roundup, I reckon."

"Howcome?"

"Bank's sellin' 'em out. Didn't yuh hear? Only a coupla weeks now till the auctioneer whangs down with his hammer. I like the way Bruce takes it, podner. I sure do. Chin up and colors flyin'."

"Where they goin'?"

"Back to Tennessee, I hear."

It gave Lantry a thought. Why not bid in the Bridlebit himself? He'd have funds to do it, and to spare, if they found the loot. In any case he'd have it when the insurance company reimbursed him. He could settle down, then, and be a gentleman rancher like Major Talcott. He'd need a place like that—if Marcella said yes. He had a feeling she would. But she deserved gracious living. A beautiful valley ranch with a fine house like the Talcotts'.

Lantry toyed with the idea, and it pleased him more and more. The bank would bid only the exact amount of the lien. They'd be glad to let Lantry bid one dollar more and take it. Just the place for Marcella. Lantry rode on, musing pleasantly.

Bruce, ahead, raised an arm to call a halt. They'd emerged on a high, cedared mesa.

The posse assembled around Bruce. "You know this country better'n anyone else," Tom told him. "So you give the orders from here on."

"We'll divide into pairs," Bruce decreed, "and scout."

For three days Lantry rode the rugged contours of the Mesa Verde. He was paired with Tom Gifford. They found many canyons, gorges, and rocky defiles. Some shallow, some deep, some with cave-pitted walls, some without. Twice they peered over a precipice to see stonework, rude ancient masonry, walling the mouths of caves. They were the habitations of cliff dwellers more than a thousand years ago. "But that's not where they took me," Lantry said each time.

Each night the scouting teams assembled at a camp on the cedar mesa. "We have to be patient," Bruce said.

"There's three hundred square miles of these interlocking mesas."

"Sure," Tod Newcombe agreed. "They stretch all the way from Mancos plumb down to the San Juan."

It was a Circle K man who, a day later, found what looked like the right canyon. He stood guard while his teammate brought the others.

Lantry arrived with Tom. The canyon seemed to be about six hundred feet deep. Looking down from its rim-rock they could see a wisp of smoke rising from its brushy bottom. The opposite wall was pocked with caves. A narrow ledge trail led from the biggest one, in a series of zig-zags, down into the canyon's bed.

Bruce and the last of the others rode up. "This looks like it," Lantry said.

Bruce posted three riflemen at the spot. "Watch the upper end. Don't let anybody get out." He led the rest of his force down the rim, looking for a place to descend.

Shod hoofs clacked on the rock, and Tom said, "We better stop and muffle 'em, fellows."

It took only a few minutes for each man to pad the hoofs of his mount. When they rode on, the clacking was less distinct.

"I can see a penful o' broncs now," Slim Borchard said.

"If their broncs can get in, so can ours."

It was three miles before they found a horse trail leading down. Bruce took the lead, and they descended single file through a niche in the rimrock. It brought them to a steep downslope twisting through cedars. Tom saw a cigarette snipe by the trail. "It's never been rained on," he reported.

Brush screened them all the way down. The canyon floor was about a hundred yards wide. Giant cedar and a few stunted sycamores grew in it. The sand of the wash was moist, indicating a spring higher up. "Get ready to shoot," Bruce cautioned.

They advanced warily upcanyon. After rounding half a dozen bends Bruce said, "We'll leave the horses here. They'll hear us coming if we ride any nearer."

Flanked by Lantry and Tom Gifford, he continued afoot upcanyon. The others followed quietly after leaving one man with the horses.

The gorge took a sharp turn, and they saw a corral. Two men were sitting on its top rail. Lantry recognized them. Dalhart and Maxie. He brought his rifle stock to cheek just as Bruce yelled, "Freeze, you fellahs. You're covered."

Dalhart and Maxie didn't freeze. They jumped to the ground, firing with hip guns. Lantry squeezed his own trigger. He saw Dalhart drop. Maxie went to his knees, still pumping bullets from a forty-five.

Then a volley from behind Lantry riddled Maxie. Gun smoke clouded the canyon. A Circle K man yelled, "Just like shootin' fish. Who's next?"

Lantry couldn't see the cabin. Cedars were dense beyond the corral. They continued on till a bullet whistled from the trees.

"Drop flat," Bruce ordered. Lantry dropped. After inching forward a little he saw a section of log wall through the skirts of the cedars. Tom's voice came from the right. "There she is, men. Spread out and surround 'em."

A rattle of shots came from the cabin. A ricocheting slug whined past Lantry. He crawled thirty yards to his left for better cover, then advanced again. A bullet kicked dirt at him. He heard shot after shot from his own side. He saw Tod Newcombe a little to his left and ahead of him.

Tod was prone, back of a rock, aiming his carbine. He emptied it and yelled, "I can see a window from here. Got one guy. Maybe two."

From off in the cedars Bruce Talcott shouted, "Come out, the rest of you birdies, with your wings high."

No one came out. At least no one emerged from this side

of the cabin. "Close in," Bruce ordered.

Lantry crawled closer, pumping bullets. Bullets hailed from all angles. The cabin door was splintered. Not a sound came from it.

"Rush 'em," Tom Gifford yelled. He stood up, rifle stock at cheek, and advanced, pumping a shot at every step. Abreast of him marched Talcott and Lantry. Slim Borchard and the Circle K men closed in from oblique angles. The door, when they arrived, was cut to ribbons.

Tod Newcombe of the Circle K kicked it in.

Five outlaws lay on the floor there. Four of them were dead. The living man wouldn't last long. He was Toby, the cook, and a slug had cut his throat.

Tom stooped over him. "Who's your boss?" he demanded. "And what did you do with the mazuma?"

Toby was past talking. Minutes later he was dead.

"Might be more of 'em in the cave," Bruce said. "Lead the way, Lantry."

All Lantry knew about the cave was that it was only ten minutes away. They were upcanyon and found a footpath in the rock wall. It looked centuries old, niched there by ancient Indians. This was sure to be the route. Lantry led the way up it, rifle ready. The path hairpinned half a dozen times, climbing steeply all the while. It brought them to a wide, deep cavern.

"This is it," Lantry said. There was the same smoked ceiling. There were the grub boxes labeled *Moab, Utah*. But no men were there.

Neither could they find any hidden money. "Seven up and seven down," Slim Borchard sang out. "Where do we go from here?"

It was plain to Lantry that at least half of the hide-out crew weren't here at all. Probably they'd taken their cut from the last big job and deserted permanently.

Tom Gifford took charge now. He kept them there all

that day and the next looking for loot and surviving out-laws. Nothing was found. The corral had only seven horses.

"Rest of 'em took off," Tom concluded.

Bruce and Lantry agreed with him. Then, with seven dead men loaded on pack mules, they hit the trail for Durango.

19

AT MANCOS THEY MET BUCK SHAW with a stranger. The stranger had a hatchet face and an accent like the east side of New York. He looked uncomfortable on a horse.

"Meet Mr. Pottifer," Buck said. "Pottifer, this here's the gent you been lookin' for. Jeff Lantry of Durango."

Pottifer, still astride a rented horse on the main street of Mancos, handed Lantry his card. It identified him as a special investigator for Metropolitan Bankers' Indemnity Corporation of New York.

"My company's holding the bag on this," Pottifer explained. "Soon as they got the first telegram they started me fast for Durango."

"I told him," Buck added, "that a posse had lit out for the Blue Mountains. He wanted to join it to see if he could recover that money. So I put him on a bronc and headed him this way."

"That's it," Pottifer affirmed. "I wanta join the hounds. Might find a loot cache somewhere. Anything we salvage'll lighten the company's loss just that much."

Bruce Talcott said, "You can forget about the Blue Mountains. We found the hide-out, and it's in the Mesa Verde. Here's the sheriff. He'll tell you all about it."

Gifford gave details of the raid and the killing of seven outlaws. "We turned the place inside out," he said, "but we didn't find any money."

The ride from Durango had wearied Pottifer. Gifford

and Lantry took him to a cantina for a glass of beer. Over it the insurance detective asked a hundred sharp questions. He drew out Lantry's complete story from the kidnaping at Chama to date.

"Everything's clear now," Lantry finished, "except two things. Who's the boss of that gang, and what did they do with the loot?"

Pottifer looked pretty glum about it. "My company," he said, "insures not only the Durango bank but two of those Kaycee banks where they cashed the cattle checks. So we take an awful beating. Worst we've had since the fall of 'eighty when a client in St. Looey got stood up."

Lantry blinked. "Seems to me I remember that stick-up," he said cautiously. "It was the Frank Foster gang, wasn't it? They got away with a coupla hundred thousand?"

Clyde Pottifer nodded. "But that's ancient history. Water over the dam. What I want to do now is make a more thorough search of that cabin and cave you tell me about. You say it's right close to Mancos?"

"Yes," Lantry said. "It's that battleship-shaped mesa you see right out there." He pointed.

"We went over every inch of that cave and cabin," Tom insisted.

"But I'm a detective," the New Yorker argued. "Searching a premises is my specialty. Can you furnish me a guide there?"

Tom could and did. He called over two of the Circle K men, deputized them, and turned them over to Pottifer.

In a very short while Pottifer set forth with his guides toward the slope of Mesa Verde. Buck Shaw resumed his homeward way toward Dove Creek. Tom, Bruce, and Jeff Lantry continued east toward Durango.

Lantry wasn't satisfied. He had a feeling they'd missed something. There should have been more than seven out-

laws in the canyon cabin. Was there an outpost some-
where? What about the leader, the man they called Harry?
Certainly he wasn't any of those second-raters who'd held
Lantry at the cabin.

The leader, Lantry reasoned, wouldn't be too far away.
To direct operations he'd need to keep in touch not only
with the Mesa Verde but also with Durango. A spy in Durango would do no good without some convenient link of
communication. The link would need to reach across the
Mancos Valley through some agent who could appear
with safety at either end.

"Look, Tom," Lantry said, "I want to hang around out
here for a while. Right here in the Mancos Valley. I had a
string of share homesteaders out this way. Far as I know
they're all on the level except a fellah named Dickshot.
Dickshot did a little wide-looping on the side, so he might
do anything else. What about me holing up for a few days
at your place, Tom? I could ride around the valley and
ask questions. Maybe I could pick up an angle."

"Help yourself," Tom agreed.

His little ranch on the Mancos River was at present being taken care of by Luke Carmody's oldest boy, Alex. Lantry dropped off there. Tom and the others continued on
to Durango.

Lantry was asaddle at the crack of the next dawn.
"Maybe I'll be back for supper," he told Alex, "and maybe not."

He rode southeast, toward Cherry Creek. He had no im-
mediate plan except to reappraise Abel Dickshot and to
quiz any rider he might meet. Of reliable witnesses he
could ask if they'd ever noticed anyone who made regular
and unexplained trips to and from the Mesa Verde.

Lantry was halfway to Dickshot's when a sound far off
to the east diverted him that way. It was vaguely like the

pop of a rifle.

Maybe it was only a cowboy potting at a coyote. It had seemed to come from the cottonwood bottom along Cherry Creek. Lantry loped in that direction. A jack rabbit zigzagged in high leaps across his path. Far ahead he saw circling buzzards.

Then, about half a mile distant, he saw a riderless horse. The horse was saddled, its reins dragging.

Lantry rode up to it and saw a Bridlebit on the hip. That meant nothing, since Talcott-bred stock were scattered by bill of sale all over the Basin. The forger who'd cashed Gerry Ashton's checks at Farmington had ridden such a brand.

But this horse, Lantry saw after a closer look, had blood on its saddle. The blood was fresh. The rider, apparently, had been sniped from ambush within the last hour.

Lantry backtracked the horse. The tracks led over a sand dune. Just beyond the dune he found a dead man. The body was still warm. He was a man of about Lantry's build and height, with dark hair and brown eyes, dressed more like a townsman than a rangeman. He wore spurs and half boots, but no gun belt. Lantry had never seen him before. His suit was tailored from darkish corduroy of expensive weave.

Something odd about that coat. It looked familiar. All at once Lantry knew why. It was his *own* coat. The one he'd worn on the train when he'd left Durango for Kansas City.

This, then, must be the man who'd changed clothes with him at Chama. The impostor who'd impersonated him at Kaycee. The head of the gang? Harry? Maybe. And maybe not.

Lantry knelt by the man and searched him thoroughly. Maybe there'd be loot on him. Or some clue to his connections.

But all Lantry found was some loose change and a scrap of yellow silk. It was the sample Marcella had given him at the Durango depot.

That made it conclusive. Here was the forger and con man who'd fooled banks and railroads and cattle agents. The same man, no doubt, who'd intercepted the London checks payable to Gerry Ashton.

But why had he been dry-gulched? After a minute's thought, a reasonable answer came to Lantry. After using this artisan, milking his skill for all it was worth, the gang wouldn't need him any more. Maybe he'd demanded too large a cut. He'd be a hazard if found with them, the only real hazard, in fact, because he alone could be identified as the impostor.

As Lantry saw it now, the man had reported to gang headquarters, turned over the loot, and had then been ordered to lie low at the Mesa Verde hide-out. On the way there, he'd been followed and shot. It made sense. Nothing else did.

Tracks of his horse indicated that he'd been riding up Cherry Creek from the south. Lantry followed those tracks in reverse. Logically they should lead to the place where the man had last stopped overnight.

Lantry, not born to the range, wasn't a skilled tracker. Twice he lost the hoofmarks in high grass. By patient search he found them again on sandy ground beyond. They continued to lead south down the creek bottom.

Mile after mile Lantry followed them. The valley narrowed to a bottleneck between buttes, then widened again. He wasn't far from the New Mexico line now. A headgate on the creek marked the beginning of an irrigation ditch. The horse tracks continued along the berm of the ditch.

Ahead Lantry saw a fenced meadow. Brown bulges in the meadow were stacks of alfalfa. Beyond them he saw the buildings of a well-equipped ranch. The Bar X Box!

The Sax Consadine place! Lantry stopped, his eyes flickering with new thought. Consadine! Was he in on it? Why would a reputable and well-to-do cattleman like Consadine consort with outlaws?

No evidence at all except these horse tracks. They followed this ditch, straight toward the Consadine house.

Lantry felt a consuming urge to search that house. For loot or for anything else which might tie Consadine to the dead man back there.

He diverged from the ditch and angled across the meadow. He mustn't let them know he'd backtracked a horse here.

The ranch yard, when Lantry rode into it, looked normally innocent. A cowboy was forking hay from the barn loft. Another was breaking a colt in the corral. Two others were lounging on the bunk-shack stoop. Lantry knew all four. They hailed him genially.

"Sax at home?" he asked them carelessly.

"Sure, Mr. Lantry. Go right in."

He dismounted at the main house and knocked. It was a pleasant rock house shaded by elders, its roof gabled and shingled. Consadine had always lived well; the best people of Durango had been entertained here. On several occasions Lantry himself had stopped overnight at the Bar X Box.

Consadine opened the door. He was in smoking-jacket and slippers. His hand clapped Lantry cordially on the shoulder. "Just the man I want to see, Jeff. Come on in and have one."

In a big living-room with a steer's head mounted over its stone hearth, Sax Consadine poured wine. "What's cooking, Jeff? They tell me somebody snaked you off to the Blue Mountains while they—"

"Not the Blue Mountains," Lantry cut in. "The Mesa Verde. We just found the hide-out there and shot it out with 'em." He watched alertly for Consadine's reaction. The man's eyes flickered, but it might mean nothing except surprise.

"Mesa Verde!" Sax gave a low whistle. "Right under our noses all the time! Who'd've guessed it? You cleaned 'em out, I hope?"

Lantry nodded. "Seven men there. All killed resisting arrest. Gifford took the bodies to Durango. That's what I stopped by here for, Sax. The sheriff sent me to round up everybody in the valley. He wants you and your crew to ride to Durango and see if you can identify the bodies. Strangers, all of them. If we knew their names, it might give us a lead."

"Lead to what?" Sax asked.

"To where they hid the money. We didn't find any of it at the hide-out."

Consadine sipped his wine. "Sure, Jeff. I and my men'll be glad to co-operate. If we'd known about it, we'd've been in that posse, ourselves. Stay to lunch with us, and then we'll hit for town."

"Thanks. I'm pretty dusty, Sax. I'll wash up for lunch, if you don't mind." Lantry went back to the kitchen, bathed his face and hands there.

No cook was in sight or any sign that the kitchen had been used this morning. And that, to Lantry, seemed to indicate an upheaval of some kind. Sax Consadine had always kept a house servant or two.

"Outfit's off looking for strays along the San Juan," Sax explained. "Cook's with 'em. That's why I'm eating at the bunkhouse right now. Come along."

Lunch at the bunkhouse exposed only the four men Lantry had already seen. Again it didn't look quite normal. Consadine had always kept a dozen or more hands. This wasn't the season to be looking for distant strays.

If this were gang headquarters, the missing men might

be off on a raid. Or after a big coup like the looting of Lantry's estate, some of the men might have taken their cut and faded to parts unknown. It made Lantry more than ever determined to search these premises.

"What are your plans, Jeff?" Sax inquired. He'd finished eating. Now he rolled a cigarette, took two golden dice from his pocket, and rolled them idly on the table.

"I thought I'd bid in the Bridlebit," Lantry said. "I'll have to wait, though, till the insurance company pays me off. I'm broke right now."

"Good idea," Consadine approved. "Just what Buck Shaw and I advised you to do, one time. Remember?"

Lantry stood up. "I've got to ride. Want to make two or three places west o' here before dark. Gifford wants 'em all at Durango to see if they can identify those dead men."

"I and my crew'll start in right away," Sax promised. He shifted the dice from his right to his left hand and looked at one of his men. "Higby, go saddle up. We're all heading for town."

Durango was northeast. Lantry took another direction, west. He rode until a ridge screened him from the Consadine buildings. Then he dismounted, retraced a few steps, and peered over the ridge.

He saw five men lope out of the Bar X Box barnyard and take the Durango trail. By his tall, creamy hat he could identify the leader as Sax Consadine. Lantry watched their dust until they were out of sight.

The coast was clear now. But it hardly seemed worth while going back. The fact that Consadine had left his ranch unguarded seemed proof enough that no fortune in cash was hidden there. Nor any incriminating evidence.

So Lantry rode back to the house with only a dim hope of finding anything. If he was wrong about the place being deserted, he'd need an excuse for going back. He decided to claim, if accosted, that he'd taken a ring from his finger while washing his hands in the kitchen. He'd say he was returning for it now.

He looked in the bunkhouse, found it empty. It was the same at the cookshack and the barn. A few loose horses were in the corral. Hens were scratching in the yard. No other life was in sight.

Lantry knocked at the house door. No answer. The door was locked. He went around to the back. The door there was locked too. Clearly the ranch was deserted.

Should he break in? Lantry thought back to the dead man up Cherry Creek valley. And to the scrap of yellow silk in a pocket. Tracks of that man's mount led straight from here. There *must* be a connection. Lantry drew his gun and knocked a hole in the pane of a kitchen window. Reaching in, he unlocked it.

After crawling through the window he listened cautiously. The house had the stillness of a ghost town. Lantry relaxed. With the crew off to town he'd have all afternoon to search unmolested. Consadine's room, he decided, was the place to begin.

The first door up the hall gave to a guest room. Lantry had slept in it himself, more than once. The next bedroom was Consadine's. Lantry opened its door, took a step inside, then froze.

Sax Consadine was sitting on the bed. He was aiming a forty-five at Lantry's head.

20

"HATE TO TREAT A GUEST THIS WAY, Jeff. But I don't like snoops. You're a dead duck."

Lantry hadn't holstered his gun after smashing the window with it. It was still in his hand, but hanging at arm's length. He knew he couldn't whip it level in time to shoot it out with Consadine.

"Drop it," Sax said.

The gun clattered on the floor.

"Now turn around."

Lantry turned his back, braced for the feel of a bullet burning through it.

"We'll do it outside, Jeff. I don't want to mess up my own house. Out you go."

Sax came forward and pushed his gun muzzle against the small of Lantry's back.

Might as well be here, Lanthy thought, *as anywhere else.* His right boot heel had a sharp spur on it. He kicked back, suddenly and hard, and the spur gaffed into Consadine's shin. At the same instant Lantry dived flat into the hall. Consadine's gun boomed, and the wall beyond Lantry splintered.

Lantry rolled over, lay on his back there in the hall. Sax was standing over him, aiming the gun down at him. "Too bad Indian Charlie isn't here," Sax jeered. "He could knife me in the back like he did Jallison. But I still don't like blood on my carpets. Get up and walk."

Lantry got to his feet. He'd gained nothing but a minute's respite. Sax marched him toward the front door.

They entered the living-room and crossed it. A heavy brass key was in the door lock. "Turn it to the left," Sax said, "and open the door."

Lantry put a hand on the key. He drew it from the lock, stooping, whirling, and hurling the key in one flash movement. There was nothing to lose. Again a bullet blazed from Consadine's gun. It smashed the door above Lantry. Lantry dived from a crouch. A third shot was even wilder —for two reasons, the heavy brass key had struck Consadine's eye, and Lantry's full, diving weight had hit Consadine at the knees. Lantry clung there like a football man tackling a dummy. Consadine went over on his back with

Lantry riding him.

A fourth wild shot, but now Lantry had a hand on the gun. He twisted desperately, his knee in Consadine's stomach. "What did you do with it, Sax? The money. Or is your name Harry?"

He was stronger than Consadine, and the wrist in his grasp gave. A bone cracked, and the gun dropped free. Lantry snatched it, leaped to his feet, and backed off. There should be two live shells left in it. "What did you do with it?" Lantry repeated.

Sax stood up. His lips took a droop of surrender. "It's your drop," he admitted. "I'll take you to it."

He walked back into the hall with Lantry at his heels. Sax turned into his own room. Lantry had forgotten his own gun, which lay on the floor there. "I want that money," he repeated.

"It's under this rug," Sax said. He stooped as though to pull the rug aside.

Then he straightened up with Lantry's gun in his hand, whirling as he fired. Lantry pulled his own trigger. Smoke from two guns choked the room. A nausea dizzied Lantry. His arm burned, but he kept his feet. He heard a thump, and it was Consadine hitting the floor.

In a moment the dizziness cleared, and he knelt by the man to feel of his heart. There was no beat. Sax Consadine was dead.

Lantry sat on the bed, breathing like a blown runner. Sweat made a stinging mist in his eyes, and he wiped it with his sleeve. Money was in this house. He was sure of it. Else Consadine wouldn't so cagily have remained on guard. Saying it was under the rug meant nothing. That, of course, had only been a ruse to pick up a gun.

Lantry searched the bed first. He slashed open the mattress and pillows. Nothing was there. Four hundred thousand dollars would need plenty of space. A trunk or a chest, more likely.

In the kitchen wood box he found an ax. Lantry went about the house with it, smashing open every locked receptacle he could find. Trunks and bins and closets. The living-room desk had five drawers, four open, one locked. Lantry cracked the lock and searched thoroughly. The drawers held a miscellany of papers and old letters. He shuffled hastily through them looking for some record of a cache or payoff—or any clue to the identity of confederate outlaws.

It turned up no worth-while find. Lantry picked up Consadine's body and put it on the bed. The first pocket he delved into had two golden dice. Lantry left them there. The other pockets offered keys and a wallet. The wallet had a few small bills, a brand certificate, various ranch memos and stock tallies, and an assortment of accumulated scraps. One of the scraps seemed to be a short letter in a semiliterate hand, signed *Gus Irvine*. Lantry couldn't imagine that honest old prospector having anything to do with crime or loot. He transferred the paper to his own wallet, too absorbed in his main search to spend time in weighing the significance of an irrelevant oddity.

Minutes were too precious right now. He must have this house ransacked to the last nail hole and be gone before those five men returned from Durango. It was clear that a fifth man had been here all the time. Under cover. Perhaps hiding in the barn all during lunch. Consadine had put his own tall, creamy-white hat on the man, sending him in with the other four, in case Lantry might be observing from afar.

Lantry pulled up all rugs looking for disturbed floor boards. He tried the fireplace, the hearthstones, the chimney flues, the guest-room bed. Room by room he covered the house.

Two hours, and he was still at it. Then he found something in a table drawer of the guest room. Not money. Just an old calendar. A name was written a hundred or more times across the back of the calendar. The penmanship was the same in every case, and the name written was Gerald K. Ashton. This, clearly, was a forger's practice exercise. As a guest long ago in this house, he'd prepared himself at leisure to endorse convincingly those hundred-pound quarterly checks from London.

Not that any more evidence was needed. Except that it definitely linked one forgery plot to another, and established beyond the last shadow of doubt that this house had been the brain center of an organized and versatile band of outlaws.

It redoubled the vigor of Lantry's search. The house had no cellar. It had a false attic, but Lantry found nothing there except cobwebs and bare rafters.

Dropping down from the attic he felt an ache in his left arm. His sleeve was red and drenched. Consadine's last bullet had nicked him, but he'd been too eager in his search to think of it. Now he took off his shirt and found a flesh wound just above the elbow. Not serious, but deep enough to bleed freely.

A washroom adjoined Consadine's bedroom. It had a bowl and a pitcher of water. Lantry bathed his arm wound and then looked for a rag to bind around it.

A laundry bag hung from a wall peg there. Lantry had already looked in it and found nothing but soiled shirts. Now he looked in it again with the idea of finding some rag clean enough to use for a bandage.

He emptied the bag on the floor. Out came a mass of soiled linen—and packets of money. Currency in hundred-dollar bills!

Jeff Lantry stared down at it, grinning sheepishly. Right under his nose all the time. Sax had merely camouflaged his loot bag by filling the top of it with laundry.

Lantry spread the money on a table, counted it. There were thirty-seven packages, fifty bills to the package, each with a rubber band around it. Each bill was for a hundred dollars. It came, in all, to $185,000.

A little less than half the missing money.

And when Lantry thought about it, it seemed reasonable enough. The many other members of the gang would need to be paid off. Then there was the spy in Durango. Whoever he was, he, too, would have a cut. Sax had done fairly well to salvage nearly half the total for himself.

His share, and his share only, would logically be on these premises. Lantry decided to take it and be gone.

He found a clean rag and wrapped it around the arm wound. Then he put the money back in the laundry bag, found a sheet of canvas, and rolled the bag inside of it. He took it out and tied it on his horse.

Loping out through the gate, he reasoned it would be too risky if he took the trail to Durango. Those five men might be returning, and he'd meet them on the way. It was late afternoon. He was far south on the state line, a little nearer to Farmington, New Mexico, than to Durango, Colorado.

If he met anyone, he was in no shape for a fight. The quicker he got to the haven of a town the better. So Lantry reined to the right and took a trail southeast toward Farmington.

His route took him through broken cedar country, with bunches of Bar X Box cattle grazing here and there. He met no one except a family of Navajos with a burroload of piñon nuts, trailing toward the San Juan Indian agency. Off to his left Lantry could see the broad fertile valley of the San Juan River, main artery of the Basin. He reached it at the mouth of the La Plata. Here was an adobe settlement with small goat herds and winter-brown patches of alfalfa.

Darkness had fallen by the time Lantry rode into Farmington. It was a quiet, agrarian town, sleepily shaded, great spreading cottonwoods hovering over the streets. Most of its people were Mexicans and Navajos. The hitchracks had more burros than cow ponies. An irrigation ditch gurgled down the main-street gutter. Soft guitar music came from beyond the blue shutters of cantinas. Nothing roaring about this place; none of the sound and fury of Durango.

Lantry stopped at a restaurant. He tied his horse where he could watch it from his table. He went in and ordered a steak. They didn't have any. He settled for mutton and beer.

There was a sprawling adobe hotel. Lantry went to it, taking his money package in with him. It made a pillow for him that night, as he slept behind a locked door in Farmington.

His dream was of a broad and beautiful place on the west fork of the Dolores. And of Marcella settled there with him. The Talcott ranch. Tomorrow, he remembered, was the auction day at Rico. He couldn't make Rico in time to bid. But no matter. The bank didn't really want the Bridlebit ranch. It wanted only to protect its lien. Crump would be glad to reconvey the property for a dollar profit.

It was on Lantry's mind all the next day as he rode north up the Animas toward Durango. What a gracious life he could build for Marcella on the Bridlebit! They'd be practical, too. They wouldn't go broke raising race horses. The thing was to get ahead. They'd stick to cattle. Thoroughbred cattle, ultimately.

By noon Lantry had crossed the state line. This trail led straight up the well-settled Animas Valley. Mike was fagged, and Lantry took it easy. He stopped for a restful hour at a farm by the river.

A light flaky snow began falling as he reached the mouth of the Florida. Beyond there the trail was slushy, slowing him to a walk. It was dusk by the time he sighted Durango.

He rode in on Second Avenue. His route to the hotel would take him right by Doctor Ed's house. Lantry decided to stop there and have his arm properly bandaged. It was paining him a little. No use risking an infection.

Should he tell Marcella about his fight with Consadine? Perhaps he'd better not. Killings, he knew, revolted her. Sax Consadine had been her friend and frequent guest. Best to let her hear the whole story later through Tom Gifford's official report. No doubt she already knew about the posse's raid in a Mesa Verde canyon. Since the posse had returned two days ago, the tale of its adventure would by now be all over town.

Doctor Ed was out. Only Marcella was there. She looked apprehensively at Lantry's bandaged arm. "But Tom didn't tell me!" she exclaimed. "I thought you got through it without a scratch. Is it bad?"

"Just a pinprick," he said. Since she thought it was a wound he'd received in the Mesa Verde clash, there was no point in telling her otherwise. That way he could avoid, for the time being, shocking her with the fact that he'd killed Consadine.

She bared the arm, bathed it, and applied a disinfectant. Her touch thrilled Lantry. Never before had she seemed quite so tender and lovely. He wanted to take her in his arms. Maybe he would, as soon as she finished putting that bandage on. Why not ask her now? When could there be a better time? They were alone. Everything was right for it.

"Those terrible outlaws!" she was saying. "Robbing people all these years! How can anyone be like that, Jeff? Snatching away other people's money. How can a man like that live with himself?"

Lantry looked into her level, honest eyes, and suddenly there was a wall between them. It was a thing he'd felt often before when he was with Marcella. Her last words echoed. *How can a man like that live with himself?*

How could a man like that live with Marcella? A man who snatched away other people's money. The haunting ghost of a memory came to Lantry. A memory of this very house. Of himself slipping up to its second-floor-rear room —Marcella's room now—to steal loot from a dead felon. To steal it and use it all these years, to get ahead, to get ahead—

How far was he ahead now? How far when he couldn't even look into a girl's eyes and ask her to marry him? When he knew the revulsion that would come to her, if and when she ever learned the truth.

How could he ask her now? *Everything was right for it,* had been his thought a moment ago. But no, *one* thing was wrong for it. That package of money on a saddle out in front. Consadine's loot! Yes, and Jeff Lantry's loot, too.

She gave the bandage a pat. "There! Make yourself comfortable now while I bring you some hot coffee. Doctor Ed will be back pretty soon. He went to the hotel to see a Mr. Pottifer. Nothing wrong with Mr. Pottifer, though, except he's sore and stiff from a long ride."

So Pottifer was back from the Mesa Verde! An idea came to Lantry. His mind clutched at it, desperately. It was a way out. The *only* way out. The only way he could *ever* make himself decently eligible for Marcella.

"I got to be shoving on," he said nervously. "There's things I need to tell Tom."

He left Marcella abruptly and went out to his horse. He swung to the saddle, dug in furiously with his spurs. Mike leaped forward. Lantry had never before spurred him like that.

And never before had Durango seen Jeff Lantry race at

a breakneck gallop up Main Street. Snow was still falling. Through a curtain of flakes both sides of the street—the good and the bad—saw and wondered.

Lantry pulled up at the Grand Central. Dismounting, he tore savagely at the knots which held a canvas-covered package to the saddle. It was bulky, this loot he'd recovered from Sax Consadine. Hefting it to his shoulder, Lantry strode into the hotel which had been his home for four years.

"Which," he demanded of the clerk, "is Clyde Pottifer's room?"

"Number two-o-seven, Mr. Lantry. And by the way, Tom Gifford reserved your old room for you. Two-o-eight. He knew you'd be plenty tired when you got in."

Lantry hurried up the steps. He was pushing himself along, desperately, before he could change his mind.

He burst into room 207 and found Clyde Pottifer getting ready for bed. The man had a jaded look. He turned stiffly as Lantry entered.

"I found the slicker who forged those checks," Lantry announced. "And the man who put him up to it. They're both dead."

Pottifer stared. "What about the money?" he gasped. "Did they have any of it on them?"

"The dead outlaw did. I mean it was in a laundry bag hanging in his washroom."

"How much of it?" the insurance investigator asked eagerly.

"All of it," Lantry said.

"All of it?" Pottifer's mouth hung open. He gaped incredulously.

"All of it," Lantry repeated. "Four hundred thousand. All the money that guy checked out of the Lantry accounts. Your clients are in the clear now, Pottifer. You don't owe them a dime."

21

LANTRY LAID HIS CANVAS ROLL ON THE BED. He untied it and exposed a laundry bag. "Take a look, Pottifer."

Still jolted half out of his wits, Pottifer reached into the bag and drew out sheaves of hundred-dollar bills.

"Listen," Lantry said. "I'll tell you what happened. Then we'll call in Tom Gifford and Banker Crump."

The story he told diverted from the exact truth only in two details. Beginning with the moment he'd left the posse at Tom Gifford's place, Lantry recited his movements until his arrival at Farmington. "It slowed me down, all that money. If I met any of those outlaws—and there's a few of 'em still loose—I'd have to ride fast. So I left all the fives and tens and twenties with a friend of mine at Farmington. The centuries didn't weigh too much, so I brought them on in."

Pottifer counted thirty-seven packets of fifty bills each. "One hundred and eighty-five thousand!" he exclaimed jubilantly. "But you recovered it all, you say?"

"That's right. And say, Pottifer, let's not tell about the part I left in Farmington till I can get it banked. There's men in Durango who'd cut a throat for a tenth that much."

From what he'd seen of Durango, Pottifer hadn't the slightest doubt of it. The only thing which interested him was his own good luck. He was here purely to reduce, or prevent entirely, a loss to his employers, the Metropolitan Bankers' Indemnity Corporation of New York. Eagerly he brought a form from his valise. "If you have no claim against our clients, Mr. Lantry, will you please sign a release?"

"Certainly," Lantry agreed. Promptly he signed a release by which he admitted full recovery from forgeries on all bank accounts in the name of Jefferson D. Lantry, both at Kansas City and at Durango.

Pottifer mopped sweat from his forehead. With this release in hand, his mission was accomplished. "I've had breaks before," he admitted, "but this beats 'em all." He went to the top of the stairs and shouted down, "Hey, you, bring me a telegraph blank."

The clerk came up with a blank telegram. His eyes bulged when he saw money piled on the bed.

Pottifer wrote a telegram to New York.

All funds in Lantry case recovered. No loss. Case closed.
Pottifer

"Send this to the depot," he instructed the clerk. "I want to get it off right away."

Lantry put in, "And send a messenger to Banker Crump's house. Tell him to come here at once."

Crump arrived promptly. He was elated at the news. Lantry let Pottifer tell it. Again he enjoined secrecy about the part of the money left at Farmington. "We don't want to start a stampede that way. I lost that money once, and I don't want to lose it again. At least five of Consadine's gunnies are, or were, right here in Durango."

Crump led the way two blocks south to his bank. He opened it. They went in and put one hundred and eighty-five thousand dollars in the vault. Crump gave Lantry a deposit slip to cover.

"What do you plan to do with it, Lantry?"

"I'm gonna buy the Brid—" Lantry checked his statement.

For a moment he wondered why. His plan to bid in the Talcott ranch had become suddenly distasteful. Marcella, he was sure, wouldn't like it, either. They'd feel just a little like they were snatching at the bones of a friend. Carey and Bruce Talcott had been staunch, loyal friends. Now they were destitute. Pouncing on the spoils wouldn't seem quite—Lantry searched for a word and borrowed one from Gerry Ashton—it just wouldn't be quite *cricket*.

"I haven't decided," Lantry corrected himself. "As you pass the sheriff's office on your way home, Mr. Crump, will you send Tom Gifford to the hotel?"

He was waiting in Pottifer's room when Tom arrived. With a happy smile Pottifer showed his release. Again the story was told. This time Lantry accurately described the spot where he'd found the forger's body. "You better pick him up, Tom, before the coyotes get to him."

Tom grimaced. "Just my luck," he complained, "not to be there for the showdown. Sax Consadine, huh? And we thought that guy was a model citizen. Head of the gang, huh?"

"No question about it," Lantry assured him. "For instance, you'll find a calendar in his house where they practiced Gerry Ashton's signature. The whole thing ties up. Sax pulled every string for the Blue Mountains gang—Mesa Verde gang, I mean."

Tom licked the flap of a cigarette. "That outfit pulled plenty jobs, these last five-six years. Wonder what they did with the dough?"

"Most of it," Lantry reminded him, "went to pay for Sax's land and cattle. And you can get that part of it back. Slap a judgment on the Bar X Box and on Consadine's account at the bank. Use it to pay off all claims from any known victims of the gang. Except me, of course. I've already recovered mine."

"Means I gotta ride." Tom stretched his arms wearily. "No rest for a sheriff. Why did I take this job, anyway? Gimme those names again, Jeff. I mean the five hands who rode off to town."

"Ad French, Les Baker, Vic Higby, a guy they call Squinty, and a fifth man we don't know. I had lunch with

them at the bunk shack just before the showdown. Told
'em to see you and identify some bodies."

"Naturally they didn't see me," Tom said. "Somebody
here in town must've tipped 'em not to. Their Durango
lookout, likely. Wonder who that guy is?"

"Better get going, Tom," Lantry said. "Me, I'm hitting
the hay. And as you go out please tell the clerk I don't
want to be wakened for twenty-four hours."

He crossed to room 208 and went to bed.

This was his old room, and he felt pleasantly at home.
It was good to lie between clean sheets again. And to feel
clean himself, inside and out. What a break that Pottifer's
company had also indemnified the St. Louis bank in the
case of that old stick-up pulled by Frank Foster!

Not so strange, though, Lantry thought. Bank indemnity was a new wrinkle in insurance. Possibly only two or
three companies in all the world handled indemnities like
that. Lloyd's of London was one. Metropolitan Bankers'
Indemnity of New York might be the only insurer of its
kind in America.

The precious fact which lulled Lantry was that his own
thievery, four years ago, had been entirely against the
insurers. They, in the end, had paid the score. Therefore
they and they only had lost. Now they were paid back,
every dollar, plus $15,000 for interest.

Because actually Lantry was still short $215,000. By sign-
ing his name to a release, he'd made the indemnity company a present of that sum. And no one knew it. Only
himself and his conscience.

Lantry smiled in the dark. He could go to Marcella with
clean hands. He was really getting ahead, now.

He closed his eyes and slept an untroubled sleep. Morning came, and he still slept. He needed it, after the long
weary days asaddle. All day he lay abed with the even, easy
breathing of a child.

Dusk had fallen when he awoke. Lantry bathed and dressed, whistling an old range song. He was ravenously hungry. He must hurry down to the Chuck Wagon for supper.

Going out he turned south along the walk. Across the way saloon row was roaring, as usual. Shouts and coarse talk and raucous music, the boastings of men and the falsetto laughter of women. This side was quiet and subdued, the shops all closed for the night. Durango, Lantry concluded, was two places. An evil place and a good place. And he himself was like it. He was an evil man and a decent man. Every time he saw himself in a mirror it was like looking across Main Street in Durango. Most men were that way, he thought. Both evil and decent. In Durango and everywhere else. Women weren't. Women were either all good or all bad. At least it was so by the standards of Durango.

Across the street everything was aglitter with lights. This side was dark except for the eating-places. The Chuck Wagon was aglow, of course, but Lantry wasn't prepared for what he found there. Again he discovered that it had been chartered for a single extravagant party.

Again a long curved table, horseshoe-shaped, filled the room. Fifty or more guests were there, the elite of Durango. At the place of honor, proud and smiling, sat Major Carey Talcott. The wheel chair of his invalid wife was at his right, while his son Bruce sat at his left. The man next to Bruce was on his feet, speaking. He was Doctor Ed Amory.

The headwaiter whispered softly to Lantry. "We saved a place for you, sir. It's a farewell dinner given by the citizens of Durango to the Talcotts. They're going back to Tennessee, you know."

Lantry nodded. Having lost their beloved ranch they'd naturally go back to Tennessee.

He followed the waiter to an empty chair. It was between Marcella Blair's and Melissa Ashton's.

Marcella smiled. "We hoped you'd come," she whispered. "We sent for you, but the hotel clerk wouldn't let you be disturbed."

"Hush!" cautioned Melissa. "Doctor Ed's making a speech."

Lantry settled himself to listen. Doctor Ed's speech was, of course, a eulogy of Carey Talcott. Lantry caught only the end of it.

" . . . and another proof, dear friends, of his grand character is the fine human way he had of dealing with his less fortunate neighbors. Major Talcott had one rule which he never broke. A hungry man must never be prosecuted for butchering a Bridlebit beef. Some took advantage of it, perhaps, but Carey Talcott in the bigness of his heart never faltered from his rule. Thus no poor settler's wife or child on all that range ever needed to go hungry. Bridlebit meat was for all who lacked meat of their own. It was manna in the wilderness. And for that, God bless you, Major Talcott."

Doctor Ed sat down. Cheers and clappings rang around the table.

Something tugged at a corner of Lantry's mind. He remembered an odd scrap of paper he'd found in Consadine's wallet and transferred to his own. Pressed for time, he'd read only the first clause and the signature. Vaguely he recalled the first few words: *To my kind and generous neighbor—*

Lantry took the scrap out now and read it in detail. It wasn't easy. The scrawl was semiliterate and barely legible. When its full significance hit Lantry, it seemed to him the last magic throw of Consadine's golden dice.

He got to his feet and shouted for the table to be quiet. "Doctor Ed," he said, "hasn't told you half of it. It wasn't only poor hungry homesteaders who ate Bridlebit beef. Listen to this. Once there was a shabby old prospector, driving three burros ahead of him, pecking at rocks through the Uncompahgres. Some years he was grubstaked. Some years he wasn't. Often he was hungry. At those times he knew exactly what to do. He could kill himself a yearling. If it was my yearling, or your yearling, he might be hanged for it. But if it was a Talcott yearling, he needed only to take the hide to its owner and hear him say, 'You're welcome, suh.'

"At last this old prospector made a strike. A rich strike worth millions. But he was sick and old by then. He lay down to die by the great golden ledge he'd struck—and he remembered the one neighbor who'd been kind to him. And so this old man—Gus Irvine was his name—wrote a holograph will. It leaves his entire estate to Carey Talcott."

The banqueters stared, breathless. Everyone knew of that fabulous strike up above Rico. It wasn't far from the very courthouse where the Talcott estate had been sold for debt.

In the hush Lantry went on. "Honest men, as you know, found his body there. But a rogue had found it first, and stripped it. A wandering vandal from the Mesa Verde gang. From Gus Irvine's wallet he took a scrap of paper which was to him worthless. He carried it to his chief, Sax Consadine. Consadine couldn't use it, either, but he kept it as an oddity. Two days ago I had a showdown with Consadine. I found Gus Irvine's will in his wallet. Here it.is."

Lantry produced it from his own wallet. He carried it to the head of the horseshoe and presented it, with a smile, to Carey Talcott.

Pandemonium erupted. For once the east side of Main Street was noisier than the west. Guests rushed to Major Talcott and smothered him with congratulations. Men laughed, and women cried. Doctor Ed stood wreathed in smiles, like a benevolent monk. "It's virtue's dividend," he said. "I've never known it to fail. Bread cast on the waters—" Lantry felt someone squeeze his arm. It was Marcella. Her eyes had tears in them. "It's like a fairy tale," she whispered.

Not till the feasting was over did Lantry see Tom Gifford. Tom had come in late, booted and gun-slung, after a hard ride to the Bar X Box.

For a brief moment he took Lantry aside. "I found everything just like you said, Jeff. Except one small detail. You say you left the golden dice in Sax's pocket. They weren't there when I arrived. And we didn't succeed in picking up those four men."

"Five men," Lantry corrected. "I don't know who the fifth was."

"The way I see it," Tom offered, "those men came to Durango, consulted their lookout here, found out they weren't expected to identify any dead men, so they knew you'd handed 'em a bum steer. They fogged back to the Bar X Box and found Sax dead. Nothin' on him but the gold dice, so they took 'em and lit out for the tall timber."

"Sounds reasonable," Lantry concurred.

He rejoined Marcella and asked to see her home.

From her doorway across the street, Ruby Costello saw the café party breaking up. The crowd came out in couples, turning this way or that. One pair was Lantry and Marcella. Sight of them strolling intimately down the walk narrowed Ruby's eyes into oblique slits of bitterness and hate.

Despair, too, harassed her. Everything was tumbling down. News had just reached her about Harry Listra. He'd been on the losing end of a gun fight with Lantry. And his death by violence, according to Harry's threat, meant that she herself would ultimately be exposed. Somewhere he had a bank box with the full story of her guilt.

She went sullenly back to her bar and ordered vermouth. Her day in Durango was done. That much was certain. There was nothing she could do but salvage as much as possible and run.

Run where? By train to the east? Or by trail to the west?

Either way had hazards. She could be intercepted on a train and hustled off to jail. But a trail escape through the mountains meant rough knocks. Cushions and silks suited Ruby best.

She'd have to desert an extravagant plant here. There'd be no time to find a buyer for the Esperanza. Otherwise most of her estate was in cash. Ready cash, because the cashiers of her gambling-rooms had to keep it on hand, ready for high stakes play. Also there was her last commission from Harry Listra. It was hidden in her room. Forty thousand dollars accruing from the raid on Lantry. So if she must, she could slip away with a cash fortune without even waiting for morning.

Two customers came in. They were in excited talk about the Lantry-Consadine gun fight. Ruby listened. She heard a man say, "Shot it out with Sax, he did, and found every dollar of it right there in his house."

The statement startled Ruby. But how could it be true? She herself had a tenth of that haul. Why should Lantry claim to find more than he'd really found? It didn't make sense.

Unless, Ruby thought with a sudden alarm, Harry Listra had tricked her! Unless Harry had palmed off some phony bills on her! Had he? To make sure, Ruby went swishing back to her quarters at the rear. She unlocked a trunk and exposed money there. Four hundred bills, each for a hundred dollars. She knew money. This, beyond any doubt, was genuine currency.

Why had Lantry lied?

As she brooded over it, Ruby heard a tap at her window. A face was pressed against the pane. It was Ad French. Ad was one of Harry's men. He motioned for her to raise the sash.

When she did, he said, "Game's up, Ruby. We're skipping out. Want to go with us?"

"Where?"

"Nevada. By the back trails of Utah. Wanta go?"

"When?"

"Tonight. They's four of us. You'd make five. Higby's got broncs waitin' down by the river."

It left one man unaccounted for. Ruby knew that *five* men had been with Harry at the Bar X Box. "Who," she asked, "isn't going?"

"Trigger Smith."

"Why?"

"Trigger's in the clear," Ad explained. "Lantry didn't see him at the Mesa Verde place. Nor at the ranch, either, 'cept from a distance ridin' off with Harry's hat on. So Trigger aims to stand pat right here in Durango. He says he'll buy himself a saloon and settle down."

"What with?"

Ad drooped an eyelid. "With his own cut—plus Alf Fontana's."

Ruby understood. She knew, of course, all about Trigger Smith. He was a specialist, a triggerman. As a killer by trade, his duties had been to enforce discipline in the gang and to eliminate dangerous witnesses. For that purpose he'd been kept well under cover. Harry had sent him to Kansas City to keep an eye and a gun on Alf Fontana, in case Alf got any ideas about skipping out. And after Fontana had delivered the take to Harry at the Bar X Box, Trigger Smith had been ordered to put him out of the way. Alf had become a hazard, because too many train, bank, and hotel employees could point a finger at him.

All that Ruby had known. What she learned now was that Trigger Smith, for his trouble, had been allowed to help himself to Fontana's cut. With that kind of money, he'd have the price of a saloon in Durango.

Why not sell him the Esperanza?

"Are you absolutely sure," Ruby asked Ad, "that Harry's dead?" She'd had no real evidence of it except bar gossip.

"Deader'n a buffalo skull. Here's proof of it. We took 'em outa his pocket." Ad French displayed two golden dice.

Ruby reached for them, balanced them in her small white hand. Harry, alive, would never have parted with them. So she knew beyond dispute that he was dead.

They were dice, tools of her trade. She was a gambler.

Nevada? A region of desert mining towns. The last and deepest hinterland of the frontier. A place to change her name and dye her hair and get a new start. Beyond a curtain of desert mountains she could build another glittering bar, another and even more dazzling palace of chance.

"I'll be ready by midnight, Ad. But first send Trigger Smith here. I want to make him a proposition."

22

YESTERDAY'S SNOW HAD MELTED from the walks. Some of its slush still lay in the gutters; and Lantry, walking home with Marcella, took her arm as they crossed F Street. She held her skirts clear of the half-frozen mud. A drift in the far gutter stopped them. It would engulf Marcella's party slippers. So Lantry picked her up, carried her across, and set her down on the walk.

Only a block up the hill, now, to Doctor Ed's. She was chattering about Gerry and Melissa. Lantry, engrossed with a decision of his own, hardly heard her. For he knew now that it wasn't enough merely to relinquish the Frank

Foster loot back to its losers. There'd still be a wall between himself and Marcella. The wall of a secret. He could tear down that wall only by telling her the truth.

"Gerry's taking her to England," she was saying, "to meet his people there."

"Are they coming back?" Lantry inquired absently.

"Of course. They'll be back late in the spring. This country licked him once, Gerry says, so he's not going to run away from it. And Lissy feels the same way. She loves the Basin, in spite of everything. And she's awfully proud of Gerry."

That was it, Lantry thought. A woman had to be proud of her man. There must never be any shadow of shame between them. Nor any false colors or shame or furtive deception.

They were at Doctor Ed's gate. Lantry opened it, and Marcella passed through. He made no move to follow.

She turned, her eyes both inviting and puzzled. "Aren't you coming in, Jeff?"

He wanted to step through that gate and sweep her up in his arms. Instead he stood stoically aloof, with the open gate between them. "Something you got to know, Marcella. Once I found some stolen money. I knew where it came from and all about it. I shouldn't have touched it."

Her eyes searched him. After a torturing moment she prompted, "But you *did?*"

"I kept it and used it," he admitted, "for a long time. Then I gave it back. Every dollar, with interest. That's the truth, and so help me, God!"

She didn't come toward him. She didn't retreat. Her face wore pallor and shock. But a look came into her eyes, and it was like Melissa looking at Gerry Ashton, that day on the porch here.

"Why do you tell me this, Jeff?"

He said humbly, "So I can ask you something, Marcella."

Her smile lighted the darkness. "Well, go ahead and ask me, Jeff Lantry."

Like a man unshackled, he stepped through the gate and took her in his arms. "I want you, Marcella."

"I hoped you did, Jeff."

"I'll never let you down," he promised.

From a dark pine in a vacant lot across the street, an owl hooted. Then Doctor Ed's voice called to them from the house. "Hey, you, out there! Come on inside before you catch your death o' cold."

As if, Lantry thought jubilantly, he could ever be cold again!

Yet almost instantly he *was*. Marcella whispered with her cheek warm against his, "I'm so glad you gave it back, Jeff. *All* of it."

All of it? Had he given it all back?

Of course he had. Principal and interest. Was there anything else?

Deep inside of him he knew that there was. There was the profit he'd made from the use of it!

Did he have a right to keep even that? By his own loose code he did. But what about Marcella's? She was part of him now. And what would *she* say? Would she shrink from profit spawned by loot just as she'd shrink from the loot itself?

Lantry didn't need to ask her. He *knew*. No use kidding himself. The line was plain, and you had to stay on one side of it or the other. It was like the two sides of Main Street in Durango.

Lantry hardly knew his own voice. He heard it say, "There's one more thing you got to know. And there's one more thing I got to do, Marcella."

Ruby sat facing Trigger Smith in her room at the Esperanza. "I'm leaving town," she announced.

"So Ad tells me." Trigger poured himself a drink. He was a lean, loose-limbed man with a blood-raw face and watery blue eyes. He wore a cartridge belt but no chaps. The holster at his hip was flapless and shallow, exposing his forty-five clear to the trigger guard.

"I know exactly what your cut was," Ruby said. "And exactly what Alf's was. Which means I know just how much spot cash you have. It's *almost* enough to buy the Esperanza."

Trigger Smith blinked. He wanted to buy a saloon and settle down. But a fancy place like the Esperanza, he'd supposed, was entirely beyond his purse.

"Almost, you said. How much more would it take?"

"Just one bullet," Ruby said, "out of your gun."

The watery blue eyes flickered. Trigger Smith sipped slowly from his liquor glass, watching Ruby over its rim. "Who's the bullet for?"

"Jeff Lantry."

Trigger took the name in stride. "When," he asked, "do I get title?"

"To the Esperanza? Ten minutes after he's dead. Come right back here and I'll have the deed ready. It's all got to be done right away, because I'm ducking out at midnight."

"Lantry, huh? Where is he?"

"At Doctor Ed Amory's. Second and F. He took the nurse home just now. When he comes out, you be waiting across the street. She'll say good-by to him on the porch. Or maybe she'll walk to the gate with him." Ruby's eyes narrowed. "Which is the way I want it. I want her to see him go down."

"That," Trigger objected, "will make her a witness."

"No. It's a dark corner. All she'll see is a flash from across the street. You'll find a pine tree in a vacant lot there. All the cover you need. Take it or leave it, Trigger."

Trigger Smith took it. Title to the Esperanza was too

sweet a prize to pass up.

"No risk," Ruby assured him. "He isn't even wearing a gun tonight. I know because I saw them come out of the Chuck Wagon."

"Have the title ready," Trigger said. He stood up and took a hitch at his belt. "I'll be back for it in an hour."

Ruby let him out at a side door, and he faded into the dark.

A glow of delight brightened Marcella's face. "Why, I think that's a perfectly wonderful plan, Jeff!" They had come inside and were seated on the sofa in Doctor Ed's little parlor.

"Would it make everything all right?" Lantry asked anxiously.

"Perfect!" Marcella insisted. "It makes everything right and just and beautiful."

They'd had a hard time deciding what to do with one hundred and eighty-four thousand untouchable dollars. Since neither banks nor insurance companies had lost anything, to whom should the money go?

Then Lantry had suggested the St. Louis orphanage from which he'd run away at the age of ten. He knew that the institution was still operating, but was pitifully under-staffed, underequipped and underendowed. "Maybe," he'd offered wryly, "that's why I got such a twisted start."

They'd decided to keep only a few hundred dollars, the exact sum, as nearly as Lantry could remember, that he'd originally brought into Durango. The best of it would be working it out together. It would be fun, really, sending that endowment to the orphanage. And fun getting a fresh start, too. Already Jeff had ideas. Maybe they could borrow a year's rent and lease the old Jallison place.

But now the hour was late, Lantry got reluctantly to his feet. "I better go before Doctor Ed throws me out."

Marcella went out into the hall with him. Lantry opened a closet and took his hat from a peg there. On the front porch he turned to kiss her good night. It was a long and precious moment. Tomorrow would be their wedding day.

Lantry's back was to the dark street. And Marcella, locked in his arms and looking over his shoulder, saw something which gave her a start. She drew Jeff quickly back inside and closed the door.

"I saw a man over there," she worried. "In the vacant lot across the street."

Lantry laughed. "So what? There's lots of men in Durango."

"But this one," she persisted, "was behind a tree. Peering out and looking at this house. Please stay all night, Jeff. We've loads of room and—"

"And so you're afraid for me to go home in the dark!" Lantry laughed again. "No apron strings, please, lady. At least not till after tomorrow. Anyway, you just imagined it. You saw a shadow, that's all."

She wasn't convinced. "It was a man," she insisted. "Maybe he's waiting for you to come out."

That, Lantry admitted, was barely possible. Some of the Mesa Verde outlaws weren't yet accounted for. "If it'll make you feel any better," he said, "I'll borrow one of those insurance policies I saw hanging in the closet when I picked up my hat just now."

He opened the closet and exposed pegs from which hung various hats and coats of patients. Also there were two cowboy cartridge belts each equipped with a holstered forty-five.

"That one's Sam Corson's," Marcella said, pointing to one of the belts. "They brought him in today with a broken leg."

"Since Sam can't use it in bed," Lantry chuckled, "I might as well let it chaperon me home." He took the gun from its holster and dropped it into his coat pocket.

Then he kissed Marcella again and was gone.

She stood in the open door, looking anxiously after him. That pine tree across the street now looked shadowless and deserted. Maybe she'd been mistaken. Maybe—

She saw the flash first, then heard the roar of a gun. It came from across the street and froze Marcella. She stood dumb and petrified, staring into the night.

Then flash after flash. Roar after roar. From both sides of the street, now, for Jeff was shooting back. He stood braced against a gate post, tripping the trigger of Sam Corson's gun. Marcella saw it all, terrified. She couldn't make out anyone over there. Just flashes from the dark.

She didn't even see the man fall. But she saw that Jeff Lantry *didn't* fall. He turned toward her in a moment, perfectly relaxed and with a warm gun hanging loosely from his hand. The gateway framed him like a tired, gaunt warrior coming home. His voice was the stern, strong spirit of Durango, calling to her, "It's all right, Marcella."

It was late spring when the Jefferson D. Lantrys drove a buckboard north across the upper Dolores. Bulky bundles in the bed of it were a tent, sleeping-bags, and other camp equipment. The team was high-stepping matched grays, a wedding present from Carey Talcott.

Lantry reined to a stop in a park at a bend of the river. It was a level, grassy spot, and the wild plum fringing it was already in bloom. The sun had just dipped behind a piney sky line. "Shall we camp here, lady?"

"It's lovely," Marcella said. She jumped down to help him unload.

They were experts by now, and the tent was quickly up. Lantry kindled a fire with last year's pine cones, and a pan was soon sizzling. This was a delayed honeymoon because they'd been too busy, as well as too poor, to make a train trip anywhere. Just why her husband was taking her in this particular direction Marcella didn't know. He'd been a little mysterious about it.

"Is it to see the Talcotts?" she asked him during supper.

He shook his head, grinning. "Guess again."

But she could think of no other guess to make. They couldn't be going to see the Ashtons, because Gerry and Melissa weren't yet back from England.

A gentle spring rain fell that night. Marcella, on her pallet of spruce boughs, heard it tapping sweetly on the canvas. Jeff was by her. She listened to the even, untroubled breathing of his sleep. He was always like that now, as relaxed as a boy. And yet with all a man's courage and strength and will to win. He'd worked so hard, these last months. They'd leased the big Jallison ranch, the Circle K, paying a year's rent with a loan made them by Major Talcott.

How wonderful the major had been. And how gallant he'd looked giving a bride away who had no father of her own. And how beautiful Melissa, the matron of honor. How sturdy and handsome the best man, Tom Gifford, waiting for her beside her own Jeff at the altar of that blessed little church in Durango. Doctor Ed, she remembered, hadn't been there. He'd been busy fighting for the life of a man they'd found under a pine tree, only the night before. A futile effort, for the man had died. A man named Smith, they said. That was all they knew about him.

But that part was a dark chapter she must never think of again. Jeff, she was sure, didn't. He'd drawn a curtain over the black past of Durango and looked ahead now, only to its shining future.

The patter on the canvas lulled Marcella, and she slipped into sleep.

When she awakened it was daylight and the rain had stopped. She could hear Jeff outside chopping the breakfast wood.

Then she heard a horseman splash across the river. And greetings.

"Hi, Tom."

"Hi, Jeff."

"Anything new, Tom?"

"Plenty. Take a look at these."

Marcella sensed that Tom Gifford was displaying some startling exhibit. She wondered what it was.

Evidently they didn't want her to know. She heard them withdraw a little farther from the tent. Their voices made only a hum now.

When she dressed and went out, Tom Gifford was gone. She looked anxiously at Jeff's face. But it wasn't troubled. "What did Tom want, Jeff?"

"Nothing," Jeff said. "He was just passing by. A sheriff has to cover a lot of ground."

"He told you something. What was it?"

Lantry tried to evade, but she was insistent. "All Tom said," he explained finally, "was that some sheepherder found a skeleton on the range. Two gold dice lay by it. The same dice Sax Consadine used to carry around. Nothing that concerns us. Now stop asking questions, lady, and cook me some breakfast."

She was glad enough to dismiss the subject. Sax Consadine, now, was only an unpleasantly dim blur in her memory. Jeff, she discovered, had not only chopped the wood but had caught four fat trout from the river.

All that day they drove north toward Lone Cone. They crossed Turkey Creek, then Beaver Creek, through a land of pine and aspen.

"Isn't Major Talcott's place near here?" Marcella asked.

Lantry nodded. "A piece off to the right. Up to his neck

in horses again, I hear. And losing money fast."

Marcella laughed. "What does it matter, so long as he's happy?"

Beyond the Beaver the pines petered out. Lantry could see the tall black spire of Lone Cone looming ahead. He was glad he'd been able to avoid telling Marcella the identity of that skeleton. It would depress her if she knew it was a woman's. And what other woman could it be but Ruby Costello?

She'd skipped out immediately after the showdown with Consadine. The railroad was positive she hadn't left by train. Consadine's gold dice had disappeared at precisely the same time. And now, months later, the dice were found beside a woman's skeleton on the range.

Most of all, Lantry was glad he hadn't told Marcella just *where* the skeleton had been found. Picked clean by coyotes, there'd been nothing to identify it except those golden dice.

Gifford's guess, Lantry thought, seemed as good as any. It was that surviving outlaws of the Mesa Verde crowd had fled west, taking Ruby with them. They'd headed for Utah and Nevada, apparently, keeping to the dimmest back trails to avoid capture. Ruby would naturally take along what money she could lay hands on. Presumably her escorts had murdered her for it. Not a pretty tale. The less Marcella knew of it the better.

Midafternoon brought them to a summit from which they could look down into a deep, steep-walled valley. Marcella remembered it well. Slim Borchard had brought her here one time, in a Bridlebit rig, taking her to Melissa's.

Below lay Disappointment Creek. What sinister memories it brought back! And why was Jeff taking her there now?

The grade down, just as it had before, seemed endless.

But this was spring, and everything was green. The valley floor was like an emerald ribbon. Scrub oak, studding it in clusters, had already put out leaves. When they came down to the creek, Marcella saw currant and gooseberry bushes overhanging its banks. It was a sizable stream now, with snow melting in high country to the east. Its riffles made a melody of whispers as Lantry turned the grays down valley.

This could only be toward the old Ashton homestead. "But they won't be back for a week yet!" Marcella protested.

Her husband smiled wisely and made no answer.

Then the valley opened, and she saw people. Wagons and teams and people. Gay talk and laughter. Right where Melissa had lived for those four terrible years.

But the shabby hovel was gone now. In its place stood a gracious house of fresh-cut logs. The house had a gabled roof and dormer windows. Two men were on it, tapping on the last shingles. Beyond, other buildings were going up. A log barn. Sheds and a corral.

"They call it a log-rolling," Lantry said.

He drove up at a trot, shouting greetings. "Hello, Buck. Need any help? Hi, Bruce, Tod, Slim!"

Buck Shaw's crew was there from Dove Creek. And people from Rico and Telluride and Dolores. Whole families were there in covered wagons. A smell of barbecued meat was in the air. It was like a great picnic and must have been going on for days.

The main house was nearly done. Some of the women had made bright curtains and were putting them in the windows.

"Hey, you Lantrys!" a cowboy yelled. "Roll up yer sleeves and get busy. Them Ashtons'll be poppin' in on us any day now. Where the hell they gonna sleep if we don't get this house done?"

Lantry put his arm around Marcella. She was crying. Just like she'd cried before when she'd come here and found Melissa. "Now brighten up, lady," Lantry commanded, "or they'll think you don't like it."

She rubbed away her tears. "But I was so wrong, Jeff!"

"Wrong about what, lady?"

"About this country. I said it was hard and cold and cruel. But it isn't at all." Her voice choked a little. "It's warm and sweet and tender." Then she was crying again, shamelessly, with her head on his shoulder.

"I guess it is," Lantry said, "if you play straight with it." He looked soberly off down the valley, to distant brown badlands where this creek made its confluence with the Rio Dolores. "But if you don't—"

He remembered what Tom Gifford had told him this morning. About the place where they'd found Ruby Costello. Right where Disappointment Creek flowed into the River of Sorrows.